Starling
Love in Los Angeles Book 1

By Racheline Maltese and Erin McRae

Avian30
New York, New York
2017

Avian30
New York, New York
Starling by Erin McRae and Racheline Maltese
Copyright 2017
ISBN 978-1-946192-03-5

www.Avian30.com

This work originally published by Torquere Press, September 2014
First Avian30 Printing: February 2017
Printed in the USA

1

After yet another fight with his boyfriend about work-life balance, Paul Marion Keane gets to the small suite of offices that belongs to the writing team of hit TV show *The Fourth Estate*. At seven thirty the lights are still off.

Between the fight with Craig and a stack of notes to go through on an episode that isn't even his, Paul is grateful for the time alone. He's got a pitch for a plotline to work on too, but suspects it will wind up relegated to a C-plot.

He punches the lights on, drops his bag on his desk, and walks into the kitchenette for a cup of terrible coffee. At which point his already unpleasant morning becomes ridiculous. Their intern Nick and some unidentified boy are making out against the counter in front of the damn coffee machine.

Paul reaches around them to grab a mug out of the cabinet. "Seriously, what the fuck?"

Nick unsuctions himself from his companion and turns around sheepishly. He's trying to shield the other guy, but he's taller than Nick so it's not very effective. The other guy is also startling in appearance: Red hair, dramatically freckled face, and ridiculously plump lips. Paul can't help but focus on him despite Nick's fidgeting.

"We didn't think anyone would be here," Nick says.

"Obviously." Paul shoves into their space to grab the carafe out of the coffee maker. "When you get caught making out with someone at work, apologize first."

Nick backs up nervously, but the other guy slides down the counter as if this absurd turn of events is merely mildly interesting.

"Also, start the coffee if you're the first one in." Paul isn't sure what to do. His emotional spoons are low and yelling seems like the best choice. "Don't you have homes, either of you?"

"He didn't want his roommates to know," Mr. Unidentified says. He blinks at Paul mildly.

"And who are you?" Paul asks.

"Production assistant."

"Right," Paul turns the sink on to fill the carafe. "Should have known from the hideous cargo shorts. Do you have a name?"

Unperturbed by the insult to his wardrobe, he grins. "Alex."

"Nice to meet you," Paul says grudgingly, but doesn't extend a hand. Under the circumstances there's only so much courtesy he can muster. "Nick, go do something useful." Despite everything, Paul can't help but smile when Nick reaches for Alex's hand and give a little squeeze before bolting.

Alex hoists himself up to perch on the counter. "I'm sorry he's —"

"A giant fucking closet case and completely dysfunctional?" Paul pours the water into the coffeemaker and shoves the carafe back in with more force than necessary. He hopes the anger hides how intensely pathetic he feels today. "Yes, thank you, and welcome to Hollywood."

"I've been here for two years," Alex notes.

"Whatever."

"Bad morning?"

Paul cocks his head to the side and considers the question. First Craig stormed out this morning and now these two? He's reminded of his mother's insistence that he's the luckiest man she knows—not good lucky or bad lucky, just *weird* lucky.

"Strange morning, as far as it's your business," he finally replies.

Alex blinks back at him.

"Piece of advice: Don't screw idiots who aren't out and have your next tryst in a different department, okay?"

Alex nods. "Yeah. No problem." He slides down from the counter. "Although, that's two," he says as he saunters out. "Hope your day gets better."

Paul shakes his head and laughs. "Yeah, you too."

When Alex is gone, Paul sighs. He has no energy for this, and Nick is an idiot with whom he should probably go have a heartfelt and sympathetic conversation.

◆

Despite the aborted morning makeout, Alex's day doesn't get truly weird until after the cast and crew of *The Fourth Estate* break for lunch. The assistant director tells him to pop over to wardrobe when he's done.

"The hell?" Alex asks around a mouthful of chicken and rice.

"It's another paycheck," Gary says in lieu of explaining.

Alex swallows. "Awesome. Explain." Too many pranks happen on sets for him not to want the full story.

"We've got a line that references a specific type. Because we occasionally work with morons, the background selection is inadequate, and you're today's lucky winner."

Alex sets down his fork. "Neat. How big's the check?"

◆

Alex only becomes clear on what he's gotten into when he gets back to set in skintight jeans and a shirt he would never wear. His buddies on the crew start ribbing him immediately. They only eventually shut up because there's work to be done. But the hundred extra bucks to do a cross and react to one of the principals reacting to him is hard to argue with no matter how many times he'd almost gotten his balls caught in the zipper back in wardrobe.

The backstage spirit that permeates *The Fourth Estate's* narrative isn't that different from the atmosphere that permeates Alex's working life behind the scenes of the show. The dramas of a ruthless, dysfunctional, crack team of reporters differ only in degree from the bullshit of a set for a highly rated nighttime TV drama. The problem isn't even *Fourth*; it's that L.A. people work long hours, are casually cruel, and relentlessly judgmental.

No one tells him is that the line meant to reference him is *Who's the twink?* Alex isn't supposed to engage with the line so the words aren't supposed to matter to him. But when Liam (who plays James, a former field reporter turned anchor) tosses it to Natalie (Marjani, James's co-anchor, ex-lover, and frequent rival) after the cross, Alex can't help but retort. Because *not likely*.

He realizes his mistake immediately but waits until they call cut before he puts a hand to his mouth to apologize. He's been on sets long enough to know better. "Sorry, sorry, I know…I'm sorry —"

"No." A voice drawls the word loudly from somewhere behind the monitors.

The objection belongs to Victor, their showrunner. Alex wants to fall through the floor. Among other things, he would really like this day's double paycheck situation not to end in no paychecks.

"I am so —"

"Shhhhhhh." The shushing sound reminds Alex of a snake. "Keep doing exactly what you're doing," Victor says.

They reset the scene and go again. This time, when Alex retorts, Liam — James — breaks off from the cross to get in his face. They start bantering. Alex has always had a retort for everything, and there's no reason for that to change now that there's a camera on him.

Alex isn't sure if Liam's words are angry or flirtatious — or quite how in character any of this is — but Liam's attentive blue eyes keep him anchored in the strange moment. In Alex's peripheral vision Victor holds up his hand and makes a looping motion. *Keep going.* Alex doesn't know if it's meant for him or Liam or the camera operator. He keeps talking.

They do several takes. Alex keeps wondering if this is what happens when you're dead: Your life, exactly as you've always known it, turned on its ear and set in endless repetition.

Between the third take and what's apparently going to be a fourth, Victor points to him and suggests he join him in his office when he's done.

Alex nods. You don't say no to Victor Salcido Santillan. Ever. Even when you really, really want to. Although, in this moment, Alex is not sure he does. He's just been effectively given a line. Or several. And that could mean far more than a hundred bucks. It could mean this month's rent, although only because he lives in a shithole apartment with a roommate. But he still thinks he might be in trouble.

"We're going again," Gary shouts as Alex rubs his sweaty palms all over the pants the wardrobe department provided.

Everyone resets as Victor walks away. As he goes, he calls out fondly to Alex over his shoulder, "Don't ever wear cargo shorts again".

Alex stands there feeling lost and cursed.

"It's okay," Liam says, with a glance towards the departing Victor. "Everything's going to be great."

♦

At midnight Alex finally pulls his car into the little parking lot behind his apartment building. He takes one last moment for himself, wrapping his hands around the steering wheel and taking a deep breath before he gets out.

There's a flight of stairs, narrow and poorly lit, that leads up to the apartment. Alex fumbles for a moment to find the right keys to unlock the multiple latches on the door. Inside, all is the same as ever — ratty couch, rattier chair, milk crate coffee table, and his roommate curled up in pajamas.

"What happened to you?" she demands when he shoves the door closed behind him and drops his keys back in his bag. "You look terrible."

"Thanks, Gem." Alex closes his eyes and wishes for more time to let the bizarre events of the day settle in. "Why are you still awake?"

"You didn't answer your phone. I was worried."

Alex opens his eyes and looks at her. "You waited up for me?" Her concern is still something he's getting used to. Back home in high school in Indiana, Alex came and went as he pleased.

Gemma is perched on their lumpy, faded couch. She's wearing her grey pajamas covered in angry clouds and her chin-length black hair is pulled back into two uneven pigtails. Her laptop is open in front of her.

"Don't you have an audition tomorrow morning?" Alex asks.

"It got cancelled." She turns her attention back to her computer. Her voice is the dangerous kind of controlled. Alex asks nothing more, lest he walk further into that minefield.

"Which you would have known if you'd picked up your phone," she goes on. "Where were you?"

Alex digs his phone out to check the alerts. Sure enough — three missed calls, including one from Nick, though that can wait. "I was at work."

"Until midnight?"

"Do you not pay attention to anything I do?" Crew days are long. Longer than actor days, which Gemma should know. Sure, Alex is usually done much earlier than this, but erratic hours are hardly unexpected in either of their lives.

"You look like shit," Gemma says bluntly.

"It's been a long day, okay?"

"Take your shoes off. There are leftovers in the fridge if you're hungry." She turns her attention back to her laptop.

"Thanks, Mom," Alex mutters on his way to the kitchen.

"I heard that!" Gemma yells. Alex hums to himself as he crouches in front of the fridge to examine the leftover options.

"Work was weird," Alex says when he's finally seated across from her in their ratty armchair, a plate on his lap. The paint on the wall behind Gemma is chipping. The lamp beside her, that they picked up from the curb one trash day, makes the cracks stand out more visibly than they do in the daytime.

"What happened?" Gemma shuts the laptop, hugs it to her chest, and waits for him to find words to answer.

Alex is grateful. He's spent plenty of time training her to be quiet when he needs her to be. "Do you want to go out to dinner this weekend?" he asks. Bribery seems like the safest tactic to hand.

She looks skeptical. "A roommate date?"

"Totally. We can get tacos. Or sushi! Or anything you want."

"Alex," she says warily. "I know you like to do the cagey thing when stuff's happening, but can you talk to me?"

He looks at her over a mouthful of warmed-up rice and tries to be the picture of innocence. "Mmm?"

"What's going on?"

He swallows. "I was an idiot at work and instead of firing me Victor offered me a part." The words come too quick, but they're terrifying.

"A part in what?" She frowns.

"*Fourth Estate.*"

Her mouth opens a little. "But you're a P.A," Gemma says slowly.

"Yes."

"You're not an actor."

"No."

"How did that happen?"

Alex sets his plate down on the milk crate stack passing for a coffee table, crosses his legs and curls up into the chair. He can hardly explain any of this to himself. None of it feels real yet, and there's a frightening ominousness to this kind of unknown.

"I told you," he finally says. "Weird fucking day."

"What kind of part?" Gemma demands. "None of this is making any sense. Like at all."

"I don't know." That, in fact, is a lie. But if he tells Gemma about the series of stepping stones Victor put in front of him — including a chance to be a principal in the magic world where it all works out and he comes back next year — he's both afraid that he'll jinx it and that Gemma will murder him in his sleep. "They're still working out the details."

"Are you going to do it?"

"I don't know."

"What!" Gemma shrieks.

Alex jumps. He's used to her volume but the explosions still catch him off guard.

"What do you mean you don't know?!"

He stretches a leg out and curls his toes against the edge of the milk crates. "I'm a P.A."

"Who just got offered a part on a major network's Thursday night anchor!"

"Yes."

"Why would you say no?"

Alex thunks his head against the back of the chair. "God, Gemma, do you really want the list?"

"*Yes.*"

"It's long," he warns.

"I've got all night. It's not like there's anywhere I have to be tomorrow."

Beyond his own reasonable fear and unreasonable guilt, Alex feels genuine sorrow for her. Auditions may be a dime a dozen in this city, but it can take thousands of them for any one person to reach their dreams. "I'm sorry," he says sincerely.

"It's not your fault."

Alex knows that's a hard kindness for her to offer, but Gemma is an extraordinarily good friend even if, or perhaps because, they met on the internet. They've been in this together ever since they moved to L.A. after high school graduation with little more than their love of stories. But Gemma is the one who wants to be a star. Alex has always wanted to make movie magic, but he's never wanted to be it.

Their apartment is the worst sort of shithole, but it has locks that work and a landlord who doesn't care that they're still occasionally, if increasingly rarely, unemployed kids. Compared to the welfare cheese of his upbringing, it's at least an adventure.

Gemma, as is her narrative destiny, has a waitressing gig and is registered as a nonunion extra at Central Casting. Alex signed up for the city's film and TV internship program as soon as he got here. It had cost him nothing and also paid him nothing, but there was a real job on the other side of it. As a P.A. he's been hired, or not, on a day-to-day basis since. It's not secure, but then, nothing for him ever has been.

"I don't even know if this is going to happen," he finally says. "There are a lot of factors in play. If I even start this process the rest of the crew is going to hate me. I'm not sure the cast is going to be thrilled either. You should have seen the look Natalie gave me. And even if it was going to happen for sure, I did not come to Hollywood to be in front of the cameras. I don't know if I can do this."

Good things like this don't just get handed to him. Anything Alex has, he's gotten because he decided he wanted it, figured out how to get it, and then put in whatever work was required to secure it. He trusts the results of his own efforts; he doesn't trust other people. A prize that comes with risks he hasn't even begun to calculate could be all sorts of dangerous. And Alex hasn't survived by not calculating his risks.

"Obviously you can, if they offered you this."

"I don't know if I want to," Alex says slowly for what feels like the thousandth time. He doesn't know how to explain his innate reluctance to someone who wants so badly what he's been handed. "They didn't pull me because of what I can do. They pulled me because I look like a twink."

"You are a twink."

"I'm not —"

"You are skinny, vaguely hairless, and young."

"Gemma," Alex protests. She may not be wrong, but getting slapped with labels she knows mostly from gay porn is completely awful. Where Alex comes from, getting labelled like that gets people beat up. Or worse.

Gemma is unconcerned with his discomfort. "Seriously, though. What happened?"

Alex stabs his fork into his rice. "They needed a certain type in background for James to rag on. Apparently even the fucking T-shirt and clipboard do not save me from resembling that particular type."

Gemma considers that for a moment. "Okay, I get that's not a typical reason to have something good happen to you, but do you know what it's like being *Gemma Hyong* in this town?"

Alex shakes his head.

"It closes a lot of doors."

"You had an audition last week," Alex says, trying to be encouraging.

"Yeah, to be a sex trafficking victim. Again. And I didn't get it, again, because my tits are too small. The doors that open for me are horrible. But they're still doors. Other people walk through them all the time."

"Yeah," Alex says cautiously. "Not like this."

"Right, explain to me how being called a twink turns into a part?"

Alex sighs. If he'd kept his mouth shut, he could have avoided this whole thing. "It pissed me off, the line. So I said something back, on camera, and Liam decided it was a great time to test my improv skills."

"What did you say?"

Alex scowls. "I don't know, Gemma. Tune in and find out while I hide under my bed with the tequila. Jesus." He tucks his knees up as close to his chest.

"Sorry," she says, although she doesn't sound like she remotely means it. "But I still don't understand."

"Victor called me up to his office after for a very long, very scary chat. He liked the moment, thought there was room for a new character on the show, and thinks, maybe — since he couldn't take his eyes off me and neither could anyone else — that it should be me."

Gemma is silent for a whole five seconds at that. "Alex, that's incredible."

"Victor is crazy."

"Victor is legendarily crazy," she corrects. She reels off Victor's back catalogue of shows in syndication along with their associated network battles from when they were in production. "But he's the best. And the people he writes are so real. You can't say no. Like, fame and money and I hate you, but art," Gemma finishes softly.

Alex mostly ignores her. Listening is way too scary right now. "What if I want to say no?"

"You don't want to."

"You don't know that!"

"Alex, you can't say no. You'll be a star! You'll be able to afford your rent! You can get cuter jeans!"

"My jeans are fine," he snaps. Saying yes for such reasons seems inherently dreadful, even if the prospect of reliably making rent is appealing.

"Your jeans are atrocious. You can get a car that works! You're Marilyn Monroe, you don't say no."

Alex sets his plate down on the milk crate. He's not hungry anymore. "Marilyn Monroe is dead."

"AND FAMOUS. DEAD AND FAMOUS, ALEX, YOU DON'T SAY NO."

Alex laughs. Gemma is actively absurd, but she's also a little frightening right now.

"I'm thinking about it," he finally says, because he is, even if not for any of the reasons Gemma is telling him to. But for all his hesitation, his instincts are telling him to do this. Alex trusts his instincts, even if he doesn't know what's going to come of all this. Besides, she's not going to stop being scary unless he assures her he's already working towards yes.

2

The house is dark when Paul pulls into the driveway. Craig's car isn't in the garage.

"Hello?" he calls when he gets in the door. There's no response, and he doesn't know whether he should have expected one. Todd, his white and tabby hodgepodge of a cat, comes trotting down the stairs and rubs against his legs. But there's no excited bark from Beau or greeting, however grudging, shouted from Craig.

Paul flicks on the lights as he makes his way to the kitchen. Todd follows, mewing piteously at his heels as if everything in the world is terrible and it's all Paul's fault. The cat isn't wrong.

There's a note on the counter written on the notepad they use for grocery lists. Craig's handwriting is neat.

I'm staying at Tara's tonight. I'll come back to get my stuff while you're at work. So pretty much anytime this week. Don't call.

P.S. Beau's with me. Good luck with the damn cat.

Paul reads the note twice, then balls it up and throws it across the room. It's not a remotely satisfying gesture.

Todd yowls his displeasure at being ignored. Paul sighs as the house settles with a creak around him. His boyfriend left and took his dog. It's an awful country song.

Paul fills Todd's food bowl and changes his water. He leaves his bag on the counter before he heads upstairs. He's not sure if he can sleep alone in the bed tonight, but he's perfectly sure he can cry in the shower.

◆

By the morning, Paul's grief is less about Craig — things had been messed up between them for a while and his schedule was probably the least of it — and more about the eerie quiet of the house. Being single has always leant him an unsettling feeling of isolation. It's stupid and unhealthy, but Paul loves being in love, and now it's down to him and the cat. Todd is awesome, but he's always been a mercenary sort of cat, more interested in food than laps.

"Maybe I can learn something from you, buddy," he says, patting the animal's side as he puts his bowl down.

Todd meows happily, and Paul zones out on watching him eat for a minute. He does this thing where he squeezes his eyes shut as he crunches his food that Paul finds stupidly adorable.

He sighs. His life is suffocating, and he can't imagine it's going to get better anytime soon.

◆

Paul knows he's right when he gets to work and finds Alex sitting on his desk, a most Los Angeles sort of changeling. Somehow, he's not surprised, even though there's little interesting or appealing about the office itself. Like all the other backstage spaces for *Fourth*, and indeed the rest of Hollywood, it's drab and involves a lot of fluorescent light and dingy white walls in need of a good scrubbing. The once-expensive but now decrepit and mismatched ergonomic chairs don't make it any cheerier.

"No sign of Nick?" Paul drops his things down like Alex isn't there. Maybe he's not. Maybe he's simply a ghost of yesterday's disasters.

Alex levers himself off the desk and follows Paul into the kitchenette. "I'm not here for Nick."

"I sure hope you aren't here for me, because let me tell you, I am some bad company right now."

"I'm hiding from Victor."

"Oh. Well. Aren't we all?" Paul says amiably as he rummages around in the tiny refrigerator for some juice that isn't the wrong type of furry. He doesn't mean it. He likes Victor more than most of his crew does. Paul doesn't mind the demands he makes of the people he's deemed worthy of his attention. Even the extent to which Victor tends to interfere with those people's lives doesn't really bother him anymore.

Alex leans against the doorframe but doesn't say anything.

"Why're you dressed up?" Paul asks. Not that he knows Alex's personal style choices, but cargo shorts and nerd T-shirts are the uniform of the P.A. unless it's cold enough for flannel. Certainly, it's what Alex was wearing yesterday. But today he's in tight, dark green cords with a long-sleeved and very fitted gray V-neck. "Are you about to quit?"

Paul watches Alex ponder the question. He looks pained.

"I don't know."

Paul gives up on the contents of the fridge and shoves the door closed with his hip before leaning back against it. "What is your deal?"

Alex ignores the question. "If you were offered an opportunity to do something you never wanted to do but maybe only because you never knew you could, and it would change your life — like in ways everyone fantasizes about but no one can really imagine — would you do it? Even if the offer was because of something stupid?"

"I'm going to go with yes. Granted, I don't know you or what the hell you're talking about, and my partner walked out on me yesterday and took the dog, so I might not be your best source of advice right now."

Alex's eyes widen comically. "Oh wow, your day did not get better."

Paul surprises himself with his own laughter. "No. No, it really didn't. Although that mess started before you cursed me with your well-wishes, so don't get cocky." He pauses. "What about yours?"

Alex shakes his head, and that startled look returns. Paul knows he's an asshole for finding it appealing.

"I don't know yet," Alex says. Then, having seemingly found whatever he was looking for, he's out the door.

Uncertain what to do in the face of that abruptness, Paul yells after him. "I'll give your regards to Nick!"

Alex doesn't respond.

♦

Alex's life becomes frightening and disorienting. That, it seems, is how fairytales work.

There are meetings and more meetings, screen tests, and all manner of awkward conversations. These mostly involve people Alex had been happy to avoid in what he's now starting to think of as his former life as a P.A.

Victor offers him a temporary gig in the production offices to shelter him from the worst of trying to do his usual job in the sea of interruptions and vanity the process becomes. When Alex says no, that he'll deal with whatever shit he gets from the crew for his sudden and possibly imminent change in circumstance, Victor nods with satisfaction. Alex suspects he has passed a test he didn't know he was taking.

He changes his clothes in the studio bathroom between work and meetings. It's a practicality but also deeply strange. Every time he walks back out the door he feels different than when he walked in.

Alex wonders if this process is supposed to teach him how to act.

♦

"We're adding a character," Victor tells Paul late one night when the writers' room is otherwise empty. Everyone else apparently has some semblance of a life. "That P.A. we pulled from the background shot. Alex Cook. Now Zach Reagan, junior reporter. New kid on the team. Young, but smart and hungry."

"Yeah?" Paul looks up from his notes. There have been rumblings, but coming from Victor like this means opportunity. It also explains some things about Alex, who Paul's been seeing around more and more in less and less explicable circumstances. No wonder his eyes are always so wide.

"Yeah," Victor confirms, but his tone is mocking. "And he's not going to be minor. So, if you want to pitch something that's not cleanup on everyone else, this is your chance, because I'm going to make you fix the rest of the cycle."

"Okay." Paul takes a breath and has ideas already. "Thank you." This is a vote of confidence and a reward for years of doing the shit work.

"You should know," Victor says, in the thoughtful voice that means he's plotting something. "He looks like a delicate little thing, but he's very much not."

"Zach?" Paul asks. "Or Alex?"

Victor just smiles. "Show me what you've got on Monday."

◆

Paul comes up with his first pitch over a weekend alone in the house, in sweatpants with the stereo cranked up. Todd protests the throbbing bass with narrowed eyes every time Paul paces in front of his chair.

On Monday Victor looks at what he has and tells him to make it happen.

Paul practically careens out of Victor's office to track Alex down wherever he might be skulking about the studios this time.

"Walk with me," he says when he's found him in an empty office, flipping through some papers. He's wanted to do that since he fell in love with *The West Wing* as a kid.

Alex gathers up his papers and goes with Paul. He's quiet, but Paul isn't surprised. In each of their strange and brief interactions Alex has used surprisingly few words while being a surprisingly massive presence.

Paul leads them through the maze of corridors, picking a route where they're unlikely to run into other writers. Or Victor. He watches the way Alex moves beside him, to understand his body and his secrets and where he hides his tension. "Victor decided it's my job to figure out who he thinks you are when you're Zach," he says eventually. "So I need you to talk to me, about anything, I don't care what. I just need to understand the rhythm of your voice."

"I don't have the job yet," Alex says.

"Victor asked me to rebuild the rest of the season around the introduction of your character." Paul feels sick as he says it. He doesn't know if he has permission to reveal this secret, even to its subject. He also doesn't know why Victor made him the messenger.

Alex doesn't react to the news. "Zach isn't me," he eventually says.

"Really? It wasn't you who was pissed off at one very choice word?"

"Can we consider that overlap aberrant?" Alex asks.

"No," Paul says thoughtfully.

"Why not?"

"Because you're twenty, don't like to talk, and tossed the word *aberrant* at me."

"So?"

"So that's interesting."

Alex makes a noise under his breath that sounds faintly like a cat hissing. "You're as bad as Victor."

Paul smiles. "Thanks for the compliment, but no. Talk to me?" He tells himself the query is about research and not his own growing interest. Or that outside of Victor the only person he's talked to in days is his cat.

"About what?" Alex looks surprised but not annoyed at Paul's persistence, which is a relief. Scaring the kid off wouldn't do anyone any favors.

"Seen any good TV lately?"

Alex stops walking to stare at him. Paul stamps down his own excitement at the attention.

Alex's eyes, a brown so dark they're almost black, fix on Paul's face. "You're an asshole."

"So are you."

Alex laughs, sudden and sharp. After a beat, he shakes his head. "I have to go."

As he walks down the corridor he gives Paul a look over his shoulder, part wary, part challenge.

Paul takes a deep breath and reminds himself firmly not to be an idiot, lest he go after Alex the way he so badly wants to. He suspects the impulse is self-destructive. Any interest in Alex on his part is inappropriate. Just because he wants a challenge doesn't mean he should inflict that desire on anyone else.

Stars have to make the first move. That's how Hollywood works. Paul makes his way back to his office. At least he has a better sense of who and what Zach can be now.

3

Alex signs the papers. He tries to read all of them first and fails, not because it's hard, but because it's boring. He worries a little bit for his soul as he scratches a pen, not fine enough for the occasion, over page after page of agreements. Victor looms from behind his desk. A network executive stand at his side. When it's all over, they both shake his hand.

As far as the union is concerned he's J. Alex Cook. There was already an Alex Cook and an Alexander Cook, and the thought of being called Jasper, as his mother named him, in *TV Guide* is more absurd than he can reasonably handle.

Work begins immediately.

Six weeks later, in the first week of September, the episode with the unintentional repartee airs. Gemma watches it and cackles loudly enough for Alex to hear from his bedroom, where he's got headphones jammed on while he goes over his lines for the next day.

Three weeks after that, Zach gets his first plot. From there everything goes crazy.

Somehow, it all harks back to that first line from Liam. The fans who always wanted James to be gay suddenly have someone for him to be gay with, which is infuriating. The actual point of that moment was that James is an asshole who doesn't view other people as real. But now that corner of the world wants a romance.

The ridiculousness manages to spread to the rest of the audience in part because Liam plays it up on his social media in a way that leads to the appallingly offensive #WhosTheTwink hashtag. Gemma sends him the link, and Alex makes the mistake of looking at it between scenes at work. He proceeds to flip out until Victor, who seems to be everywhere these days, asks him why he cares.

"You're gay, you're young, and you're beautiful, Alex. Why does this bother you?"

"Other than the fact that the straight internet is tweeting it 'til it trends?" Alex snaps.

"Yes."

"I'm smarter than that," Alex tells him. "And I'm from Indiana."

He's grateful that Victor takes that for the answer it is. The thought of trying to articulate it further is painful.

◆

As they wrap a few days later, Victor beckons Alex over with a crooked finger and invites him up to his office.

No matter how many times Alex has seen the inside of this space over the last few weeks, he can't feel at ease here. He stays standing as Victor settles himself behind his desk, sitting only when Victor gestures for Alex to take the chair across from him.

The office is intimidating by design. Unlike the functional shabbiness of the space Paul shares with the other writers, Victor's office is sleek and pristine. The walls are white, and the glass shelves built into them glitter in the light. The shelves themselves are full of the awards Victor and his shows have won. The desk, in contrast, is a glossy black, solid and sharp-edged like the shelves. Scattered across its surface is the detritus of the day-to-day business of running his empire: Scripts, a laptop, two tablets, a voice recorder, and a notebook. No technology is beyond or beneath him.

"How are you?" Victor asks. Victor is no less intimidating than his office, surely also by design. He's not tall or particularly muscular, but he's solidly built. His skin is a warm golden brown, his hair jet black. Alex doesn't find him attractive, but that's because Victor exists beyond such questions. His charisma is overwhelming and more than slightly frightening. He commands attention simply by doing nothing so much as sitting behind a desk. Alex shakes his head. "People keep asking me that. But I'm pretty sure they don't want the answers."

"Because they're being disingenuous or because the answer is terrible?"

Alex's smile is all teeth. Something about Victor makes him profoundly aware of his canines. "Yes."

"I can assure you," Victor says. "I don't ask questions I don't care about the answer to."

Alex collects his thoughts. Victor waits. He'll wait for any answer he wants for as long as he has to.

Alex is surprised he doesn't fear Victor more. Everyone else seems to. But while the focused attention of other men has always felt like danger, with Victor he is, he thinks, safe. And if not, at least he's protected from anyone outside the room. Alex knows to take a bargain when he sees it.

"I'm in over my head. And I'm lonely," he says.

He hadn't meant to say that second part. But that's what Victor does: force everyone he encounters to confession.

Alex understands why his buddies on crew are either awkward or awful with him and he should have expected the volume of people in the audience who hate Zach vociferously. The faux enthusiasm from people who are now his cast mates is harder. If Gemma isn't jealous, he can't understand why they are. Then again, they don't know Gemma. Before he can manage any of that aloud, Victor speaks again.

"Did you think it wouldn't be lonely?"

Alex blinks at him slowly. He can play the waiting game too.

Victor picks up a paper clip from the surface of the desk and uses his thumb to pry it open. "Weren't you lonely in Indiana?"

Alex isn't sure if the fidget is supposed to convey boredom or what Victor likes to do to other people. "I was all sorts of things in Indiana."

"I'm sure." Victor's voice isn't sharp, but he's definitely scolding. "Now. Let's talk about all the sorts of things you should and shouldn't be here."

"Like what?" Alex asks warily.

"Like don't be the twenty year old star that gets caught having a drink at a bar. Don't do drugs, either, but you're not the type. Don't fuck fans, prostitutes, or anyone who will blackmail you. Don't get your heart broken, because no one here has any time for that, and don't —"

"I *know* all that," Alex snaps.

"Do you?" Victor raises his eyebrows in a mockery of innocence. "You'd be the first of many."

"I'm not an idiot."

Victor leans forward over the desk. "You don't even know what you are."

"And you do?"

"I know what you can become. And I have no interest investing time in something that's going to blow itself up."

"Has that happened before?" Alex isn't sure what he thinks of Victor calling him a thing. He is, however, sure he wants to know whether Victor has a habit of breaking his new toys.

"You're from Indiana, what do you think?"

Alex doesn't want to talk about Indiana. He also doesn't want to rise to the bait. Victor hasn't said *don't fight,* but he's pretty sure punching his showrunner is off the list of things that are allowed to him. "Fine. Any suggestions on what the hell I should do?"

"You need a team. Lawyer, accountant, agent, manager, publicist. I trust you're smart enough I won't have to explain why. And," Victor looks Alex over with an appraising eye, like he's a statue the man is considering adding to his collection. "A personal trainer."

"Fuck you."

"No?" Victor purses his lips as if in delight that Alex is pushing back.

Alex wonders why people don't hate the man more than they already do. "Why are you like this?" he blurts.

"Because I enjoy it, and it's useful." Without dropping Alex's gaze, Victor twists the paper clip until it snaps.

◆

Victor gives Alex a list of names and phone numbers. When Alex asks if his own team should be so blatantly comprised of people with loyalties that lie elsewhere, Victor smiles his shark smile and says to consider it a starting place.

Alex goes to Liam the next day. This new life of his is at least somewhat Liam's fault, and he's never seen him be cruel to anyone, only at times clumsily unaware of other people's boundaries. Alex is by far the baby of the cast, and Liam has the fewest years on him of any of them, allowing Alex to feel a little less like a kid who needs handholding.

Liam is surprisingly helpful. His dark curls bounce as he nods thoughtfully. He understands the problem immediately, although he seems unduly amused by it. But a few days later he gets Alex a list of names that don't represent a conflict of interest with anyone else on the show.

Putting his script aside between takes, Alex drops into his director's chair and scans over the names, not that he recognizes any of them. "How did you come up with this?"

"I know a lot of people. All of whom are too nice to me."

◆

Margaret, the woman Alex settles on as his manager because she seems as judgmental as he is, tells him to lock down his Facebook. He doesn't use it because he doesn't like anyone from high school enough to keep in touch, but locking it does at least put an end to the friend requests from people he doesn't know.

Alex looks forward to their first full business meeting. No one recognizes him as he takes the elevator up to her office in the nondescript Beverly Hills office building. Margaret's office is decorated in mint green and white, with a plush couch against one wall and framed abstract prints in pastel colors. The effect is soothing — nothing like Victor's stark office — and very Los Angeles.

He sits in the chair across from her. Margaret asks, as she chews on the end of a ballpoint pen, if the green cords are the only nice pair of pants he owns.

"I have the same pair in gray," he tells her.

She frowns. Margaret's a tall woman with rich brown skin. Her hair is twisted into innumerable braids and wrapped, crown-like, around her head. Alex has never cared much about his appearance, but he is very aware that Margaret is a hundred times more elegant than he could ever hope to be.

"We need to do something about that." She shuffles some papers on her desk as if she's flipping through some sort of new celebrity checklist. "Next up. You can't get caught having a beer — you're still only twenty — and you can't get caught having a fling."

"Yeah, I know. Victor already told me."

"Did he? Good."

Alex wonders how many more lectures on these subjects he's going to get from people who should have no place to tell him what to do. "I don't like people and I don't have any free time."

Margaret gives him a skeptical look. "You live in L.A."

"My entire social life revolves around hanging out with my roommate and talking about the sort of hot boys neither of us will ever have a chance to get near."

"I don't believe you." Margaret twirls her pen across her fingers. Alex finds it far less unsettling than Victor's paperclip.

"Why not?"

"I can't speak for your roommate, but you're one of the hot boys now. Also, you need to move."

Alex is outraged. "Why?"

Margaret glances down at his paperwork. "Because you live in a shitty part of Little Armenia, and there's no reason to do a job this hard if you can't live somewhere wonderful. You'll also probably want some security soon."

He takes a deep breath. Then a second. He's gotten so used to his crappy apartment and his routine with Gemma. Even now that he's filming regularly for a big deal TV show, he never considered that the job would necessitate a change to his home.

"You should probably let your roommate know."

"I'll bring her with me," Alex blurts. The decision as snap as it is absolute, although he can see by the flicker across Margaret's face that maybe it shouldn't be.

"Is she going to be your girlfriend?" Her voice is full of judgment.

"I — no…I…oh God. No," Alex stammers. He's not going to be in the closet and he certainly wouldn't admit that he would consider using Gemma that way if he were. His heart starts to race. While he knows this isn't quite a panic attack, he has the suspicion one might be waving to him from across the street.

♦

The panic attack arrives when Shawna, a grip who works on a show two stages down from *Fourth* and who he's been friends with for years, insists they go out dancing. Alex isn't sure if it's to celebrate or let off some steam, but the idea of *do this now while you still can* is definitely clear.

Normally Alex would flatly refuse. He doesn't like other people, and he's really not into having other people's bodies near his. But if this is the last time he'll be able to do anything like this, he'd be a fool to say no. He can spend the night drinking soft drinks and being Shawna's wingman.

But it's already too late for anything so simple. Within an hour of getting there, a man dances up close to Alex and slips his arm around his waist. While Alex is pondering whether Victor would approve, the guy calls him *Zach*. It's way too uncomfortable and invasive. Alex tries to bolt but the guy grabs his arm and pulls him back in until their bodies are flush against each other. The man's breath is hot on his neck.

Alex is lithe and clever and strong enough to handle himself — he wrestled in high school and men bigger than him should never, ever grab him in ways he doesn't want to be grabbed — but his arm is at a bad angle and all he can hear is Victor's voice in his head that he *can't*.

Alex can't get angry; he can't throw a punch; he can't even shove his way free. He can't, he realizes, decide he doesn't want this man touching him and do anything about it any more than he could have decided he wanted him for five minutes and done anything about that either.

The horror freezes him in place. Shawna has to rescue him by stomping a spike heel into the guy's foot. She grabs Alex's hand and runs them out into the breezy and too bright L.A. night.

4

The first time Paul sees Alex act he understands what it is about him that fascinates Victor. There's something about Alex — and therefore Zach — that makes him seem like he's never been owned, not by a job, a religion, or an ideology, and certainly not by a person or a relationship. That's so unlike most people that it makes him irresistible as puzzle to solve or a toy to own. Paul's not unaware of the irony, but he's also not immune to Alex's pull.

Now that everything is official, he aches to write for Alex, to solve with his words the mystery of who he will be as a performer. The work makes everything else in his life a little less awful, even when writer's block keeps him up too late. Paul's alone. His own projects outside of *Fourth* aren't getting any traction. Craig still has his dog. But the ring of Alex's voice when he speaks as Zach makes the words come a little easier.

While Zach isn't his and Paul's not the only one writing for him, he feels possessive of the character. He can't write a scene for him without remembering the clever, fearless kid he once chased out of the writers' room for making out with their intern.

♦

There are a lot of things Zach does that Alex would never in a million years do. Some are little things, like how he dresses. Some are bigger things.

Like voluntarily visiting a prison to interview inmates.

Alex thinks he's going to be fine until he gets to set and finds a reasonable replica of a prison visiting room. The fluorescent lights, metal chairs, phones, and Plexiglas panes are all too spot-on for his comfort. But there's no way to say that or show that he's ill at ease. Not without raising questions Alex doesn't want to answer about his sister and Indiana and weekends spent driving to Putnamville with his mom until he finally refused to go anymore. He takes a breath the way he used to on those not-long-enough-ago trips and braces himself.

When he has the mechanics of the scene and the equipment of filmmaking to focus on, he's fine. It's during the frequent stops and hurry-up-and-waits that the institutional setting starts to get to him. The minutes tick by with excruciating slowness. After three hours, Alex can't take it anymore.

"I'm sorry, I need a minute," he says when they're called back to start the next page. He needs to get out in the hallway at least and breathe something like fresh air.

"You just had a break, we don't have time to wait on you," someone from the crew snaps.

"Then make some," Alex snaps back. He knows he shouldn't even as he speaks. He is talent; it's not his job to make anyone else's more difficult. Lashing out is also a very good way to show exactly where his vulnerabilities lie. But he feels like he's suffocating, and his rational mind is not in control. He has his limits, no matter how often he gets the message that such things are, for him, not allowed: Because he's not a *real* actor and because America thinks it owns anything it can see on its TV screens.

Before the guy can say anything back — or Alex can dig himself any deeper — Victor is there. He doesn't look at Alex as he pulls the guy aside.

To tell him what, he doesn't know and is afraid to contemplate. Victor knows about his sister; there is no information about any of his people Victor doesn't feel entitled to. Despite his apparently uncontrollable little outburst, Alex doesn't want that information to spread further or get more attention than it already has. It's bad enough being the gay kid from Indiana. He doesn't also want to be the gay kid from Indiana whose currently incarcerated sister tried to stab him in the ramshackle kitchen of the ramshackle house they grew up in. Twice.

His mom only knows about one of those times. Victor had somehow gotten both out of him.

After Victor releases the guy — looking shaken and subdued, back to the crew — Alex expects Victor to round on him next. Victor does meet his eye. But instead of crooking his finger and telling Alex he had better come with him, he nods and moves along.

Somehow, Alex manages to get through the rest of the morning. Once they break for lunch he peels away from the group headed for catering. He needs some time alone and to be nowhere near anything that resembles an institutional setting.

He finds a nook behind a bunch of the set flats, out of the way and certainly out of sight to any casual passersby. He sits down with his back against the wall, puts in his headphones, and closes his eyes.

Five minutes later he's startled out of his solitude by a shadow. Someone has rounded the corner of the flats and is now looming above him. Alex opens his eyes, fully ready to snap again, only to find that it's Paul.

"It's you." Alex hopes he'll go away.

"It's me." Paul smiles and sits down on the floor next to him.

Alex pauses his music and looks sideways at the other man. He can't help but wonder if he's been sent by Victor and, if so, for what incredibly intrusive purpose.

"I need to talk to you," Paul says. "So I can write for you."

"Again?" Miserable and shaky as he might be right now, he doesn't want to offend anyone else by being today's bad attitude bear.

"Mhmm."

"We already did that."

Paul smiles. "I know."

"Did you need something else?" Alex still doesn't get why Paul is here.

"It's been a while. I wanted a refresher."

Paul doesn't look like he's being deceitful, but still, Alex is twitchy and annoyed. "Why? If you need to watch me, you can stream the episodes now." It's an obnoxiously cocky thing to say, but it's true, and Alex would really prefer to be alone.

Paul frowns in thought. The gesture makes his forehead crease and his eyes look even kinder. He might be a writer but he's built like the guys Alex and Gemma still only talk about. He's fit, with pale skin a little tanned from the sun. His hair is blond and his gray eyes are completely intent on Alex.

"That's not remotely the same. You're more than some small talk and a collection of edits, no matter what marketing tells you. People change and grow all the time, show me how that works for you. Or, you know, be grumpy," Paul says with a shrug. "It's all data."

Alex doesn't quite know what to do with any of that, so he snarks something about clichés. Paul snarks right back, smiling the whole time. Like everything else for Alex lately, it's a dare, but it feels different — and better — than most of the others.

When Paul gets up five minutes later, Alex feels more like a real boy than he has in a while. Maybe he can resume this day from a place resembling neutral.

Also, Alex notes after Paul disappears around the corner that for a writer, Paul has a great ass.

◆

Gemma doesn't ask Alex if she can come visit the set, but Alex knows what such a visit would mean to her. Both because of her professional ambitions, and because of how much she loves *The Fourth Estate* and indeed all of Victor's work. Plus, Alex owes her. Not only for putting up with his surliness at home, but for her support and encouragement ever since they first met online and started talking about moving west. It's a small gesture to make in repayment, but it's what Alex can do right now.

Seeing the two parts of his life — one almost old, one still very new — interact is strange. He watches Liam and all his clichéd black Irish charisma shake Gemma's hand. His gaze is like the beam of a lighthouse, all focused on her. His smile is warm, and Gemma glows with the attention. Alex is good and doesn't roll his eyes when Liam winks at her. It's profoundly surreal.

He nods Gemma — and her incredibly loud yet surprisingly tasteful high heels — down a hallway in front of him. This may be his life now, but there's absolutely nothing about it that feels normal.

When *The Fourth Estate* first aired three years ago the critics had ignored it as an unexpectedly soapy backstage drama from Victor, from whom everyone expected something better. But it had claws and stars, so people watched it, even if just for the occasional partial nudity.

But somewhere towards the end of the second year, things on the show had shifted, and what had seemed disjointed and incoherent started to reveal itself as part of a much bigger plan. The audience realized its shallow, trashy drama was no more shallow and trashy than their own lives before the critics did. Now it's event television, pulling in everyone from teenyboppers to their grandparents.

Alex had watched it before he started P.A.ing for it. The glamour and thrill of working on a show — either as crew or as an actor — isn't what most of the audience assumes that it is, but it's still magic. The work of storytelling is incredibly satisfying, at least when he's not terrified he's going to fail. He'd forgotten that, these last few months. There had been so much to be frightened of. But now, seeing his work and his world through Gemma's eyes, he can feel his perspective start to shift. He *is* lucky to be here. Even if that luck comes with so many downsides.

As he and Gemma run into people, Alex makes introductions and Gemma holds her own, happily chatting about plots and arcs and relationships in a way that hews a surprisingly gracious line between fan and aspiring professional. He's proud. And grateful.

Alex is fascinated by watching Gemma get to see how the real people of the cast and crew intersect with the characters they all carry around with them. Some, like the irritatingly extroverted if friendly Liam, are far from their alter egos. His character James is reckless as hell, eagerly facilitating everyone else's inevitably awful choices. Marjani — Natalie's character — on the other hand, is almost as much of a diva as Natalie is. The only one of the cast Alex is sure he likes is Raphael, who plays the star member of their fictional journalism team. The character is a mess, but Raphael seems well-adjusted. At least for L.A.

Gemma floats through it all. When he walks her back to her car before the afternoon's shoot, she kisses his cheek.

"Thank you for a peek at the dream," she says.

◆

The network, Victor's people, and Margaret all try to start Alex off small with the media. Margaret assures him over and over that they're always going to say *no* a lot. That's not personal; it's not even about the fact that Alex has no idea what he's doing.

Instead, she says that the secret to success is to always leave everyone wanting more. Alex nods. He understands; it's obvious and in the very way *The Fourth Estate* is written and structured. No one but Victor could get away with doing that to an audience for over a year before they understood what they were watching.

Alex tries his best to follow Margaret's advice and Victor's example. He never mentions his family in interviews if he can help it, but there are two weeks where every gossip show is obsessed with the idea that he doesn't know his dad and that there's some drama involving his sister. On the days when how hard it is for him must seem obvious, Margaret asks Alex why he's doing this. He says that Gemma told him he's Marilyn Monroe and not allowed to say no.

"Sometimes, on TV, it's important to be less strange," is her only response. She doesn't even blink.

Alex laughs and crinkles up his eyes.

"That," she exclaims, "is your secret weapon."

◆

Alex's first TV interview that matters is a late show after the late show. Paul and Victor watch it together on the shitty first generation flat screen with the dodgy cable connection that lives in the writers' room. In television no one sleeps.

When the host finally asks Alex if he's gay, Alex giggles, squints, and smiles sly. "Is this something we didn't know?"

"America just fell in love with him," Victor breathes, leaning back in a chair with his feet on a desk, beer bottle halfway to his lips.

"America's not the only one." Paul murmurs. He's not sure if he means it as a jibe at Victor, who is notorious for his fascination with his stars — rumors have been going around about him and Liam forever — or his own personal moment of realization.

◆

In January Alex wins a People's Choice award for Best Newcomer.

Liam gives him a bright *Congratulations!* when Alex slides back into his seat at the awards show. As is usual from Liam, it's both sweet and excessive. Alex finds it faintly irritating. He has never believed in the myth of the perfectly kind and utterly humble star. The day-in and day-out of *The Fourth Estate* largely hasn't changed his mind. Liam is trying to be that guy all the time and Alex doesn't get it.

"You know, that category is new," Liam says, nodding at the trophy in Alex's hand as they leave together for the after party. Alex doesn't want to go, but Victor had sternly instructed him to be there and even Margaret had reminded him that he's contractually obligated to attend.

"Mmm?" Alex says vaguely. He never paid much attention to awards season as a civilian. He always cared more about the stories people told than the glamour of the red carpet. That's still true.

Liam nods. "It exists this year because of you."

"Oh?" That's a disturbing thought. Alex didn't come to L.A. to be an actor. For L.A. to be rewriting its rules for him seems a break in the order of the natural universe. Who knows what calamity could come from that.

"People — and advertisers — are hungry for you. And your Cinderella story."

It sounds like something Victor would say. Alex has another disturbing thought. How much time does Victor spend talking about him to Liam? To anyone?

He's going to demand more information on that subject from Liam but they step outside. There are fans staked out. The noise and the shouting and the flashes are overwhelming. He takes a deep breath and, along with Liam who loves shit like this, handles it as best he can. He signs a few things to be gracious, until a girl grabs his arm and pulls him way too close. Then the person next to her grabs him too, fingers digging into his shoulder. More hands reach out to him, landing on his sleeves and even in his hair. Alex feels like carrion being fought over. He doesn't hear what any of them are yelling, but disentangles himself as politely and quickly as he can. He seethes internally that his gratitude must extend to what no real person would be expected to bear.

When the Emmy nominations come out that summer, *Fourth* is up. One of the nods is for writing; it's not for an episode that has Paul's name on it, but Alex finds him the next morning to give him a high-five anyway.

5

Awards season, which seems to take up half the year, is tense and exhausting for everyone. The airing structure of *Fourth* may be quasi-groundbreaking, but one of the downsides of not shooting on a normal schedule is that major writing times overlap with days the rest of the industry takes off to party. It doesn't make any of them live quieter, more responsible lives. Combined with the last minute changes that are part and parcel of the very chaotic *Fourth Estate* beast, Paul can't wait for everything to calm down and go back to normal.

They win at the Emmys for Best Writing and Best Directing, although they miss Best Dramatic Series. Victor grumbles in a manner intended to be entertaining all through the celebration. Once the hangover from the celebrations wear off, Paul starts planning the real victory party.

He's almost not surprised when Alex is in the writers' room the morning Paul invites everyone over to his house the next weekend. Paul's seen him moving in and out of the different spaces at the studio when he's not on set. Like an unsettled cat, Alex seems to be trying them out for comfort. More and more, though, he's been landing here.

"Don't you have a trailer?" Paul asks as he squeezes by Alex and starts unpacking his laptop bag.

Alex is squinting at the massive bulletin board that takes up most of one wall. Cards scrawled with notes on character arcs and plot beats are thumbtacked to it. Alex must know it represents a map of his future. "Am I in the way?" he asks, not taking his eyes from the cards.

"Not yet," Paul says like the question is reasonable. No one complains about Alex regardless of where he lands. He's a star now, and no one complains about stars to their faces. "And I'm glad you're here. There's going to be a party next week, you should come."

"Another one?" Alex is already dressed as Zach for the day — at least, Paul feels safe assuming Alex would never choose an outfit that makes him look so delicate. The way Alex carries himself when he's off duty doesn't suit the pale blue shirt in an almost feminine cut, much less the scarf he has looped around his neck or the pants that might have been painted on for how tight they are. Not that Paul is looking.

"At my house and for fun," Paul reassures him. "Totally off the clock. No cameras and no official business. Work people, but what can you do? It's not like any of us have lives."

"I don't know." But when Alex bites at his lower lip just so and smiles, Paul knows he'll say yes. "You guys should celebrate your win. I wasn't a part of that."

"We were writing for you," Paul says. "You were it."

Alex turns to look at Paul over his shoulder. His lips part slightly in wonderment and he looks startled in a way Paul knows isn't a reaction to a simple compliment. "Okay."

◆

As people start to pile into his house, Paul realizes he's hosting this party not only because he can, but also because he must. When they had been together, Craig had always resented these events. No matter how many times Paul tried to explain the subtleties of becoming a team leader in the high-stress hothouse of a Hollywood writer's room, Craig was never willing to hear it.

Despite hosting a party to pull the team together being work for Paul, he wasn't lying to Alex. This isn't putting in face time for anyone else. But Paul has built his career — slow and steady will one day win the race — by taking Victor's benevolence and mentorship and trying to be the most diligent and loyal guy in Hollywood. He hasn't hopped from job to job. And, no matter how many times he's wanted to, he has never abandoned a gig or a crappy fix-it job on someone else's shitty script for a better opportunity.

If he's allowed Victor to always count on him in ways that make other people in the writers' room think he's weak and Craig think he isn't any good, Paul has done it because he knows that one day, Victor will pay that debt. The agreement between them is mostly unspoken and deals with Victor may smell faintly of sulphur, but Paul believes in his choices. He's been part of Victor's nearly inner circle for a long time. He trusts the man, such as it is, and the dividends are finally starting to come due. Paul being allowed to write for Zach is going to change everything.

Which means Paul has to hold up his end of the bargain more now than ever before. Victor isn't kind in a way other people easily understand. So keeping everyone human and happy has always been one of Paul's jobs.

Alex shows up later than Paul expects, apparently happy to nab a beer from the kitchen and drift through a party where he runs no risk of being the man of the hour. He's wearing a plain black T-shirt and jeans. When he slides out onto the small second floor balcony with the smokers he looks almost like what he once was — a random P.A. none of them had ever noticed before. But now, in a room full of people, no one can look at anyone else.

That magnetism a strange gift, one that Liam and Natalie both have as well. Everyone on the show possesses an eerie charisma of one form or another. Paul's always wondered what that's like; to trail such a wake or to expend whatever massive energy output it takes to dampen it. He assumes he'll never know. Having watched Alex wrestle with it in himself these last months makes him almost glad of it.

Alex's silhouette through the glass, the orange embers of cigarettes, and the lights of the city combine to tell too much of the story of L.A. It's a place for fallen things, Paul's family had warned him when he'd first come out here. He can't imagine what Alex's must have said.

He reaches for the door handle but thinks the better of it. Alex is a big boy and can get his bearings at a party without Paul's help. They'll find each other later, he's sure.

♦

The room is easy, no one is trying to impress, and Alex feels unexpectedly comfortable. He's aware of Paul's steady presence as he moves around the house and feels safe in the knowledge that no one here wants more of his time, attention, or body than he's willing to give. He doesn't have to be on, and that's a relief; other people are never easy. In that regard, he finds L.A. harder than Indiana. Alex is fairly certain everyone in this city is always auditioning or rehearsing, no matter what they do or what they aspire to.

Alex doesn't understand it. If L.A. teaches anyone anything, it's supposed to be the scope of dreams and the limits of opportunity. He transcended the limits of his own life, the one he was raised in, the day he got in his car and drove to L.A. For him possibility should have ended there. But everything that's happened in the last year is a new sort of vastness. What's happening to him now isn't supposed to happen to anyone.

He has another drink and, as the room watches him, he watches Paul.

♦

Alex finds him alone, eventually, in the kitchen, restocking the beer in the fridge.

"I'm glad you came," Paul tells him, offering him a cold bottle.

Alex takes it. "Thanks," he says, both for the drink and for Paul meaning it.

Paul regards him in silence for a moment. "How are you?"

"Here." He doesn't know any other way to articulate his current state of being in all its forms.

Paul laughs, loud and surprised like he sometimes does. Alex grins back at him. Paul's smile stays and his eyes meet Alex's and linger. Alex knows he's doing the stupid squinchy-eyed thing that so many people apparently find attractive. He turns his head away a little, not sure what he should be expecting or wanting out of tonight yet.

"Hey, no." Paul raises his hand and presses two fingertips, dry and warm, against Alex's temple. He turns Alex's head back until their eyes meet again. With a question in his eyes he drops his hand slowly, from Alex's face to his side. Alex knows it's to give him a chance to stop him if he wants.

He doesn't, and Paul's hand settles on his waist.

"Party's out there," he says and tips his head back towards the living room. "Want to go join?"

"Not really," Alex says. Not only because there are people out there. He'd much rather stay here — with Paul — and see what happens next. It's a new sort of thrill, not one he's used to at all. But it doesn't feel bad.

Paul smiles at him, delighted and maybe a little surprised. "Well then." His fingers tighten on Alex's waist and he draws Alex closer to him. There are fine striations of brown and blue in his gray eyes. As Alex watches, Paul's eyes dip to his mouth.

It's not an invitation Alex has any interest in saying no to. But before he can do anything about it, one of the grips appears in the kitchen doorway, laughing and saying something to someone over his shoulder. Alex jumps back; Paul lets his hand drop from Alex's waist. Alex appreciates it. There are witnesses to nearly everything Alex does now; whatever is starting with Paul, he'd rather not have an audience.

The grip doesn't seem to realize he's interrupted anything. Paul leans close again and whispers in Alex's ear, "Now do you want to go back out there?"

Alex nods. Paul takes his hand and leads him out of the kitchen. Alex hides his smile in his shoulder.

♦

Paul keeps a hold of Alex's hand until they're at the side of the room. There he tugs him a little closer, sliding his hand back around Alex's waist. He starts moving his hips to the beat.

"Really?" Alex cocks his head questioningly, though he doesn't step away. "We *just* almost got busted in your kitchen."

"Do you mind?"

Alex shakes his head, looking perhaps a little surprised at himself as he does.

"Then c'mon. I know you can," Paul tells him. He puts his other hand on Alex's waist too. No one who can control their face and body they way Alex does when he acts can't dance.

Alex smiles that small, dangerous smile of his and puts his hands on Paul's shoulders. "Okay."

Game on. Alex moves beautifully, easy and strong to the beat. Paul can feel the power of him under his hands, the physicality of his magnetism. It's extraordinary. Paul imagines this is why Alex doesn't like to speak; maybe he simply doesn't need to, his body a more faithful storyteller.

When Paul had invited Alex to this party, he'd entertained vague fantasies of getting to talk with him meaningfully and maybe making out with him in a corner. But Paul has been thinking about Alex as desirable and intriguing for so long that with him in his arms now Paul wants nothing more than to go big with that desire. He can't imagine a few kisses being enough.

Songs pass and they keep moving closer to each other until they're far too close. Paul hopes Alex knows he can do what he wants here; sure they're still being watched but it doesn't matter. This feels way too good, and Paul pulls them together until their thighs are brushing and his arms are snug around Alex's waist.

Their eyes keep catching in the dark. More than once Paul's gaze drops to Alex's mouth. Alex tightens his fingers on his side when it does, his eyes flickering between Paul's lips and his eyes. When the song shifts again to something heavy and slow their foreheads brush together. Alex's nose touches Paul's cheek.

They both hesitate, and Paul sways in a little before he steps back and asks, "Do you want another drink?"

"Sure," Alex says, breathless like the movies.

"I'll be right back." Paul finds his hand and squeezes it before threading his way back through the room.

♦

As the night goes on, the crowd thins out and Paul and Alex switch from beer to mixed drinks. It's one of those innocuous, unspoken things Gemma would define as a sign, and Alex is pretty sure is them egging each other on, step by tiny step. Whether that's towards oblivion or a hookup, he refuses to let himself be sure.

They drift apart and together over and over, never dancing again. Sometimes they stand too close, Paul whispering harmless conversation in his ear, and sometimes too far, Alex calling something sharp and funny across a room, not for the purpose of saying *I'm still watching you* but rather, *you're all I can see.*

Which is not good. Alex is smart enough to know that as cool and hot and seemingly lovely as Paul is, a lot of Alex's feeling towards him is likely rooted only in timing, or the fact that Paul never changed the way he spoke to Alex when his circumstances changed. Both magic and normal are sexy.

But his opportunities are far and few between in his new life of look but don't touch anything. Yes, maybe it would be awkward or dumb, but on some level he knows that Paul's just a writer. If things go wrong for some inexplicable reason, he's not someone with any authority over Alex, and he's not someone he has to see on a daily basis. There's no reason that a drunk and friendly grope could somehow cause more drama than everything that's happened to all of them in the last year.

If he has this opportunity, he's damn well taking it.

◆

Paul starts to tidy up at one. It's not as harsh as turning on the lights to kick everyone out, but it does the job. His hands are full of other people's beer bottles when Alex finds him again but says nothing. Paul asks him to stay, despite every instinct telling him that he has to let Alex run the show. But this is, after all, his house, and Alex can perhaps have no power over him if Paul doesn't invite him in first.

Alex nods, and for a moment says nothing. Then, "Do you want some help?"

Together, the task goes faster. When they're more or less done, Paul is happy to show the last stragglers out the door and note that Alex's is the only car remaining besides his. Paul smiles to himself. He won't have to deal with hungover colleagues coming to retrieve vehicles in the morning.

He turns around from the door to see Alex halfway up the stairs, a hand on each banister and with a smile far more shy than the rest of his choices suggest.

"Are you inviting me upstairs in my own house?" Paul laughs.

Alex backs up the flight, disappearing out of sight behind the wall when he gets there.

Paul bolts up the stairs after him, laughing again when he finds Alex still hidden behind the wall and biting his lip.

"What?" Paul asks,

"I'm an idiot," Alex says. "Which one's the bedroom?"

"The one with the cat," Paul murmurs. But instead of opening the door he closes the distance, savoring again the bare inch he has over Alex and rubbing their faces together until they slide into a kiss neither can be blamed for.

He snakes one arm around Alex's waist and hitches him closer, his other arm stretching out to fumble for the door.

It opens, and Todd darts out with a sharp meow and runs down the stairs.

"He has to stay in for parties," Paul says, breaking the kiss but still breathing right against Alex's mouth, "else he drinks all the beer."

Alex laughs, crinkles his eyes up, and this time doesn't look away.

Paul kisses him again, slides his hands up under Alex's shirt, and murmurs into his mouth, "Should have done this that first time I caught you with Nick."

Alex shivers. "But then what would have happened?"

"Everything." Paul turns them so he can back Alex into his bedroom and skims his hands up his sides until Alex takes the hint and gets his shirt off.

"Fuck," Paul breathes at a body somewhat more built than he expects. He's wiry without being delicate and freckled *everywhere*. "You are beautiful."

"Don't," Alex says, but it's distracted and out of breath. Paul lets it go. Alex thanks him by grabbing his face and shoving his tongue in his mouth. Eventually he pulls back, worrying his teeth over Paul's bottom lip as he goes.

They pause briefly, looking at each other, taking stock of the moment and what's about to happen. Paul hurries to lose his shirt too.

"What do you want? What do you like?" he asks, fascinated by the prospect of being able to make Alex speak. But Alex doesn't answer, distracted by tracing his fingers up Paul's stomach and over his abs.

"Jesus," Alex says.

Paul doesn't say anything. It's nice to be appreciated but it's not like he works out for reasons of sanity and health.

Alex hums and scratches his nails across Paul's side.

Paul stills his hand, squeezing it in his own. "Get naked," he says. "Let me take you to bed already."

There's a moment where Alex falters. It's small, barely there, but Paul sees it, and it makes him doubt the assumptions he has about Alex's history. He does his best to brush past the doubt and the guilt it brings him. If nothing else, it can wait until tomorrow.

But then Alex is naked, in his bed, propped against the headboard, and saying something smart about

Paul not moving fast enough to take either of them anywhere.

Alex takes himself in hand and jacks himself slowly. As Paul gets out of his jeans he tries to remember what it was to be that young and fearless and terrified.

He gives up, instead crawling onto his bed and licking a long stripe up the pale and freckled inside of Alex's left thigh. He holds eye contact with him as best he can and smiles when Alex shoves a hand into his hair.

When he doesn't drag Paul's mouth to his dick, Paul has to take a moment to remind himself of *twenty, famous and odd*, before saying, "Do you want to fuck my mouth?"

"God yes." Alex lets go of Paul's hair to go up on his knees.

Paul, in turn, slides onto the floor. His own knees will survive. He blinks up at Alex, coltish and powerful and strange above him.

"So, show me what you've got," Paul teases. That's enough for Alex to get his hand back in Paul's hair and feed his dick into his mouth.

Alex is gentle with it at first, but it doesn't seem to be out of caution. Paul does his best to work with Alex's rhythm and swirl his tongue around the head of his cock, as Alex is, quite obviously, uncertain and trying to read his reactions.

He puts a hand to Alex's hip to push him back briefly. "Whatever you do," he says, his lips wet with him now, "don't take your eyes off us." Paul dips his head back in, blinking up through his lashes at Alex, as he wraps his lips around the head of his dick and sucks hard.

◆

Alex cannot believe this is happening. But his own shock has become such a constant state of affairs he's starting wonder how severely his perception has been altered. If his fairytale has stunted him, though, he's grateful for it, especially if it'll mean he'll last a little longer because *oh God*. There is no way he's going to be able to keep his eyes open — right now, he's not convinced he's not going to tip over — and Paul's going to have to live with that.

At least that's what Alex thinks until Paul pinches the inside of his thigh sharply every time his eyes roll and flutter closed. He wants to be more outside of his own thoughts than he is, but Paul's not letting him.

"Too much," he eventually manages to choke out.

Paul pulls off. "Good." His fingers knead at Alex's ass and delve between his cheeks.

That's the point Alex decides he should probably freak out except for the fact that it feels spectacular, fantasy and reality colliding perfectly. Alex takes a deep breath and runs his hand through Paul's hair. One more sharp learning curve with no warning won't kill him. This one feels better than most, and Paul doesn't even push. Literally.

Eventually Paul drops his hands from Alex's ass and takes his cock back into his mouth. Alex smiles to himself and hardens his gaze. That's all about self-satisfaction until Paul's eyes go liquid, and, wow, that's a lot.

"Fuck, you have no idea, do you?" Paul pulls back enough to say.

Alex keens.

"Spoiled," Paul says, jacking him hard and sliding his other hand between his own legs.

"Yeah," is all Alex manages until his mouth becomes frozen open in pleasure in those few moments before he comes across Paul's face. His stomach muscles contract so hard with the force of it he suspects he'll be feeling it tomorrow.

When Alex falls onto his side on Paul's bed they're both a mess, Paul scrambles up to rub every inch of himself against Alex, and they kiss wet and messy, filthy and desperate. Somehow it's this moment, not when he came, that Alex feels like is the first time he's ever really understood sex. He sees his ability to form thoughts and judge circumstances for a brief instant before it leaves him.

Alex flips them, startling Paul. Alex cackles. "High school wrestling," he says before he slides down Paul's body, scraping teeth over muscle.

"Oh my God," Paul laughs.

The blowjob isn't expert, but Alex can't help but award himself points for enthusiasm. Paul doesn't seem to mind, either. He gasps when Alex moans around him and, when Alex's fingers stray up to Paul's nipples, his back arches off the bed with it.

♦

Alex and Paul lie together, tangled on their sides, foreheads touching. They stare at each other, and it feels magical and terrifying.

Alex's brain comes back online slowly, swimming up through the haze of pleasure. He wishes it wouldn't, even if there's a relief in taking himself back under control. He's cold and needs to pull up a blanket, put his shirt back on, or press closer into the heat of Paul's body. But he has no idea which of those options is appropriate. He's naked and in another man's bed, anxious with uncertainty and vulnerability. This is part of learning curve, but as much as Alex wants everything his life has to offer now, he has no idea how to move through this moment.

"Hey. Are you okay?" Paul's voice is gentle and low. He gropes between them on the mattress for Alex's hand.

Alex is more than okay, though he doesn't have the words for what, exactly, he is right now. He opens his fingers so Paul can interlace his.

♦

Paul smiles. Watching Alex blink in his bed, heavy-eyed, strong-limbed and — for once — relaxed, feels like a privilege. Instinct and Alex's eyes tell him this is a rare moment and, as with all rare and fragile things, care should be taken and gratitude given.

Alex fidgets with Paul's hands. When he finds the ridge of scar at his wrist, his eyebrows pull in a little, and he presses his thumb hard against it. His fingers go searching for its twin on Paul's other arm. "Where did you get these?"

Paul is not remotely prepared to answer that question, and the shock of it throws him. He doesn't think of them that often.

"Where do you think?" He lets the South Carolina come through in his voice more than it usually does. Alex's eyes flick up to his face. He doesn't look contrite, merely surprised. Paul should be offended; the rudeness of the question in any circumstance aside, it's the worst pillow talk he's ever encountered.

Instead, he's fascinated. It's almost an act of vulnerability for Alex to touch Paul's wrists like this after putting himself in Paul's hands; to admit, in such a bald attempt to right the scales, how badly tipped they'd been.

Paul wants to keep doing this — pillow talk, sleeping together, spending time with each other — to see all the ways Alex will find to shock him and all the ways he can keep Alex in his hands.

When Alex says nothing and the silence stretches out, Paul kisses him again.

♦

Alex begins to feel the first stirrings of claustrophobia. It's not an unfamiliar feeling — it comes in crowds and at events and sometimes from being in front of the camera — but here he has no defenses against it, not with the additional vulnerabilities of being naked and in Paul's bed.

He pulls back and sits up. "Where's your bathroom?"

Paul points over his shoulder at the door.

"No identifying animals?"

Paul shakes his head. "Not this time."

In the bathroom, Alex blinks against the brightness. He adds the fan for the blissful wash of white noise. It doesn't shut up his brain the way being with Paul had, but it at least makes it harder to concentrate on the roil of thoughts that has started up again.

He washes his face because he needs to and because he feels like he should do something other than hide in here while he collects himself. When that doesn't take long enough, he fidgets with his hair, which is a predictable, glorious mess. He breathes deeply until he feels sure of the limits of his own skin again.

Once he feels stable he runs a washcloth under warm water for Paul. His face is even more of a mess, not that he seems to care. Which is hot in its own way.

When Alex returns to the bedroom, Paul is lying on his side under the covers with his arm crooked under his head. "Stay the night?" he asks.

Alex reaches the bed and remembers that he knows how to be brave, because he wants this too. "I would have anyway," he says and tosses Paul the washcloth.

"Thanks," he says with a surprised breath. After he's scrubbed his face he adds, "Just wanted to be sure."

Alex slides under the blankets and into Paul's warm and welcoming arms. For the first time since his arrival in Los Angeles, he's sure he's made the right choice.

6

Paul wakes up first. Alex's face in sleep is lovely; younger than it looks when he's awake, relaxed and at ease except for the way his brow furrows when Paul disentangles their limbs. As much as he would love to stay in bed with him, Paul remembers his brief flight the night before and wants to give him whatever space he'll need when he wakes up.

He leaves the bedroom door cracked open and goes downstairs to tackle the last of the cleanup from the party. Todd is sprawled blissfully in a puddle of midmorning sunshine, and Paul stops on his way to the dishwasher to rub his belly with a foot.

Most of the mess left in the kitchen is dealt with by the time he hears movement from the bedroom. He takes a last private moment to smile to himself before the footsteps start down the stairs.

He turns around to see Alex hovering at the bottom of the flight, one hand on the railing.

"Good morning," Paul says. Alex bites his lip before he smiles. He's in his clothes from last night but still barefoot. It's absolutely adorable.

"Hi," Alex says. He sounds almost shy again.

"How did you sleep?"

"Are you always so polite to your guests?" Alex asks as he leaves his perch by the stairs and comes into the kitchen.

"Southern hospitality," he says with a shrug. "Do you want anything to eat?"

"No. Thanks." Alex steps into his space and kisses him.

Paul expects a quick peck; instead, he gets pushed up against the counter with Alex's hands in Paul's hair and his tongue in his mouth. Alex swings so quickly between shyness and boldness that can't get a handle on what to expect from him. He's fascinated.

He grabs Alex's hips to hold him there. When Alex tries to pull away, he follows. Alex's eyes are unnervingly dark with the rest of him so fair. He blinks them open as he presses a last, soft kiss to Paul's mouth, and they catch and drink the sunlight in a way that makes Paul need to take a breath.

Alex asks, "Can I invite you to take a shower in your own bathroom too?"

Paul laughs and tightens his hands on Alex's hips. "Yeah. *Yes.*"

◆

Paul's body is glorious — lean but thoroughly muscled, with good abs and strong thighs. Alex savors the opportunity to get his hands on it again, this time in the light and under soap and water. He marvels at himself as he does. He's never spent time with someone like this before. Never had anyone he wanted to spend time with. Or anyone he trusted.

Paul washes his back for him. Alex closes his eyes and rests his forehead against the cool tile while Paul's hands, firm and sure, knead their way across his skin. His brain is still churning, wanting to analyze every one of Paul's movements and find the correct response, but it quiets as Paul keeps touching him.

Alex feels lazy, heavy with the heat and with arousal, but eventually he pushes Paul out of the way and rinses the last of the shampoo out of his hair before reaching for the tap.

"I should get going," he says regretfully and shoots Paul a smile when he pouts.

Paul presses his fingers to Alex's naked side before grabbing towels for them both.

"Thanks," Alex says, as he starts scrubbing out his hair.

"Anytime." Paul kisses him again before wrapping himself in his own towel and disappearing into the bedroom.

Alex feels satisfied with himself as he gets dressed. The lessons Margaret and Victor both repeat to him of storytelling and fame — leave everyone wanting more — apply to real life, too.

Paul teases him at the door when Alex worries about having to go out in last night's clothes and then offers to lend him something. Alex makes a face at him and turns him down. Leaving Paul's house wearing Paul's clothes would leave even less doubt as to what he's done.

Paul holds Alex around the waist. "Can I call you?"

Alex doesn't know what to say, but Paul seems determined to wait him out as Alex flicks his eyes over his face. The answer is obviously yes, but Alex feels paralyzed at the idea. Other people learn this part of the process in high school, but he's never dated anyone and doesn't know what happens next. Eventually he nods.

They trade numbers, and Alex has his hand on the doorknob ready to go when Paul catches him for one last kiss.

If Alex puts his dumb victory playlist on and sings along as he drives home, there's no one around to judge.

Gemma is worried and loud when he gets back to their apartment, even though he texted her the night before. She wants to know *who* and if it was a good idea with the *you know…and all* because she can almost never bring herself to say the word *fame* without whispering. Mostly, she doesn't even do that.

She also wants to know *what*, in a blow-by-blow (and, oh, how accurate that request is) way, until Alex retreats into the shower again to get space from her. He feels ridiculous, he only just got out of the shower at Paul's and is hardly dry from that. But desperate times and all that. He's fairly sure that, unlike his bedroom, she won't barge into the bathroom.

He stares at the dingy and cracked tiling of the shower stall where a splash of plum memorializes one of Gemma's more unfortunate hair color experiments. He's going to have to look for a new place soon. It's way overdue, but he's used to this crappy little apartment; he's already had enough change for a lifetime.

Alex's assumptions about privacy prove wrong. Gemma does have the audacity to join him in the bathroom while he's under the water. He's glad their current shower curtain isn't clear like the last one, which mold and mildew destroyed; their apartment is inherently gross and he and Gemma are both terrible housekeepers.

Even with the shelter of the opaque curtain, Alex feels uncomfortable. He doesn't want her here as he checks his body for marks. Alex feels like there should be some, but there aren't. If she doesn't leave soon, he's not sure he can stop himself from talking to her about the roil in his head regarding last night.

"What are you doing in there? Your hair was wet when you came in," she demands.

He speaks as authoritatively as he can. "I will have this conversation with you later."

"Why not now? Is it because you need more private time?"

"I am late to brunch and in the shower, not trying to jerk off," Alex says sharply. Shawna had invited him earlier in the week, and if he doesn't get there soon she's going to want to know why he was delayed. Alex doesn't want to answer any questions about that at all.

He shuts the water off aggressively. "Tonight, okay? Sunday. HBO and all that?" He holds his breath as he waits for Gemma to retreat. Amazingly, she does.

Paul arrives early for weekly brunch with his friends. The house had felt too empty after Alex's departure. He tells himself to stop moping over him being gone. Getting used to having someone around after only one night is not going to lead anywhere good.

Besides, brunch brings with it friends, mimosas, and the prospect of his dog. Beau is still in Craig's possession, though it's been months since they last fought about him. Thank God for restaurants with outdoor patios.

When Paul gets there he crouches next to his chair to rub Beau's ears. He's carrying on a conversation half with Craig and half with Josh on the other side of the table when Shawna says, bright and excited, "My darling Alexander, you made it!"

"Yeah, sorry, couldn't find a parking spot."

Paul's heart jolts. That's Alex's voice and he's here, in one of the last places Paul would have expected to encounter him.

He gives Beau a last distracted pat between the ears and gets back up in his seat. Alex stares at him for an instant before he turns, obviously tense, to say something to Shawna.

Alex is no longer wearing the T-shirt he left Paul's house in. He's replaced it with a tight dark green V-neck. Sunglasses are shoved up on top of his head over a knit beanie that hides at least most of his distinctive hair. Paul wants nothing more than to get up from his chair and round the table and kiss him, but even if Alex weren't someone who gets an enormous amount of attention in public, they haven't talked about this. They haven't talked about anything. Whatever happens here needs to be Alex's call.

Since Alex looks even more startled than he usually does, his call is, apparently, to pretend last night didn't happen. Paul understands there are any number of good reasons for that. But he wishes they were at least sitting next to each other.

Shawna puts a hand on Alex's shoulder until he sits down. "Hey, so, I think you know most of these guys —"

"I'm Brian." He interrupts her because that's the kind of thing Brian does.

Paul watches as Alex turns to look at him, a faint frown creasing his eyebrows as he judges the weedy-looking guy with the obnoxious moustache. Paul approves of the reaction. Brian goes around the rest of the table introducing everyone. He ends with "and that's Paul, Craig, and Divorce Dog."

"Excuse me?" Alex asks.

"Honey, there have been custody battles waged over actual children of actual marriages far less ugly." Brian says.

Alex's eyes go from Beau, whose ears have perked up in hope of a new friend, to Paul. Alex stills for an instant before he gives Paul a small, sweet smile.

"His name is Beau," Paul tells him, after a pointed look at Brian.

Alex leans out of his chair and offers the dog a hand to sniff. "Hi, Beau."

"If you had been subjected to their shrieking on the matter, he'd be Divorce Dog to you too," Josh supplies helpfully.

Paul laughs. So does Craig. Alex sits up again, smiles sharply, and focuses on his menu.

♦

Alex is grateful when the food finally arrives. It gives him something to concentrate on other than not doing what he wants to do, which is to share a private smile with Paul and nudge their feet together under the table.

If the damn dog (he's a really cute dog) is anything to go by, Craig is the same ex who walked out on Paul the same day Paul walked in on him and Nick; the day Alex's life changed forever. He can't help but take a moment to look over Craig appraisingly. Attractive, athletic, clearly a bit of a gym rat, and a couple years older than Paul if the lines on his sun-weathered face and the little bit of grey in his short black hair are anything to go by.

That they're all at brunch together the morning after he and Paul have hooked up is bizarre, spooky, and awkward. Alex isn't particularly superstitious, but he is starting to wonder what it is that Paul's doing to him — or what that one day over a year ago is doing to all of them.

As the conversation spins around him he feels increasingly out of place. Not because of what he does or how many people know his face. But because he's twenty and lives in a tiny apartment with a roommate he met obsessing on television shows via the internet. He still can't order a drink in public.

Alex vaguely remembers that Paul turned thirty — there'd been a party; any excuse for a party at work is taken — a few months back. The table laughs over his and Craig's 'divorce,' and someone else starts talking about a play date they had with their nephews and starts showing photos around. As Alex passes the phone with the pictures of two little toddlers along the table he feels miserably young.

Young and impermanent. Paul has history with Craig; however painful their breakup was, they have a dog and seem easy enough together now. Alex wonders if, like the story of his fame, his story with Paul will be about how he didn't exist and was never supposed to, and, one day, how he didn't anymore.

He's pulled out of his thoughts by someone yelling "cheese!" and laughing as they hand a phone to Paul, who starts typing on it. Twitter, or maybe Instagram, because someone else takes a picture of their plate and Paul is laughing about hashtags and *New mystery members of #TeamBrunch!*

Alex doesn't get caught in any of the pictures, for which he is grateful. It's hard enough to be in the world as it is. Margaret — with no small amount of exasperation — always assures him that he can go out for simple things like meals without the world ending. But it's hard to be stared at and interrupted on the street and harder still to be put on the internet he once loved so much too.

As the meal winds down Paul catches his eye more frequently. Alex doesn't know what to do, so he doesn't do anything.

In his car, he pulls his sunglasses down to see his phone over the top of them and texts Paul: *Sorry that was weird. It was good to see you.* The car starts to heat up as he waits for a reply. He turns the engine on to get the AC going.

What are the chances we both ended up at the same brunch?

Given Shawna, apparently pretty good, Alex texts back.

I didn't put her up to that.

I know.

Come over for dinner sometime this week? Paul asks.

Alex bites his lip to check his growing smile. *When?*

Friday?

◆

Monday morning Alex feels like he's dragging. He's not alone; the whole of *Fourth*'s crew seems slow and cranky. For Alex, though, it's not because he's tired, but because he's distracted. A weekend without alone time is not a weekend. And now he's back at work he both wants to run into Paul and wants some distance to collect his thoughts. They spent the night together and now have a dinner date; one more new thing in Alex's perpetually changing life.

Liam, meanwhile, is working his last nerve. He seems to think the solution to everyone's Monday blahs is to actively badger them between takes about how awesome their weekend must have been for them to feel this awful.

Alex gets what Liam is going for, even if he wishes Liam would take his enthusiasm somewhere else. Liam can grate, but he's also one of the people Alex feels easiest around, an unexpected outcome of the way they have to interact in front of the camera. But Alex doesn't want to tell anyone about hooking up with Paul, and he particularly doesn't want to tell Liam about it. Not only is he a gossip, he's casually graphic about anyone and everyone's sex lives regardless of his own involvement in them. Alex doesn't feel able to be casually graphic about his own sex life at this point.

Alex isn't actually sure he wants that to change, either. He likes having a secret that's actually, he hopes, a good thing. A delicious thing. A thing he wants more of. But it's so goddamn distracting. Which is bad. There's work to be done, and the cameras never miss distraction. What Alex needs to be thinking about isn't his relationship with Paul, but the relationship between his character on *Fourth*, Zach, and Liam's James.

"So I heard a thing," Liam says in between scenes. He bounces a little on the balls of his feet in front of Alex's chair, where Alex has his headphones on and is trying to refocus before the next material.

"What?"

Liam either doesn't hear the annoyance or chooses to ignore it. "Apparently someone had a very good time at the party on Saturday."

Alex gives him a glare that Liam pays not the least attention to. That's frustrating if unsurprising. For as good and expressive an actor as he is, Liam is often awful at picking up other people's body language. Alex is going to have to resort to chasing him off with words.

"There were a lot of people at the party. I'm sure somebody enjoyed it," he says.

"Were one of those somebodies?" Liam asks, scrubbing his hand through the back of his slightly too shaggy curls.

"What I do in private is not your business. Or anyone else's."

"Dude, hanging all over each other at a party with half the crew around is not private."

"Liam —" Alex starts. They have always had very different levels of comfort with aspects of their lives being made public. Alex wants to make very clear what is and is not acceptable for Liam to talk about Alex doing anywhere near a camera. Before he can get any more words out though, Liam's eyes light up.

"It wasn't just the dancing! You hooked up with him!"

Alex drops his head into his hands. How can Liam be so bad at social cues and yet pick up on *that?*

"Don't be like that! This is amazing! Paul is awesome! Alex! How was it?"

"How do you know it was Paul?" Alex hisses from between his fingers.

"I have sources."

Alex tips his head back and stares at the ceiling in lieu of committing murder. He wonders who talked and why. Given that half the crew had been there, the list of suspects — and motives — is discouragingly long.

"So how was it? Is he good?"

Alex snaps his head back down. "No!"

"No, it wasn't any good?" Liam's eyes are wide, concerned, and utterly insincere.

"No, I am not having this conversation with you!"

Liam pouts.

Alex laughs. "Do you think that's going to work?"

"One of these days, something's going to get you to crack. When was the last time you even got laid?"

Just then they get called back to start shooting again.

"Working now!" Alex sings. He kicks up from the chair to push past him.

Liam jogs after him. "We're not done with this."

"Find someone else to bother!"

When lunch comes, Liam decides to follow Alex's advice and find someone else to pester. *The Fourth Estate* shoots on the lot's least far-flung stage. It's easy enough for him to jog past the courtyard with the shitty coffee place and go poke around the boxy office building where *Fourth's* writers have been cruelly, yet conveniently, consigned.

He never gets there. Victor intercepts him, hooking elbows with Liam as their paths cross on the asphalt.

"And what are you doing?" Victor purrs as they walk.

Liam laughs. That voice is Victor's bored voice, and Liam — more or less like everyone else on *Fourth* — serves at the pleasure of his amusement.

"I was about to seek out some gossip, but apparently you've come to deliver instead?" he asks hopefully.

"Not likely. Does anyone know where you are?"

"Crew's on lunch. We're on lunch. And they totally have to lay track before the next shot. I have time." Liam's not supposed to stray so far from set in costume without a P.A. at hand to fetch him back, but if he can't help himself, he at least tries to choose his moments. He doesn't like disappointing Victor.

Victor doesn't agree. "Mmmmhmmm."

"Alex wanders off all over the place all the time."

"Liam, Alex is a cat," Victor says in a voice that's supposed to make Liam focus but is, in actuality, as interesting and distracting as nearly everything else. "He knows where and when his dinner is served. You, on the other hand, are a dog that chases squirrels in the neighbor's yard for days at a time."

"Ow. Ow! That is harsh." Liam laughs and presses his free hand to his heart.

"Would Carly tell me I'm wrong?"

"Fine." Liam concedes. His girlfriend and Victor agree on most things, especially those that regard him. "But you still want to know the thing I was on my way to find out about."

"Really? And what's that?" Victor's voice is gentle but Liam knows he has not yet succeeded in making his case.

"Alex and Paul."

Victor squints. "Alex and Paul what?"

"Sitting in a tree, K-I-S-S-I-N-G," Liam hisses with glee.

Victor stops dead, causing Liam to trip over his untied shoelaces. "Repeat that."

"Alex and Paul. Isn't that totally awesome?"

Victor stares at him.

"Is that not totally awesome?" Liam deflates a little.

"Who told you and who knows?"

"Alex confirmed it by yelling at me when I mentioned half the crew saw them hanging all over each other at Paul's on Saturday."

"Happy Monday to me," Victor murmurs. He disentangles himself from Liam and pats his cheek.

"Be a good boy and eat lunch. I'm going to ruin someone's day."

◆

Paul's glad to stay back when everyone else in the writers' room goes to eat. He's been distracted all morning and the usual banter and grumbling of the office is getting on his nerves. With the place to himself, he can sit with his laptop on his thighs, his feet up on someone else's chair, and his mind on Alex.

Suddenly someone touches him. Paul jumps, but it's only Victor, lifting the headphones away from Paul's ears.

"Lunch time," he announces.

"Jesus, Victor." Paul puts his feet back on the ground, his heart pounding. "What's up?"

Victor drops the headphones unceremoniously onto a table. No apology for scaring the shit out of Paul is forthcoming. Paul's pretty sure Victor wouldn't even understand why there should be.

"Come with me," he says. Paul follows obediently as Victor sets out on the long way around to catering. Once the hallway is relatively clear Victor says, "So. You and Alex."

"How do you know about that?" Paul is surprised — although he probably shouldn't be — that word has already managed to reach Victor.

"Liam told me."

"Liam wasn't there."

"And?" Victor asks.

"Oh." Paul has long had — from multiple sources — more information on Victor's relationship with Liam than he wants. Paul has never been able to make sense of it. Victor's magnetism, he gets. And Liam is pretty and can be charming, when he wants something. But how they could possibly work together is baffling. Mostly, Paul tries not to think about too much.

"Oh. Yes. Exactly." Victor mocks; Victor always mocks. "Would you like to explain to me why you felt the need to take out your dysfunctional singlehood on Alex of all people? He's ten years younger than you."

Paul is affronted. Usually he's fine with Victor's encyclopedic knowledge of the one-night stands and personal debacles of his staff. But Victor's desire to comment on this suddenly strikes Paul as even less appropriate than the Liam thing.

"I didn't take anything out on him," Paul protests. "Alex is a big boy, he can handle himself."

"When it comes to this, I wish he didn't have a need to. Do not fuck with him."

Paul has dealt with Victor continuously for years, ever since he first hired him as an intern on a show now long gone but still much loved. Still, Paul feels a little thrill of animal fear at that particular tone. Not that he's inclined to give into it. Most things with Victor are a test anyway.

"It's not like that," he says easily. "It was good. It *is* good."

Victor looks skeptical. "This is not all in the past tense?"

"We've got a date on Friday."

"Do you now?"

"Yeah. He's coming over for dinner."

"You're serious right now." Victor sounds appalled.

Paul gives a little shrug and refrains from reminding Victor that he's known Alex a while. Or that it was Victor himself who assigned Alex to Paul. This isn't just a blowjob and a bucket of inappropriate workplace romance. Even if he is self-aware enough to know it's definitely all that too.

Victor narrows his eyes. "All right," he says finally. "This could be good."

Paul is amused, now that he's sure he's not getting shouted at, how everyone is always merely a character in Victor's world.

Victor goes on. "You're way more functional when you're not alone —"

"Thanks, Victor," Paul says. Because *really*.

"It's true; don't start. And I'd worry a lot less about Alex if he wasn't single."

"What are you worried about Alex for?"

"Many, many things." Victor nods to himself. "All right. But be careful of him. He has his own mind. And you front well, but we both know you were a mess long before Craig and you're still a mess now."

"Once again, *thank* you." There are days when Paul can't believe someone hasn't hauled off and hit Victor long ago. Despite the debt Paul owes him, this is one of them.

"I came to find you to yell at you, you know" Victor's voice gentles.

"I know," Paul says. "It was hard to miss."

"I feel like I should go yell at Alex instead."

"Are you going to?" Paul asks, some mixture of curious and cautious. He's not sure what Victor wants from Alex beyond better ratings. The possibilities are almost enough to make him worry.

"No. You know what you're getting into, or at least you should. And Alex…." Victor trails off before spreading his hands expansively. "Alex always lands on his feet."

By the time they get to catering, there's a bustle of people. Victor steps out of the flow just before the door. Paul stands aside with him.

"Did you know his birthday is on Thursday?" Victor asks.

Paul ducks his head, a show of self-consciousness for Victor's entertainment. "No, Victor, I didn't IMDB him." He had a while ago, back when Alex first started acting on *Fourth*, but Paul hadn't retained the birthday details. He's a little surprised that Alex is only turning twenty-one; he's far more sane and put together than Paul was a decade ago, although that may not be saying much.

Victor grabs his upper arm and squeezes it in approval, possession, and maybe even comfort. "You're terrible. Go eat. And tell him not to freak out about Liam."

◆

You didn't tell me your birthday was Thursday, Paul texts Alex later that afternoon as a way to open the topic.

He doesn't get a response for hours. *Keep forgetting, and I don't want it to be a thing.*

Actual convo for later? Paul tries.

I guess. It's not like I've never had tequila before.

If Friday's gonna be too hungover for you, just let me know.

No, Alex replies. *Looking forward.*

"Aren't you always," Paul murmurs before he sets his phone down and gets back to work.

9

The week between his hookup with Paul and their planned dinner date is long. Alex is working five full days in a row, which means he has very little time to do anything outside of work. The ten-hour turnaround he's guaranteed feels a lot shorter with each passing day. Besides work and sleep, he has a meeting and a few phone calls with Margaret. She's found a movie opportunity for him, if he's interested. Given how reluctantly he accepted the part on *Fourth*, he's surprised to find that he is. No TV show lasts forever, and whatever Alex is going to do with the rest of his life, he'd be foolish to limit his options.

Aside from work and meetings and planning, there's also Paul. Alex doesn't see him much on the lot but Paul texts him throughout the day and in the evening. He's never pushy or intrusive, but he is quietly insistent about his interest in Alex. It's yet another new experience to have someone other than Gemma to communicate with who is always willing if not eager to talk to him. Slowly and carefully, Alex lets himself enjoy it.

On Wednesday, Liam sheepishly admits that the gossip about Alex and Paul had made it to Victor…somehow. It's not hard to wring out of him that it was Liam himself who talked. Alex is thrilled when his reaction to that not-quite confession makes

Liam feel guilty enough to not badger him for a record forty-eight hours.

Thursday they make a big deal of his birthday on set. There's cake and booze and more attention than Alex wants, but less than there could be. Besides, the thought is nice. Birthdays were never a big deal when he was a kid.

Paul is there, to say hi or Tweet semi-officially for the show as is his habit. Alex isn't sure which, but decides to enjoy it regardless. He laughs and poses for a picture for him after Liam puts a plate of cake in his hands and pushes him forward. Paul winks when he lowers the phone. Alex smiles back. Even if it's not entirely a secret at this point — Liam is definitely giving Alex knowing looks around Paul's shoulder — it's still fun.

Alex's mom calls while he's driving home. Traffic as usual is awful; the mess that is the L.A. highway system never ceases to amaze Alex or to piss him off. But today it means they get to talk for forty-five minutes before Alex pulls into his parking lot and has to think about going inside and dealing with dinner.

But even then he sits in his car in for another fifteen minutes while they finish catching each other up on everything going on in their lives. At least, almost everything. If Alex can't figure out how to talk about Paul with Gemma or Liam, he sure as hell doesn't know how to talk about him with his mom.

Eventually he says *I love you too* and hangs up. It takes him a couple of tries before the odd homesickness for a place he never liked subsides and he feels ready to go inside. Every thought of home is hard for him. He misses it and his mom, even as he doesn't miss growing up in Indiana at all.

10

Friday drags as Fridays do. Paul is tired but excited by the time he finally gets home. It's only been a week since he had Alex here, but it seems longer. He can't wait to see him again away from work. Alex is clearly, maybe even calculatedly, a compendium of stories that he might one day tell Paul, but only if Paul very, *very* lucky. Now that the weekend's here Paul doesn't just want him, he wants to earn those tales.

He turns on the iPod player in its dock on the counter. He hums along as he cooks, stopping from time to time to take a disgruntled Todd down from the counter when he gets too bold in exploring what's on the stove. He's in the middle of setting the table when his phone buzzes with a text. It's Alex saying he's almost there.

Paul sees his car pull in the drive from the window and meets him at the door. He leans against the frame and grins when Alex gives a little wave as he comes up the walk.

"Do you always wear that hat out?" he asks. Alex has on the slouchy brown knit beanie from brunch.

Alex lifts the strap of his messenger bag over his head and sets it down by the door. "Only when there are people. A fan made it for me."

Paul shuts the door. "You wear a hat a fan made you to hide from your fans?"

"She was very sweet."

"You are very strange." Paul raises a hand with a questioning look on his face. When Alex doesn't back away he tugs the hat off, smiling at the way the red strands spike up in every direction. "I like you better without it."

When Alex doesn't step away, Paul combs his fingers through his hair, smoothing out the worst of the tangles. Alex watches him with that stillness of his until Paul curls his fingers around the back of his head. Alex takes the hint and leans in to kiss him.

Alex deepens the kiss and digs his hands into Paul's hips. That's new, and Paul smiles against his mouth. When Alex breaks the kiss he doesn't pull back, but leans his forehead against Paul's shoulder. Paul, after a shocked second, realizes that Alex wants a hug. He wraps his arms around Alex's back and is rewarded with the feel of Alex's arms around his waist. Alex's hair is soft against his cheek.

They stay like that for Paul doesn't know how long. Then Alex's stomach growls.

Paul chuckles. Alex laughs sheepishly and disentangles himself.

◆

"I never had Thai until I got to L.A.," Alex says as Paul passes him a plate. "I still can't get my mom to go out to anything other than Italian or Mexican when she's here."

Paul reaches for the corkscrew and tries to mask his excitement over Alex volunteering information. "I suggested Mexican one time when my family was visiting. There was an uproar," Paul says.

"God bless America." Alex watches Paul's hands as he opens the wine. "Land of the free, home of the narrow hick palate."

"How long did it take you to try sushi?" Paul asks. It's been a long time since anything other than meat and mashed potatoes had seemed unfamiliar and intimidating. But sushi had been his own personal barometer of *Oh, I'm in a big city now* way back when.

Alex wrinkles his nose. "Embarrassingly long. Gemma finally made me, which…awesome. Unlike the kimchi she told me was coleslaw."

"It's effectively coleslaw," Paul points out.

"I like it now! But it was my first night in L.A. and I was not prepared. She's sort of a food menace. Day two was kale chips, for which I was also not prepared."

◆

"Since you're officially legal now," Paul says as he pours wine for them both. "Also, happy birthday."

"Thanks." Alex takes a tentative sip of the wine. He's not used to being served dinner like this, not by a man interested, apparently, in wooing him. Business dinners with expensive food and wines he can't pronounce are becoming somewhat of a norm for him. But this — sharing food in someone's house — is not. Alex's life jumped from one extreme to the other. In those moments where he lands in the middle — in what might be called *normal* — he has no idea what to do. It can't be harder than anything else he's dealt with in his life.

"Have anything fun planned?" Paul asks.

Alex plays with the stem of his glass. "I got six different offers from three different clubs wanting to host a party for me for free. Great publicity for them. Strange for me. So, no." Not that he'd had any interest in a big industry party. There aren't enough people he'd want to invite. Or enough that he'd trust to even consider drinking around. No, that list for now is limited to Gemma. And now Paul.

"Doesn't sound too festive." Paul sits down across from Alex and reaches for his napkin. Belatedly, Alex remembers he's supposed to put his on his lap.

"Home, Gemma, and nothing to do for a night is plenty festive." He's been looking forward to it all week. Almost as much as this date. Which he should probably let Paul know. Alex nudges Paul's foot gently under the table. "So is this."

Talking to other people is something that Alex has struggled with his entire life. In Indiana, there was no one — besides his mom — who he could talk *to*. He was too different and life was too hard. Then he'd discovered the world that existed on the internet, outside of the bounds of Paragon. He'd met Gemma and other people who were, more or less, like him. Or at least were not like the people he had grown up with and who he saw at school and work every day.

Moving to L.A. had opened the world to him all over again. He didn't have to be wary of everyone he passed on the street or saw in the store. Except then he'd become J. Alex Cook and he did. Now the internet isn't a refuge anymore either. He has work to distract himself with, and Gemma of course, but aside from her — and Liam's gregarious attempts at bonding — he doesn't really have friends.

And now here's Paul, who can carry on a conversation in a way that makes Alex want to talk. He's smart and thoughtful and asks Alex questions about himself and offers information about his own life in a way that makes it clear that he's interested in Alex, not in scoring some sort of celebrity points.

It's scary, but no more so than the night when they'd hooked up. Giving someone information about himself is a way of giving them power over him. But he trusts Paul. Has, for some reason, ever since Paul caught him making out with Nick back before everything changed.

They have more in common than Alex expected. For one, their families. Paul talks about his mom and his sister, but makes no mention of his dad. For another, they both have work commitments beyond being average L.A. workaholics.

There's *Fourth*, obviously. Paul talks about some original pilot scripts he's working on, but doesn't seem to want to dwell on that topic. When Alex mentions *Paradise Square*, Paul eagerly asks about it.

"Historical drama," Alex tells him. "Immigrants and poverty and gangs and disease in Five Points. It's going to be filming in New York this winter. What days I'm needed is still getting sorted, but I wanted to see what it was like doing something I asked to be in."

Paul smiles. "You're spoiled for choice, aren't you?"

"Terror of the fairytale," Alex says. He tips his glass, watching the wine slide over the surface of it.

"Disney or Grimm?"

Alex considers it. "Andersen," he says.

"I look forward to seeing you in it. You'll be beautiful."

"The princess is always beautiful," Alex says derisively.

"Not in your fairytale. In New York."

"Is there a difference?"

Paul takes some time to think the answer through. "New York is temporary."

Alex traces his fingers over Paul's. "So am I." He doesn't know how to explain that that's not about the fact that he's not going to live forever, but that he hasn't been alive for longer. There's hardly a moment with Paul that he doesn't feel young and impermanent. "And so is the story."

Paul flips his palm up and smiles when Alex laces their fingers together. "You're going to have a busy winter. We're working on something now that'll put you on the road too."

Alex looks up from their intertwined hands, curious.

"Exteriors in D.C. And then some stuff here, but out on location."

"What's that?"

"So you know the thing where Zach can speak Farsi and *really* wants a story?"

"I don't know, tell me more about my character," Alex says drily.

"He's going to get himself into Iran. Details TBD. But word on the street is you're going to be spending some time in the desert this winter."

Alex knows he should be excited. New York, then D.C., then whatever southwest desert they'll use. It's more travel than he's ever done before, and he feels embarrassed and awkward. He's been to New York City and doesn't love it — the buildings are too high, the streets are too dirty, and there are too many lights and too much media attention. D.C. is completely new to him and therefore intimidating. Whatever he'll be doing in the desert won't be as bad, but it's one more unknown on top of the rest. Holding it all in his head at once is hard. Alex knows he should be grateful for these opportunities, but what he really wants is six months in L.A. with time to get used to all the other new things in his life. Like moving. And Paul.

"Well then," Alex says, holding up a pale, freckled arm. "I recommend buying stock in sunblock."

◆

They talk so much that dinner takes forever. Eventually, though, they manage to push back from the table. Alex is keenly aware of the heaviness of the moment, even if it's clear that they both know what they want.

"Am I taking you to the couch or the bedroom?" Paul asks as he takes their plates to the sink.

"Bed." At least in bed, Alex won't have to think. For now he distracts himself by crouching down to pet Todd who's flopped on the floor and looking hopefully at him.

After a moment, Alex looks up to see Paul watching him, an unreadable expression on his face.

"Sorry." Alex stands, not sure if he's overstepped somehow.

Paul shakes his head. "Glad you're making friends. Let's bring the wine upstairs, too, okay?"

◆

They're quiet on the stairs, and Alex feels no less awkward when they get to Paul's bedroom. The room, now that he's letting himself look at it, doesn't give much away: pale yellow walls, dark blue comforter, white trim around the windows and doors. The airiness of it is all California, but it lacks the blunt excess of his costars' massive and ugly houses. He likes it. Even so, the contrast to his own apartment remains immense and fills Alex with a certain degree of shame over his choices. Alex thinks about the nights Paul spends alone. He's fascinated by the mystery of normal adult life.

Paul sets down the wine and glasses on the little table next to the armchair that resides in the corner of the bedroom. The silence stretches, snapping only when he finally takes a step toward Alex.

Alex closes the rest of the gap and kisses him hard, pressing against him. Paul slips his hands into the back pockets of Alex's jeans and kneads at his ass.

"Clothes," Alex mutters as he starts frantically trying to pull Paul out of his.

They break apart only for the logistics of it all. Getting socks and pants off is tricky, especially when they're both so eager to get to each other's skin that hands keep getting in the way.

Once they're both finally naked Alex pushes Paul into the armchair, which faces the bed and gives Alex a million ideas that range from sitting there getting a show to simply relaxing with a book while watching Paul sleep.

Right now, though, he wants his hands on Paul. He straddles Paul's lap, wine glass in hand, and offers him a sip.

"No," he says, when Paul tries to take the glass from him.

"All right. But you may regret this," Paul says with a wicked smile, before he lets Alex hold the glass to his lips again and tilt.

The second the glass is out of the way, Paul fists a hand into Alex's hair. He kisses him hard and, when his mouth opens, feeds him the wine he's let pool on his tongue.

Alex moans, hips grinding against Paul, and almost drops the glass.

Paul laughs, breaks the kiss, and catches it just in time.

"Do that again," Alex says breathlessly, wiping wine from his chin and loving the mess of it all.

"Sure, but I hold the glass."

By the time they've finished the wine, Paul has his arm tight around Alex's waist as he shifts and grinds over him. He whimpers softly into Paul's mouth.

Somehow, Alex feels drugged by less than half a bottle of wine and the miracle of Paul's kisses.

♦

Paul nips at Alex's lower lip. "You good?" he whispers. Alex is so damn lost to it. A frantic nod and a whimper before Alex wraps his hand tightly around Paul's dick is all he gets in response.

Paul lets his head fall back against the chair, drops the now-empty glass out of his hand onto the carpet, and lets Alex drive until Paul comes all over the both of them.

"Hold on to me," he says once he's caught his breath. Alex is still shifting, restless and desperate over him.

With an arm under Alex's ass and another across his back, Paul gets them to the bed, barely. It's only a few steps, and he is happy to leave Alex's ass hanging off the edge, his legs in the air. Paul kneels again — there's something about Alex that just does that to him — and this time licks over his hole.

Alex whines and twists.

"Okay?" Paul asks. They've been taking risks together that aren't entirely stupid, but aren't particularly responsible either.

"Don't talk, don't stop," Alex gasps.

For a moment, Paul only obeys the first command because Alex tortured, unable to stop moving and unable to get or give himself relief, is the hottest thing he has ever seen. His spent dick twitches in sympathy. He'll be jerking off to this all week.

"Come on, come *on.*..."

"Patience," Paul breathes. The sound Alex makes is hopeless. Paul's body tries so hard to react to that it hurts. He presses an arm across the back of Alex's thighs, folding him in half, gets his other hand on his dick, and licks until Alex comes so hard he's pretty sure the neighbors hear it.

After, he somehow winds up pulling Alex down onto the floor and into his arms.

"What the fuck happened there?" Alex sounds dazed.

Paul laughs and quickly finds himself unable to stop from sheer delight.

Alex smiles and his eyes crinkle but he doesn't seem to have enough of himself together to laugh yet. He loops his arms around Paul's neck and slumps his head against his shoulder.

Paul wraps his arms tighter around his back. "You are unbelievable."

"Not just me," Alex says.

Paul laughs again and kisses the side of his neck. He strokes his back gently as Alex breathes into his shoulder.

"Everything okay there?" Paul finally asks, when a couple of minutes pass with Alex saying nothing at all, just growing steadily heavier in his arms. Paul's starting to get cold and his leg is a bit numb because it's tucked under the weight of both of them and they're *on the fucking floor.* Alex is warm against him, though, and Paul is happy to stay here as long as Alex needs them to.

"It's too much," Alex says into his skin. He sounds small and far away.

It's not a yes, and Paul goes still, afraid suddenly that maybe he has pushed Alex too far. The idea of letting go of him now or ever is devastating.

"Do you need to stop?" he asks, although there's nothing to stop right now except their strange cuddling in the possibly even stranger afterglow.

"No," Alex says and finally lifts his head to look at Paul, blinking like he's just becoming aware of where he is. "No, it's good." When he smiles, Paul relaxes. "I liked it," Alex adds. In another breath the smile turns wicked.

"Good," Paul says, relieved. "Because you have an amazing ass that deserves to be appreciated." He lets his hand drop below Alex's back and squeezes at it.

Alex giggles, before he blinks up at Paul through his lashes with a look that's so dangerous Paul groans.

Despite that moment of boldness, once they finally get themselves untangled enough to stand up, clean up, and stretch out on the bed for a nap, Alex stays pressed close to him. He's even quieter than usual as they lay side by side, their breaths syncing up almost immediately.

Paul rubs a thumb absently over Alex's hip until they both slip into a doze. He wonders, if Alex always lands on his feet, exactly how far he's falling right now.

When Paul wakes, it's to Alex hovering over him, happy and looking like he's about to get in trouble for something. Paul's first random thought, after *thank God* that he looks okay now, is that Alex's dark eyes are mesmerizing.

"How are you?" Paul lifts a hand to brush at Alex's cheek. His skin is so tempting.

"Hungry." Alex turns his head to kiss Paul's fingers, then sucks at the tips of them.

Paul presses his thumb to the corner of Alex's mouth. "Do you want to eat, or do you want to fuck again? Because if you keep doing that, your options are going to be limited."

Alex pulls away from Paul's hand with a last nip to his fingers. "Eat."

◆

They eat on the couch, passing the container of cold leftovers back and forth and gossiping about everyone they know on *Fourth*. They don't talk about what people on the show might be saying regarding them. Alex feels, in spite of the complications sex supposedly brings, like he's hanging out with Gemma. Being with Paul is easy and fun. But more than that, it's comfortable. Alex has never been completely at ease around anyone. But with Paul, he feels muscles that have been tight for years relax. And Paul seems to enjoy him, too. He's attentive and eager to listen to Alex, no matter what Alex is saying.

Alex doesn't know what time it is when he finally retrieves his bag from where he left it sitting by the door and follows Paul upstairs to fall back into bed again. They don't stop talking when Paul turns out the light. With Paul's voice quiet and intimate in the dark, Alex feels his universe expand.

In the morning Paul is still in bed when Alex wakes, though he's sitting up and has his tablet on his knees.

"Hey you," he says.

Alex mutters and pulls the blanket over his head and presses closer to his thigh. It's bright in the room.

Paul touches his hair gently. "Not a morning person?"

"It's Saturday," Alex complains. If days off are for anything they for getting caught up on sleep.

Paul chuckles. "You're welcome to stay in bed all day."

Alex battles internally over the offer. In the plus column is a day in bed with Paul, with nothing to do except share space and time and the very high likelihood of more sex. He's eager to get all of it for as long as he can. That said, he's starting to feel restless. He's too much in his own head even with Paul right here beside him. Alex worries this might be both too new and too much of a good thing. Perhaps there's a compromise to be reached. He pushes back the covers, sits up, and smiles into it when Paul leans in to finally kiss him good morning.

Paul sets his tablet aside. "Shower?"

"Not yet," Alex says. It's warm in the bedroom with the sunlight coming in, and he's still a bit sticky from last night, but getting up for a shower will mean the end of this extended and glorious date. Wary as he is, he's not ready to go just yet, so he pushes down the blankets and slides down the bed to settle between Paul's legs. Just because he's not willing to spend the day in bed together doesn't mean it can't start it on a high note.

They eat breakfast downstairs. Todd decides the new human is a sucker who will share the milk at the bottom of his cereal bowl. Alex and Paul talk about going to brunch with the crew tomorrow, and Alex and the cat reach a compromise: Todd gets the dregs of the milk, but with the bowl on the floor.

Alex asks quietly if he can come back later tonight, too.

"Stay here today, save yourself the trip," Paul offers.

Alex rubs Todd's ears and wonders how he used to get along with Beau. "I have some work I have to do," he says. The statement is only partly a lie. There's a call to his agent he needs to make, emails have been piling up that need answering, and he pretty much always has lines to learn and research reading to do. "Ask me again next week?"

"Will do."

When Alex is ready to leave Paul drags him into a kiss by the door. It takes effort not to let himself get lost in it. If he lets go completely he's not sure he'll ever leave, and he needs to.

As usual, Alex is a relieved to be alone in his car. Once he gets a few blocks away, he has to remind himself not to pull over to take a few deep breaths. L.A. cops are assholes, and he's way too recognizable. He knows he should head home; Gemma's probably going to be annoyed if he's out too long. But he wants some more space and time to himself first, so he drives down to the pier and parks in one of the awkward public lots off to the side of the highway that are always a little deserted because the tourists don't realize they're there.

He's been coming here a lot in the last year. The beach is one of the only places he doesn't get recognized. He looks like one more pretty kid in a stupid beanie nursing unlikely dreams in Santa Monica — no one notices and no one cares. He pays the muni meter, takes off his shoes, and sits cross-legged in the sand far enough from the water that no one gets within twenty feet of him.

The ocean is good for feeling small. Sometimes that's overwhelming, but today it feels grounding. One thing he wishes Victor had told him before his life blew up is that fame mostly will make you feel like less than you have ever been.

He wonders if fame, or the age difference, or his own lack of experience with other humans is what's making everything going on with Paul feel so good and so temporary. Alex is pretty sure Paul will show him things, and then he'll be gone into some real relationship, with a real adult who's a real person all the time; they'll even get another real dog. Todd probably misses having a dog around; Paul probably worries about that. Alex laughs to — and at — himself. He's already in deep if he's worried about the cat.

While he's stewing, Gemma calls to complain of boredom. Instead of telling her to fuck off, he convinces her to come meet him.

She shows up an hour later wearing cut-off jeans and a loose white shirt that ripples in the wind. She sits down silently in the sand next to him.

Alex surprises himself by saying, "I think it's time to start house hunting."

Because she's Gemma — and because they've talked about it faintly in the past — she starts listing her requirements before Alex has a chance to ask her if she wants to move with him. The presumption is annoying, but not unexpected.

Eventually, he makes her run up to the pier proper to get them beach fries and lemonades, because the one time he tried that since *Fourth* he got mobbed by a bunch of tourists. When she comes back, he asks her if she's ever had anal sex. He regrets the question the moment it passes his lips. He knows it's his own fault, but she manages to overshare, tell him nothing useful, and make several sets of unpleasant assumptions about his life in the process.

While Gemma babbles, Alex stares at the ocean from behind his sunglasses and eats his fries. When he can no longer avoid some sort of response to her monologue, he says, "So rimming's good; you should try that."

She tackles him into the sand, laughing, when he refuses to say anything more. Alex wonders if this is what college would have been like.

He feels sad when he has to get back in his car to follow her home. The drive is lonely, but once there he happily face-plants on his bed and takes a two-hour nap. When he gets up, he emails Margaret — his favorite source of advice on how to be an adult.

Having an attack of the grownups. I need to buy a house, and I need an assistant. Probably not in that order. Help?
She drops him a note back from her phone reminding him he has a financial advisor he should talk to about the first, but that she'll see what she can do on the second. Alex looks around his room. He wonders if, when he and Gemma move out, he should leave a note in the crevice by the window jamb. He wants whoever the next tenant is to know that yes, there are cockroaches and the faucet drips, and the tiling in the kitchen is super ugly, but this place, small and terrible, may just treat them kindly.

11

Paul has work he should be doing, but he procrastinates for hours before he makes himself face it. When he eventually does, he sits with his laptop and his notes and tries not to be too aware of the spaces where Alex isn't, or the clock and how slowly it's moving. In the afternoon, when the space and the quiet finally get to be too much, he puts his iPod on and loses another hour running.

He showers again when he gets back and feels a pleasant burst of satisfaction when he sees Alex's toothbrush, forgotten or deliberately left, by the sink. Eventually he calls his sister, Sarah, but that turns out to be a mistake. She keeps asking him how his weekend is going, and he can't give her any detail without admitting he slept with J. Alex Cook. Sarah watches *The Fourth Estate* and knows who he is. Paul doesn't want to contemplate how awkwardly she might take this news.

When Alex finally texts to say that he's on his way over, Paul sends back an invitation for sushi.

Instead of a text in return, he gets a call.

"I can't go out for dinner."

"Why not?"

"Because I'm me, and people are assholes. I want to spend time with you, not have fans taking photographs or trying to touch me like I'm some good luck charm."

"You went for brunch," Paul reminds him He wonders how fucked up Alex — or Alex's life — is if he's balking at a late-night run for sushi.

"Strength in numbers and also gays," Alex says flatly. "I can't, Paul."

"It's a little place." He wants Alex in his home and his bed, of course, but he wants to be able to go out with him too. "You're allowed to go out and do things in the world."

"Most people disagree."

Alex's words make little sense and feel frightening. Sure, fans can be weird, but the house arrest mentality is unsettling and, Paul thinks, paranoid. "No one will bother you. Code of the native Angelino and all that," Paul says carefully. It's the truest of Los Angeles's theoretical and unwritten laws: No one ever bothers a star while they are eating.

He can practically hear Alex thinking about it. When the quiet drags on, he can't resist the urge to push. "Do you not have your hat?"

Alex laughs. "Okay. Fine."

◆

Alex has only been away from Paul for a few hours but, as he pulls into Paul's driveway, he feels like he's been gone a lot longer. Paul is waiting for him at the door, a dark silhouette against the cozy glow of light inside. He kisses Alex as soon as he steps across the threshold, warm and easy. Paul's mouth feels more familiar to Alex than two nights together would seem to allow.

"Ready to go?" Paul asks, when he finally pulls back, reaching up to straighten the beanie on Alex's head.

"If there are fans I'm blaming you."

At the restaurant while they wait for the hostess, Paul puts a hand on his back. All else being equal, Alex would quite like for him to keep it there. But they're in public and a gesture witnessed is a gesture that other people get to own. Alex doesn't want other people to have this part of him too. He steps away.

Paul gives him a look, confused and a little hurt.

"Sorry," Alex mutters. He's not sure how to explain himself in words. "I —"

"It's fine. I forgot," Paul puts his hands in his pockets with an apologetic smile. "Sorry."

Moments later a girl approaches. Phone already in hand, she asks for a picture. Alex says no to her, sweetly but without apology. He doesn't feel remotely guilty for it. Paul said he's allowed to have a normal night, so that's what he's going to try to do.

As the girl walks away — at least she was polite; some of them aren't — Paul murmurs, "I see what you mean."

"The internet's not going to like that," Alex observes.

"What's the internet going to care?" Paul asks.

Alex gives him a condescending look.

"Okay, why are you going to care that random people you don't know on the internet care?"

"Wait and see." Alex is slightly more amused at the potential headache ahead than he would be otherwise. At least he'll get to make the point to Paul. The other man may have a house and a cat and an ex who took his dog, but Alex has fame. Adulthood, apparently, does not automatically allow another person to understand the price he pays for living in the public eye.

♦

Alex says he doesn't want to wait around and get spotted again, so Paul suggests they get their sushi to go rather than bailing. Alex agrees, looking relieved and grateful. Paul wonders at that; it doesn't seem hard to be kind about whatever reservations Alex fairly has about being in the world. Paul is starting to recognize that there may be a learning curve here for the both of them.

In the car he hands Alex his iPod and tells him to pick the music. It works reasonably well to distract Alex from his funk. By the time they pull into Paul's street they're arguing over the merits of various shitty country-pop bands. Paul mocks Alex's selections while Alex cackles mercilessly at some of Paul's playlists.

The internet, it turns out, cares. Alex was apparently right. Paul should have known — he does after all tweet occasionally about the show and has interacted lightly with some of the fans. But engaging fans about his job on the internet is light years away from strangers on the internet caring deeply about who Alex is having dinner with. While Alex sets out plates and chopsticks Paul checks his own phone and is shocked to find hundreds of replies to Alex's little-used Twitter account.

Despite Alex's refusal, there is a picture. Taken from behind and with only a sliver of his profile showing but still, there's still no mistaking him. His distinctive beauty is his blessing and his curse.

What surprises Paul most, though, is that he's in the picture as well. The fans desperately want to know who is out on a Saturday night with J. Alex Cook.

I dunno! Whoever posted the picture — presumably the girl who asked Alex for a photo — has responded to several inquiries of varying degrees of intrusiveness. *Some guy. I think they were there together.*

Ohmygod is he there on a date? Does Alex have a boyfriend??

The conversation devolves quickly as someone shows up convinced, and apropos of nothing, that Alex is, in fact, involved with Liam and couldn't possibly be with any other random guy. After that, the whole mess of speculation and anger spins so far away from reality that Paul doesn't know how to process it now that it touches his own very real life.

Alex looks up from unpacking the food and sees Paul staring at his phone with a mix of bewilderment and horror. He asks, his voice mild, "Was I unspeakably rude to say no to a picture, or a cheating lying whore for not being with Liam?"

"I suppose I should have seen this coming." Paul admits. He doesn't know if he's supposed to apologize — for the internet or for the fan or for suggesting they go out in the first place — but Alex doesn't ask for anything. He clucks at Todd and nudges him away from where he's eyeing the takeout bag.

"And people wonder why I never tweet," Alex mumbles.

◆

Alex doesn't mention the Twitter explosion again. Still, Paul keeps rolling it over in the back of his mind while they eat and play Trials Evolution for a couple of hours, whooping and laughing whenever one of them finds a new and spectacular way to crash. Eventually, their laughter peters out.

Paul looks at Alex, leans against him, and says, simply, "Bed."

Upstairs they're domestic. Paul swaps contacts for glasses while Alex smooths on moisturizer.

"Rules of the game, huh?" Paul wraps his arms around Alex from behind. He dips his head to rest his chin on Alex's shoulder and looks at the image they make in the mirror. They look good together. Paul's mind is running ahead of the situation, surely, but he can't help but imagine them in pictures like this.

Alex smiles into the mirror. "Gemma's fault, actually."

"I'm starting to get the impression most things are."

"She's the loyalest friend I've ever had," Alex says tightly.

"How many people from high school are you friends with on Facebook?" Paul asks, even though he's just been given a pretty clear *do not go* signal.

"I don't use Facebook." Alex twists out of Paul's arms.

Paul wants to talk more about that, to explore explicitly how lonely Alex is even without worrying about getting photographed at restaurants and gossiped about on the internet. But Alex clearly doesn't. Paul leaves the subject alone for now. He follows Alex back to the bedroom and catches him in a kiss which turns to laughter as they fall onto the bed.

The sex is easy. Alex's responsiveness in bed draws Paul in and makes him want to stay here forever. When he looks at Paul down the length of his own body, Paul can't look away. He uses all the things he's learned from watching Alex — both at work and now in his home — to coax out reactions. Alex hides his secrets deep and well, but Paul wants to reveal them all and make Alex tell him everything he's not saying.

After, they press their foreheads together to stare at each other for far too long until Alex says, "You're not very attractive as a cyclops."

◆

In the morning, they drive to brunch together. Alex is nervous on the way over, but when Paul asks if he's okay he nods.

"I'm fine." In truth, he has any number of questions, none of which he knows how to ask. Are they going to brunch *together*-together, or as two people sharing a ride? Surely the group will know their arriving together isn't purely platonic or innocent, and maybe they should talk about that. But Alex doesn't know how to begin to ask the question without sounding like he's asking for some kind of declaration from Paul.

He probably should have thought this through better.

Conversation stops at their already mostly-populated table for twelve when they walk onto the patio together.

Brian twists around in his eternal seat at the head of their table. "Well, well, well."

"Hi Brian," Paul says benignly.

"Am I correct in assuming we're supposed to change our usual seating arrangements based on this development?"

"How do you know we didn't park at the same time?" Alex says at the same time Paul says, "We don't *have* usual seating arrangements."

Brian ignores Paul. "That you said that, for one," he tells Alex. "For another, that we all know Paul."

"Don't," Paul and Shawna snap simultaneously. That earns a few chuckles as seats get shifted around so that Paul can be in reach of both Alex and Beau.

Alex is glad to leave Brian to Paul and takes shelter in conversation with Shawna. He's still painfully aware of every time the larger conversation turns back to him and Paul. Every so often Paul squeezes his knee under the table when it happens, a little gesture of solidarity. Alex appreciates it, even though

Paul touching him in public is risky, as last night at the sushi joint demonstrated so well.

Alex is more than aware of how often he's probably going to have to say no to what he is learning is Paul's propensity for public displays of affection. Paul touches everyone, all the time. Even innocently, Alex can mostly never have that. The mess of yesterday notwithstanding he still wants something for himself.

Eventually, somewhere in a side conversation Alex isn't paying attention to, someone must say something they shouldn't. Paul's voice goes sharp.

"Hey, I get that you're all being my awesome asshole friends, but can we maybe do that regarding someone less likely to wind up on TMZ or at least about someone we don't actually like?"

Alex turns his head to focus on Brian, who pulls back in his chair.

"Do we like Alex? I didn't know that had been decided." The obvious pleasure he's taking in making everyone uncomfortable shocks Alex. Before Alex can say something sharp that would likely necessitate a quick and awkward exit, Shawna balls up a used napkin and tosses it at Brian.

♦

"So you know what the oddest thing about that was?" Paul asks as Alex pulls out of the parking lot.

Alex considers his options. There are a lot of them. "Your creepy hipster friend literally twirling his moustache at me?"

Paul laughs. "No, but fair. Not being able to hold your hand."

Alex hadn't expected that. Paul's sweetness takes him by surprise. Not that he didn't know Paul can be sweet. But that Paul seems to want to keep being sweet to Alex.

"Thank you for not," Alex says, then frowns at himself. He does want Paul to know he appreciates whatever sacrifices of PDA he's is making on Alex's behalf. But that didn't come out right. "That felt weird for me too."

Paul's relieved breath is audible. Slowly, almost shyly, Alex reaches across the console and takes Paul's free hand where it lies in his lap.

Their plan was to go their separate ways after brunch. But when they get back to the house Paul has to look in on something in his email. While he gets that sorted, Alex gets out his tablet and curls up next to Paul on the couch. Soon Todd comes to join them, stretching out at their feet as they deal with the administrativa of their lives.

When the room loses the sunlight in the late afternoon, Paul turns to Alex and says, "Stay?"

"My call's at six," Alex warns.

"I'll live. And if you need to go to bed early —"

"For sleep?" Alex asks, all perfectly plausible and full-of-shit innocence.

When they do turn in, after catching up on the latest Sunday night prestige show over a pizza, Paul makes a point to suck marks into every part of Alex's body the camera will never see.

12

The morning is harsh. Paul considers getting up with Alex and going for a run, but gives up the idea for the thrill of Alex, dressed for the day, sitting on the edge of the bed and kissing him before he goes. It's warm and sexy and domestic. The two extra hours of sleep after Alex leaves, in a bed that smells of him, aren't bad either.

There's a writers' meeting first thing at work. Paul pitches an idea while Victor watches him with his fingers steepled in front of his mouth. The concept has nothing to do with Zach, but Paul had finished this outline sitting in bed Saturday morning watching Alex wake up beside him. There's a prickle at the back of his neck telling him that Victor, with his eye and memory for the personal affairs of his people, knows that.

His suspicions are borne out when, after the meeting, Victor beckons Paul to follow. Once they're in the kitchenette, Victor closes the door behind them. "I saw you were out with Alex this weekend."

"Yeah," Paul says, a little cautiously. He'd thought that Victor was okay with this. But maybe now that the situation is somewhat public knowledge he's going to get yelled at.

"And things are okay?" Victor asks sternly. Paul feels like he's being drilled by a cross between a doting parent and a hostile prosecutor.

"They are." Paul wonders where this all is going.

"I'm glad you got him out of the house. I'm assuming that was your idea?"

"Did everyone see that picture?" Paul asks. Is there any element of this thing with Alex that Victor won't take notice of?

"Get used to it or become hermits together." Which option Victor favors is obvious. He has never picked favorites to let them languish in the shadows, onscreen or off.

"He doesn't like the attention." Paul's not sure if he's defending Alex's choices, which seem so justified in the face of the bullshit that comes with his life, or lamenting them. Paul doesn't want to have to live like that himself.

"Alex wants a normal life so badly he's never going to get one," Victor says, "because he's never going to do anything except go to work and sit at home so the crazies can't get him. You're getting him out of his cave and his comfort zone. That's good."

"I don't know what to say to that," Paul doesn't know how to articulate the scope of the things he's starting to learn Alex is uncomfortable with. He is also uncertain about where those boundaries lie. As much as Victor's insight might be of some use, he very much does not want to risk touching on something Alex might not want him to share.

"You don't have to say anything. You're being good to him," Victor says smugly. "Is he being good for you?"

"He is."

"Good. Keep that up."

Paul nods. He feels strange with the weight of a promise made about Alex, but not to him. "I will."

♦

"I heard you were cheating on me again," Liam says at lunch.

Alex doesn't look up from his phone. Paul is texting him about his latest shitty Facebook game addiction. *I'm stuck on level 65. Tips??*

"When aren't I?" Alex chooses distraction over annoyance as he types back, *Better reflexes. And younger fingers.*

"You weren't this year at the Emmys when you sat next to me all night," Liam points out. The fans had an absolute field day with that one, and Liam hasn't yet gotten tired of teasing Alex about it.

"I didn't pick the seats," Alex says as his phone buzzes again with another text from Paul. *Are you volunteering your services?*

"But you gave me a hug!" Liam protests.

At work. As are you, Alex thumbs into his phone. "Because you hugged me and there were cameras. Slapping you would have been bad press. Also, Victor would have yelled."

"Ouch. Wounded," Liam says.

Alex ignores Liam's hand-to-heart melodrama to roll his eyes at the latest text from Paul. *It's lunchtime! And I'm stuck now!*

Alex hesitates only a moment. The fantasy of what might happen if he went and found Paul in person is nice, but it's only a fantasy. Even if he were brave enough to consider it, Alex can't imagine it would be possible to have a quickie on the lot and not get busted. He texts back *Patience*.

Paul's disappointed response comes almost instantly. Alex laughs to himself as he sticks his phone back in his pocket.

"Who are you texting?" Liam asks as if he can't guess perfectly well.

"Someone by the grace of whom I am not putting you in a headlock right now."

"Damn, that's some good sex if it's got you this chill."

"Am I?" Alex asks. He's never quite sure what to do with Liam and his persistent attempts at whatever friendship he's after.

"You're talking to me and haven't yelled yet?"

Alex considers how much energy he's willing to devote to being offended by Liam right now and decides not much. The return on investment is guaranteed to be low. "Do you ever stop talking?"

"Not when it gets me good details, no."

"What details are you getting?" Alex asks, exasperated.

"That you're having sex, that the sex is with Paul, and that the internet knows about it, which means that the gossip is, for once, based in fact."

"The internet knows nothing."

"It knows you got sushi with Paul. How is that place, by the way? I've been meaning to try it."

Alex kicks Liam's shin under the table. "How come every time you're out with someone the internet never decides you're a slut and a cheat?"

"Because I'm poly and the internet decided I was a slut and a cheat a long time ago. Not news anymore. Doesn't make it true — I mean, I am a slut, but.... They still know a lot more about me than they do about you. Downside to your air of mystery, J. Alex."

Alex suspects the real reasons are more gross than that. Liam is the handsome straight TV star heartthrob. The general public may not understand the consensual non-monogamy thing, but that's not Alex's problem. Being the pretty twink is.

"Please don't," he begs.

Liam perks up even more. "Hey, what does Paul call you in bed? He's a writer, he must be great with all sorts of words."

Alex can feel his face go scarlet. The memory of Paul's breathy, wrecked *Alex* in his ear right before he'd come Sunday night is remarkably effective at turning him on, no pet names required.

"What the fuck is wrong with you?" Alex demands.

Liam looks like he's just getting started. "Because Carly and I —"

Alex reaches across the table and claps a hand over Liam's mouth. "Stop! Stop talking! Now!"

Liam cracks up. After a horrified moment Alex registers the joke and drops his hand; he's still learning how to laugh at himself. He's still pissed about the maniac fans. Liam can shrug them off in a way Alex can't, but he's also good at distracting Alex, even if it's with his own ridiculousness.

♦

That week the official casting decisions for *Paradise Square* get announced and Alex's busy life gets a lot busier. There's press to do. The movie needs to start the cycle of advance hype and the general public wants more about how J. Alex Cook is going to play some historical, non-gay character. Margaret is a lifesaver of organization and efficiency, leaving Alex to do his job of taking calls and doing interviews as the wry, sharply charming young star he's expected to be.

In between conference calls he flips through his phone to look again at a picture Paul has sent of Todd curled up on a hoodie Alex left at his house. *Somebody misses you*, the accompanying text reads.

Alex replies with *Give him a pet for me ;)*. Later he has to delete the message thread that follows. The horrors of getting caught sexting are too terrible to contemplate.

The new project creates a nightmare of scheduling to work out. *Paradise* wants him to film in New York the same month *Fourth* wants him in D.C. By the time those negotiations are settled Alex feels like he — and not his time — is the commodity being haggled over.

When, tired and annoyed in between takes one day, he says as much to Liam, Liam asks him why he ever expected anything different.

The only involvement Alex has in his schedule is signing off on how few work-free days he's going to get over the holidays. He has a stab of regret about that. He'd been looking forward, in a vague sort of way, to spending a more or less 'normal' Christmas with Paul. Except, now that he thinks about it more, Paul is probably going to be out of town with his own family. So that hardly matters, he tells himself. Though there's a pang of regret about that too.

On the faintly bright side is the fact that Alex won't have enough time off to make going back to Indiana for Christmas worthwhile. He sends an awkward email to his mother. He doesn't think either of them are used to the idea that he's the kind of person who's spending Christmas in New York City and can easily afford to fly her out and pay for a hotel room for her. Her response is immediate and enthusiastic, though. So that's one thing to look forward to.

Otherwise, Alex isn't sanguine about the future. He finds it almost impossible to imagine leaving at the end of November and coming back at the end of January without finding Paul wrapped up with someone else. Someone real, whose hand he can hold. There's so much Paul wants, and Alex can offer him none of it. And while he trusts Paul — his loyalty seems beyond doubt — Alex knows how much he needs companionship, a partner in life as well as in his bed. Paul won't want to go two months without that just for Alex's sake, and Alex can't blame him.

When Paul calls later that night, Alex answers eagerly. If the expiration date of this thing is approaching, Alex wants to get as much out of this while he can.

13

Margaret finds Alex an assistant named Yancy Eckert. She's in her early thirties and is an actual professional, not another one of those barely organized recent L.A. arrivals doing the work for the money or the connections. Alex tells her point blank that he's glad they're not peers — not in age or circumstance — because it means they can be friends. He also asks her to remind him when stuff is going on he's supposed to go to her for help with, because of all the things he's done in L.A., having an assistant feels the most morally dubious. Certainly, it's the thing that would most puzzle and possibly upset his mother.

At least Paul approves, happily telling Alex it's about time. He confesses that he's teetered on the edge of hiring someone himself for years, what with the hours he works and the ambitions he has. Alex has to stop himself from offering him Yancy's services in response. He processes that for an evening of curious confusion with Gemma as she paints her nails a particularly off-putting shade of pale blue.

Of all the things of his that Gemma has always helped herself to, she makes no assumptions about Yancy's time or interest in picking up her dry-cleaning. Alex is puzzled enough to ask for an explanation, but Gemma brushes off the question, saying he'd understand if he were a girl.

♦

The next time Alex stays the weekend Paul watches him, amused, on Saturday afternoon as he pulls a notebook and a battered textbook out of his bag and cracks them open.

"What's that?" He squints at the cover, but can't make it out. It's in a non-Roman script.

"Farsi book."

"You're learning Farsi?" Paul isn't completely surprised. Studying is exactly the kind of thing that Alex, intellectual and inexperienced with acting, does. But he's still a little stunned. This is no small commitment of time or energy, and Alex has boundless reserves of neither.

Alex flips the book open to a dog-eared page. "Zach speaks it, so I need to — want to — at least a little. If he took it on at random, so can I. Especially if he's going to get his ass into Iran in the next couple of months."

"Why didn't you go to college?" Paul asks. It's a thought that's been worrying at him for months now, since before they started this thing. Alex is so sharp and takes such obvious pleasure in using his mind. Fairytale aside, what Paul knows of his path makes no sense to him.

"I didn't go to college because three weeks after high school graduation I got in my car and drove to L.A."

"But before that?"

Alex leans over to fish a pen out of his bag, then looks right up at Paul with a gaze that's loaded. "Don't think that just because you went to college and I didn't doesn't mean we're not both from some hick-ass towns in the middle nowhere."

"I know where I'm from." Paul doesn't know whether he should be offended or amused. He's only named the town that he grew up in, not told any stories about it. Paul wonders if Alex went ahead and researched that, too, or is making not entirely incorrect assumptions about Southern and gay. But Alex sounds upset, and this goes on the list of things Paul's going to have to pry out of him, someday, when Alex is ready.

"And where are your wrists from, Paul?" Alex singsongs under his breath.

Paul sighs. They haven't talked about that since their first night together. Paul's going to have to tell him eventually, but that isn't a conversation that needs to happen in a pissing contest of *my life was worse than yours*. Especially when he still doesn't know all — or even most — of Alex's story.

He lets it go for now. "What does your name look like in Farsi?"

Alex looks as wary as he does pleased.

"Like this," he says. He tears out a page of his notebook and starts to write. On the line below it, with a glance up at Paul that's a little bashful and incredibly gorgeous, he writes something else and spins the page around so Paul can see. "And this is yours."

♦

"You know Alex is going to be gone for, like, two months, right?"

Paul regards Liam over both the top of both his laptop and his glasses — it's been that sort of week — and is glad the office is empty aside from them. "Are you supposed to be here?" he asks. He knows Liam's situation with Victor gives him free reign of anything involving *Fourth*, but he also knows Victor has strong feelings about Liam's tendency to wander.

"Relax, I'm off the clock. Also, I know he was just in here, so spare the lecture."

Alex was in the building for a meeting and had stopped by to say hello. His appearance had been surprising and brief, and Paul is now trying to finish his work so he can go home and spend another weekend with him.

"Consider it spared," he says, wanting Liam to get to the damn point.

"Mhmmm. But yeah, he's —"

"I know what his schedule is, Liam," Paul says.

"Oh. Oh, Great. What are you going to do about it?"

"What do you mean?"

"He's going to be on location for a long time. And I know how gone you are over him, so. He's got a couple of days free in New York. Even if he didn't — you should go see him."

Paul sits back in his chair and flicks a pencil between his fingers. "You think that's a good idea? And you think you're the person who should be telling me it is?" Usually it's Carly who calls him out on his shit, if she believes there is shit to call him out on. Since it's highly unlikely she's subcontracted her advice giving to her ridiculous boyfriend, this particular brainstorm is all Liam's.

Liam shrugs eloquently. "Dude, if you don't, I don't want to deal with your pining."

"You also don't need to spend time in this room," Paul points out, although they do see each other socially often enough.

"Yeah. Well, or his, 'cause I have to put up with him in D.C., and comforting the lonely and lovelorn is not part of my job description."

"Really?" Paul says. He knows damn well that comforting the lonely and lovelorn is in fact one of Liam's many hat tricks. He points the pencil at Liam. "And is this part of your job description?"

Oddness of the messenger aside, Paul's thrilled at the idea. Those two months are approaching quickly. The idea of a separation that long has been daunting — too daunting for him to try to think about a solution other than enduring it. Miserable schedules are, if nothing else, the nature of their business. Paul is aware he's being more than a little pathetic considering that right now he and Alex have hardly been together for two months.

"Oh, no, man," Liam gushes. This is just 'cause you're awesome together."

"Thank you," Paul says cautiously, still not quite sure what Liam is up to. He may be sincere, of course, but he may be here at Victor's request or out of some misguided thing because of Carly, and wow, Paul's life is awkward. Alex may not know the half of it yet, but Liam sure as hell does.

"So, you'll think about it?"

"I am going to think about it a lot," Paul says. "Now get out of my office." Paul waves a hand at him and returns to his computer.

Liam laughs as he goes. "Not your office, Paul," he calls back. "Yet."

14

House hunting is peculiar.

Gemma gets mistaken regularly for Alex's assistant or girlfriend; sometimes both. Realtors speak down to him more than once. Alex is never sure if it's because he's so damn young, or if they assume that all actors are stupid.

He's deeply irritated by it, in part because of the truth in the assumptions. He has no real idea what he's doing. Having houses talked up to him as investments or party spaces isn't useful. What he needs is a place to live that's extravagant in terms of what he's come from, but not extravagant in terms of what he is.

When he tries to articulate this to Gemma it comes out as, "I don't care about hot tubs."

Gemma, in turn, informs him that she totally cares about hot tubs.

♦

Eighteen prospects later, Alex finally finds a house he's interested in. It's on a dead-end road, has some awesome outdoor space, a decent but not military grade security system, and a massive living room and open kitchen. There's a loft-like space at one end of the common area that contains another, smaller living space and a bedroom and bath that would be perfect for Gemma.

Aside from that, there's a proper — and separate — second floor with a master bedroom and bath.

More importantly, he can afford it without freaking out. No matter that his financial advisor tells him he can easily go for seven figures, no fucking way. The thought gives Alex hives, even more than that he's looking at a house on foreclosure. He feels shady about it, as if he's betraying being from Indiana and poor.

He tells Paul as much that weekend, as he gets ready to start the process of buying the place on Monday. Paul answers carefully, and Alex can understand that. He considers how awkward a position he may have put Paul in by talking numbers. Paul may already own a house, but Alex makes way more than he does.

"So," Paul says as they make macaroni and cheese for lunch. "Want to know more about the onscreen adventures of Zach and James?"

"Do I?" Alex asks, dubious, as he cubes Velveeta.

"I suspect it's the kind of thing you might want preparation for."

"That doesn't make me feel better. But go ahead." If Paul wants to share it's probably a good idea to listen.

Paul takes a deep breath. "The long-awaited romance plot is about to begin," he says in a dramatic TV-announcer voice.

Alex's heart sinks, but he has to laugh at Paul's ridiculousness. Which maybe was part of the plan.

"That's going to be…fun." He's going to have to deal with the renewed enthusiasm of the fans, and, for that matter, Liam. Alex is continually appalled at the existence of his own public life. Liam, though, will flirt with furniture if it'll get him petted and cooed over by yet another talk show host or hostess delighted to be anything but impervious to his charms.

"Yeah," Paul agrees.

"I mean, I knew it was coming."

"The entire fan base and most of the TV-watching public outside the fan base knew it was coming."

Alex smiles ruefully. "Yeah. I'm going to assume you're not responsible for any of said romance plot?"

Paul shakes his head. "I write what Victor tells me to write. But none of this was my idea."

"I mean I guess it could be worse," Alex says, trying to put the best spin on it, for himself and for Paul who clearly feels bad about all this, his fault or no. "It makes sense within the story. And Liam and I have good chemistry together. Horrifying as that is." What he doesn't say is that even with his relatively limited data on the matter, he knows that the way he connected with Liam on camera is part of why Victor reordered the world for him.

Sometimes it's heartbreaking for Alex to know so much more about the future than his character does. Alex muses about it as Paul puts the macaroni and cheese in the oven and Alex starts washing dishes. It's one of the costs of table reads and understanding how made up stories work. Zach doesn't know it, but he's about to get played out of a story. Again. He's not as vicious as he likes to think he is, and because he's so focused on the little scandals — mismanagement of military contracts in D.C., who cares? — he's always missing the bigger story unfolding much closer to him.

James is starting to see it, but James is more worried about Zach at the moment than whether rival reporters' stories are all based in fact. Alex almost feels jealous, not of the circumstances or the people, but the clarity that a life written to forty-seven minutes plus commercials on a weekly basis necessarily provides.

Paul gently hip checks Alex aside so he can wash his hands at the sink. "Those can wait," he says of the dishes. He dries his hands on his jeans and wraps his arms around Alex's waist. "And we have half an hour 'til food is ready," he adds with a suggestive look.

Which isn't to say that Victor's creations don't still have ridiculous blinders on, Alex thinks as he follows Paul to the couch. Not just about the futility of their schemes — any plan that requires another person to do exactly what you expect is a bad plan — but about the gravitational pull they increasingly exert on each other.

15

Despite upcoming drama in the script, Monday morning Liam is as cheery and chipper as ever in between takes. Alex wants to kick him as he paces by his chair *again*, because his constant need to move is distracting as fuck.

"Stop," he says shortly when Liam circles him on his third time around a winding, circuitous, and strangely unwavering route.

Thankfully, he does. Less thankfully, he stops right in front of Alex.

"You're not in a good mood," Liam says carefully.

"Is that a statement or a question?"

"What's wrong?" Liam asks.

"Nothing's wrong," Alex says shortly.

"Bullshit. You've been glaring at me for like the last twenty minutes and I don't think I did anything wrong?"

Alex sighs. "It's not you," he admits, as fun as it would be to blame this day on Liam.

"Boy troubles?" Liam asks ridiculously.

"No," Alex lies. He doesn't want to discuss these things with Liam on set of all places. Things with Paul have been so good, but Alex can't stop looking at the calendar and counting down the days he has left. They're getting close to the middle of November, and the prospect of the end is starting to wear.

"You know you can talk to me if you want." Liam puts both hands on Alex's shoulders and squeezes affectionately. Which is as annoying as hell. Alex has gotten used to people's hands on him for the sake of getting him dressed and made up as Zach, but he still doesn't like to be touched in most moments. Like this one.

"Liam? Personal space," he snaps irritably.

"Oh. Sorry man." Liam shuffles back and looks sad.

Alex sighs, exasperated now. "Don't do that."

"What's that?"

"Look like a wounded puppy when I yell at you."

"I am sorry," Liam insists, but then bounces again, all concern apparently gone. Alex wonders how Carly puts up with him. He knows how incredibly unkind, not to mention unfair, it is to wonder if that's why she and Liam have the arrangements that they do.

♦

Paul does his research and talks to Victor — who is more than enthusiastic about the idea of him taking some time to be with Alex on his next adventures — and makes a good chunk of the necessary arrangements. He can be in New York the week before Christmas with Alex, and as he marks the dates on his phone he thinks about the new year and everything after that. He can't wait for any of it.

Now he just has to tell Alex it's going to happen.

"Let me get this straight," Gemma says, sitting cross-legged on Alex's bed. Alex is packing neatly for D.C. and New York and utterly randomly for staying with Paul over Thanksgiving because one is work and one isn't. "You're spending Thanksgiving with the guy you're convinced is going to dump you the second you leave town —"

"It's orphans' Thanksgiving; if we're actually dating he hasn't said so; and maybe, just *maybe*, I'm wrong about everything and we can all die happy."

"There's no need to be snippy," Gemma tells him. "Next, you're going on location for two months, but when you get back you'll hopefully sign some papers and then we'll own a house?"

Alex side-eyes her, even though he knows she's trying to provoke him. "Apart from the fact that I will own the house and you will be paying way-below-market rent for our new and improved lifestyle, yes."

"Cool," she says. "Should I assume I'll never see you anymore when you get back, too?"

"Well, if I'm wrong, since we'll have a nice house, I'll be able to invite him over." His tone is condescending, but he's too nervous to be able to fix it.

"I don't know, Alex." Gemma is perfectly capable of matching his tone. I think we'll have to have a talk about you having strange boys up in your room with the door closed."

"Not even." Alex frowns at his suitcase. "If I decide I need another pair of shoes can you FedEx them to me?"

"Right. Because there are no shopping opportunities in D.C. Or New York."

Alex doesn't respond to her, staring blankly at his suitcase instead. He feels overwhelmed and now embarrassed. He's still not sure he likes having a life where he can buy another pair of shoes just because he packed poorly. Everything in his life feels like excess now.

"Are you nervous?" Gemma asks.

"Terrified," Alex admits.

"Why?"

"Because I'm going to New York to prove to everyone I can do something I never wanted to do in the first place," he sighs.

"Do you like acting?" she asks. "You've never said."

♦

Paul has taken to leaving the door unlocked for Alex. When he walks in that night, the lights are all on, music is playing, and Paul meets him in the foyer to wrap him up in a kiss. It silences his fears, at least for now.

"Help me finish the grocery list," Paul whispers in his ear when they finally break apart.

Alex snorts. "Sexy."

Paul kisses him again, then drags him into the kitchen by the hand.

The evening feels like the first night of summer vacation as portrayed on screen and not in the reality of a poor part of Indiana. But tonight all responsibility is gone for now and all the world seems to offer to possibility and adventure. They sit at the kitchen table for hours, drinking spiked cider, checking recipes, and talking as they knock knees under the table. Alex keeps looking up from writing things down to see Paul looking at him with a soft expression. He always smiles back.

"Do you want me to go to the store with you tomorrow?" Alex asks.

Paul looks surprised. "Are you sure? You don't usually like doing things in public."

"If we go early enough there won't be anyone there," Alex explains. "Plus it's the day before Thanksgiving. All the fans are going to be too busy travelling to make my life stupid."

♦

They go up to bed soon after they eat dinner but don't sleep until late. Paul takes Alex out of his clothes and pushes him into the armchair. He spends a long time working him into incoherence and then desperation, licking over his cock and his balls and his hole until Alex finally grabs his hair and fucks his mouth.

Paul keeps waiting for Alex to ask for the things they haven't done yet. As much as Paul wants those things (and *fuck* he wants them badly), they need to be Alex's call. Alex doesn't ask, though, and so Paul doesn't push. It's not like he ever stops craving the things Alex does let him do.

After Alex comes, laughing through the breathlessness, he stands, pulls Paul to his feet and goes to his own knees, back straight and posture perfect on Paul's bedroom floor. Alex has no trouble holding eye contact now when he looks up at Paul through his lashes, his eyes strange and dark and his tongue wicked. This is a boy, Paul thinks — right before he comes with a particularly clever twist of Alex's hand — to whom it's dangerous to teach things. He never wants to stop.

In the morning Paul coaxes Alex out of bed with coffee and the temptation of a hot shower. Then they go shopping, Alex in his beanie and Paul with his list.

"I can't believe I forgot to get canned pumpkin earlier," Paul says as they wander the aisles. "They're completely out."

"It's the day before Thanksgiving. Of course they're out." Alex crouches down to check the very back of the shelf.

"Maybe if someone had been less distracting, I would have remembered earlier."

"So sorry," Alex says in a song-song.

"No, you're not." Paul savors this little bit of utter normalcy, grocery shopping with an Alex who is happy and relaxed. He still won't hold his hand, but he does take an almost childlike delight in running down the empty aisles with the cart. Paul is content.

◆

Back at the house they start cooking. Paul is charmed and delighted that he gets to teach Alex this too. It feels significant, letting Alex handle the recipe cards Paul's grandmother wrote out years ago. He's glad not to be caught out as he watches Alex squint over measuring spoons and the spice rack.

"Who all is going to be here?" Alex asks as he balefully regards a pecan pie crust he can't get to lie right in the pan.

Paul squints at the pot he's stirring as he counts off on his other hand. "Most of the brunch crew. Shawna. Brian." Paul chuckles when Alex makes a face. "Craig for sure. My damn dog. Josh might be coming, Liam and Carly —"

"Liam's coming? Why does no one tell me these things?"

"You work with him every day. I assumed he'd mentioned it." Paul says

"He never did. Doesn't he have somewhere else to go?"

"Why are you so freaked out?" Paul asks. Liam isn't Alex's favorite, but he surely likes him better than Brian. Alex's reaction seems out of proportion to the situation.

"He's exhausting," Alex says. "And he's going to have opinions."

"Well. Yes." Paul sets down the spoon and looks at Alex for a moment. "Okay. This is a story you should hear. Because it's hilarious and because you need to know it."

"…Okay," Alex says nervously.

"So, Carly's my ex-girlfriend."

Alex stares at him. "But you're gay." He hesitates. "That probably wasn't a useful thing to say."

Paul lets it go. "We met at UNC, she was a couple of years behind me and crewed some of my projects. When she moved out here we got in touch again and one thing led to another and —"

"You *dated* her?" Alex struggles to absorb that piece of information.

"Yeah. She wasn't like…I wasn't using her to hide anything, I guess is what's important. I mean, not from anyone else."

"Then — what — what were you doing?"

"I'm not unattracted to women," Paul says easily. "They just don't rock my world like men do." He turns around to see Alex staring at him and gives him a pointed look up and down in reply. "Case in point. Anyway, when we broke up, that was why, and Carly was the one who helped me figure that out. There was a lot of honesty in that breakup. And we're still close."

"You didn't know?" Alex's face is twisted with disbelief. "I knew I was gay in middle school! You were older than I am right now when you figured it out. What the hell is that?"

"South Carolina, Alex," Paul says gently as he can. "Small town — God, not even a town. Middle of nowhere. Old family. I mean, home is a run-down farm house. It used to be something grand, but. It's not a place where stuff like that gets talked about. I knew…something, at least. But being queer wasn't something it could be, and I liked girls enough, so it wasn't."

"I don't understand."

"Yes, you do." Paul touches his shoulder on his way to the cabinet for the salt. "Even if it wasn't exactly the same for you — and I still don't know what it was for you. But I was a good kid. I played sports, I got good grades. But by the time I got to high school things weren't good anymore. My grades dropped. I was pissed all the time. I started getting into fights. I got busted for drugs once. Just pot," he says at Alex's expression, as if that's the important thing to clarify in all of this. "Nobody could figure out what was wrong. *I* couldn't figure out what was wrong. But I got called names and got into more fights because my father was very clear that no son of his was going to be a sissy fag."

"Oh."

Paul measures out salt into the palm of his hand and shakes it into another pot. "I told my sister. Swore her to secrecy. She promised never to tell our parents, then told me to never, ever tell either. She wanted to protect me," he says. "And I'm still not sure she was wrong to. I can't imagine what would have happened if I'd been able to make myself come out while I was still living at home."

"What did happen?" Alex's voice is timid.

Paul says nothing. He knows he's going to have to tell this story eventually, but he's not there yet, despite his best efforts.

"This feels like a movie, and I don't like it. I want you to be happy."

Paul continues as if Alex hasn't said anything. The story is hard enough for him to tell without having to deal with someone else's reaction to it. "By the time I did, it almost didn't matter anymore. I know that's anticlimactic." He grimaces. "Mom and Dad separated my senior year of high school. Which was…awful for a whole lot of reasons. At least after that there wasn't anywhere to go but up. Not that it made it any easier to be honest to myself. College was good. Better, at least. Getting out of the house was good, even if my father wasn't living there anymore. Sometimes you just need to get out."

"I can imagine."

"No kidding." Paul lets the conversation hang there for a moment.

Any hopes Paul has that Alex is going to say something about how the hell he landed in L.A. vanish when Alex asks, "So you finally — what? After college and after Carly?"

"After Carly," Paul nods. "Most of that is to her credit. She spent a lot of that time teaching me that as good as maybe we were together, it wasn't good enough for me, and that I deserved better than that. She spent a lot of time keeping me out of the worst of my brain too. Wasn't fair to her, but I still appreciate it."

"Sounds like a fun time."

"I've had worse. By the time I finally did come out, I think exactly no one was surprised. Word made it back to my dad — of course — and he wanted to disown me. According to my sister, Mom called him and yelled at him for an hour, then told him she'd already disowned him instead, and he could continue to stay the fuck away."

Alex laughs, "You mom sounds awesome."

"She is. You'll get to meet her tomorrow. Her and my sister. We always Skype on Thanksgiving."

"Things are okay with them?" Alex asks. "Like, is that going to be weird?"

"Things are great. They'll just never be good with my father."

"I'm sorry." Alex goes to where Paul is standing at the stove. He wraps his arms around Paul's waist and presses his face into the back of his shoulder. "You didn't say anything about the scars."

Paul closes his hands around Alex's to silence him. It feels less peculiar and awful that he's mentioned the scars this time, but Paul still doesn't want to talk about them. "It is what it is," he says, while Alex holds him tighter. "I'm here now. And so are you." He turns around in Alex's arms. "What about you?"

Alex chuckles damply. "It's a lot to process," he says. He works his fingers in and out of one of Paul's belt loops.

"I know. Take your time. It's the past, it's not going anywhere."

"Deep," Alex says.

"Writer." Paul kisses Alex's forehead

"Wait," Alex says, grabbing his arm with a look of alarm on his face. "Awful question: How did Carly meet Liam?"

"Not through me, thank God. That incestuous plot point is completely random."

"Okay, good. Good. Does Liam know?"

"Oh, Liam knows," Paul says dryly. "Liam thinks it's hilarious."

"Of course he does," Alex mutters. "Liam's capacity for delight in the absurd is boundless when there's sex involved."

They're cheerful but quiet after that, focusing on the work of cooking. Paul appreciates it. The quiet gives him time to think about what it means that he's told that much of his story and that Alex seems so comfortable sharing space with him.

When Paul mentions the latter, Alex says, "I don't hate spending time with everyone. Gemma's great when she's not asking for details about my sex life. My mom, too."

"What about me?" Paul asks, fishing.

"And you," Alex's tone more serious than Paul expects. "You don't ask me to do anything other than exist. Which assumes that I actually do. You are exactly the opposite of everything else in my life right now."

♦

In the late afternoon, pies done, turkey brining, and several funny discussions about whether marshmallows go on candied yams or not, Paul insists they go out for salads and smoothies. "We're going to be eating starch for days," he says.

"You want to pregame a holiday event with health food," Alex deadpans.

"Yes?"

"Oh my God. I wish I could say no."

In the car they discuss workout habits and neuroses. Alex for once gives up on avoiding mention of his life to talk about the inappropriate interest fans take in his physical shape and what they conclude it means about his value as a person.

"God forbid I wear a T-shirt that doesn't fit," Alex gripes.

"At least a little bit of beer won't make anyone think you're pregnant. Carly's life? Actual hell."

When they get to the place, it's filled with rollerbladers and joggers eating outside at picnic tables with umbrellas. The atmosphere is all wrong in Alex's head for November, but that's why the world was built in L.A., he supposes. Weather-wise, at least, it's Camelot.

"Can I stay in the car while you grab the stuff to go?" Alex asks. Beautiful as the day is, there are plenty of people out there, and Alex doesn't feel like being spotted or photographed.

"Uh, no?" Paul replies. He says it so easily Alex knows it would be churlish to argue further.

They eat outside at one of the picnic tables. There's a nice breeze and the sky is bright, so Alex's beanie and shades look almost seasonal, rather than like the camouflage they are.

◆

Back at the house that evening, Alex makes Paul drill him on his Farsi, handing him a stack of handmade flashcards. They lie at opposite ends of the couch, legs tangled, as they chat about *Fourth* and the language and Zach, and what the hell the character is thinking in the material on the other side of D.C.

"No prison," Alex says.

"What?"

"I don't care if he gets captured or tied up and held for ransom or whatever, but don't put Zach in prison."

"Okayyy," Paul says cautiously. "You know that's not up to me, right?"

"Victor knows," Alex adds, trying to warn Paul off with a look. "At least, I told him."

To Alex's relief Paul nods and changes the subject to why Zach thinks he'll be able to pass anywhere in Iran undetected.

"Not like he's inconspicuous," Alex agrees, gesturing to his face and hair.

"Some people are too smart to be safe."

"That could be the tagline for this cycle, you know," Alex points out.

"Maybe we should change the name to *The Zach Show*," Paul suggests.

Alex laughs and kicks at him. The flashcards go flying, but neither of them move to deal with them. They stare dopily at each other until Todd decides to investigate the new toys.

♦

They leave the flashcards on the floor when they go to bed. Despite it being with intent, once they hit the soft surface of the mattress they realize how tired they are from a day mostly spent in a too-warm kitchen. Paul is the first to complain aloud, rolling his shoulders and giving Alex a look that is both hungry and pathetic.

Alex shoves at his shoulder. "Stomach," he says. When Paul complies he straddles him to knead at his shoulders.

"You are the best," Paul mumbles into his pillow.

"I have no idea what I'm doing."

"I don't care. You're naked and bringing about a cessation of pain."

Alex works in silence, hands slipping lower as his dick fills against Paul's ass. He can't help but bring his hips into it, thumbs dragging up the long and knotted muscles of Paul's back.

Paul moans.

"Like that?" Alex asks.

"You should fuck me."

"I should," Alex says, even as he knows he shouldn't. He wants to, and he can almost bear the thought of this weekend as a fabulous parting gift in his too-young-for-Paul life. But there's only so much loss he can recover from and still be able to throw himself into work Monday night when he'll be in D.C. and Paul will still be here. He also has no idea how to say no.

Paul can't see him though and blows right by any hesitation in his voice, telling him what it would be like, how tight he'd be for him and how big Alex would feel inside of him as he fucked into him.

"Yeah, just like that," Paul breathes when Alex can't help but snap his hips forward, cock pressed tight against his ass.

"You make me crazy," Alex says, knowing it's true in more ways than one.

"Good."

"Fucking back like I can't do the job myself," he says a little breathlessly, because clearly, rutting against Paul is exactly how he's getting off tonight.

Paul laughs with delight. "Then show me what you've got," he says. "Make sure everyone knows."

"I wish I could." Alex says as leans over to rummage in the bedside table for lube. He squeezes some sloppy over his dick and Paul's crack; it makes the slide even better.

But in the back of his mind, Alex knows everything else is about to be a mess.

17

They wake up late, drifting comfortably in the warmth of the blankets and each other before they have to get up and finish the rest of the meal prep. The prospect of two months away from home and from this — particularly after Paul's unfulfilled request last night — is starting to loom unpleasantly.

Alex gets dressed thoughtfully. He knows everyone who's going to be here and doesn't have to worry about good impressions. But he's here with Paul in an odd, undefined role somewhere between co-host and principal orphan. Even if he's not sure how he could, Alex doesn't want to screw it up.

"Oooh, soft," Paul mutters approvingly, when he wraps his hands around Alex's waist and smooths the fabric of the gray wool sweater down with his thumbs. He kisses Alex before he goes to check on the turkey. It feels like reassurance, and Alex is grateful.

People start to arrive in the early afternoon. The house has been such a refuge for Alex lately, and he can't quite get a handle on the noise and the babble of the group. Having Carly and Craig and Beau — who curls up on one corner of the couch like it's his old favorite spot, which it probably is — here makes everything more fraught. Alex can't help but look at them and think about the lives they had with Paul before Alex existed.

He wonders who will succeed him in this place once he's gone. In the middle of his musings Paul catches his eye across the room and beckons him with a tip of his head. Alex goes and Paul wraps an arm around him. He kisses the side of his forehead, an indulgence of public affection that Alex, here, can let stand, if only for the novelty of it.

When Paul murmurs "I'm glad you're here" into his ear, Alex can't help but be happy, whatever may come.

"Me too," he says.

♦

Alex accidentally winds up in a corner with Craig.

Alex feels like a deer caught in the headlights. Craig says, "Hi."

"Why are you here?" Alex asks. "I mean. Not *here*." He tries to backtrack and flails his eyes around the room in search of Paul or any other plausible escape. "I mean, why didn't you go home? Where are you from?"

"Hawaii," Craig tells him. "It's a long, overpriced way to fly just for a few days, so I usually stay here. Not *here*, here."

"Oh. Okay." Alex tries to ignore the obvious fact that Craig is mocking him.

Awkward quota of socializing fulfilled, Alex is more than ready to move on, but he has no idea how. At least in the midst of this mess he can take a moment to enjoy the fact that he's a couple of inches taller than Craig.

But before Craig can move off graciously instead and presumably award himself points for a minimal level of awkwardness with his ex's famous boyfriend, Alex blurts, "Why didn't you take the cat too?"

Craig starts laughing and can't seem to stop.

Alex feels too horrified to speak. Into his silence Craig says, "He doesn't like the beach."

♦

Getting the turkey out of the oven and onto the platter is nearly as awkward. It takes both Paul and Alex, a great deal of chaos, and Paul possibly burning his leg through his jeans on the pan. At least he swears a lot, but he waves Alex off when he offers to go fetch him a Band-Aid or something. But when they get it to the table, it looks beautiful, and Paul offers Alex the honors of carving the bird. Alex may never have had a father at home to know what the gesture means, but he knows it means something.

After dinner, Paul video calls South Carolina. Everyone gives the screen a wave, and Paul tugs Alex forward for a proper-if-via-internet introduction.

"This is Alex, Mom," Paul says over Alex's shoulder while Alex waves at a camera that has nothing to do with his job. Paul has her eyes, he notices. When she beams and waves back at him — he has her smile, too.

If Paul were Alex's boyfriend, this would be a significant moment: meeting his family. But Paul isn't his boyfriend. Still, it's almost easy to imagine how he could be. Especially once he meets not only Alex's mother and sister but his brother-in-law and his adorable baby nephew.

He knows Paul's sister Sarah watches the show, but she's not shy at all about calling him *honey* and asking him what side of the marshmallow-on-yams debate he's on. It all feels good. If Alex can somehow stick around in Paul's life until he returns from New York, maybe the boyfriend conversation is one he can think about having.

For now though, the prospect still feels so terrifying and so adult, that on top of everything else it's too much. After the excessive consumption of pie, Alex finds himself hovering between spaces, trying to escape the crowd in the living room. But like any good party, the kitchen is also full of people looking for alcohol and scavenging food.

He startles when Carly approaches him from behind, her fingertips playing at the inside of his arm.

"Not like what you grew up with, is it?" she asks.

Alex feels odd not knowing what to say to her when they've already met so many times. But now that he knows she dated Paul, he realizes she may well know things about him.

"Default question," he says. "It's not personal," she says. "It's odd for everybody. The only one here who grew up in L.A. is Brian."

Of course it's Brian, who is, as far as Alex can tell, not just mean but the absolute worst sort of hipster. Alex is fairly sure that Brian makes up random bands to say he's into just to be sure no one else has ever heard of them.

"Nothing's ever personal," Alex says.

"Everything's personal," she counters with a toss of her hair.

Alex squints at her. "Are you trying to figure out if I'm going to be a jerk about Paul being your ex?"

"Are you?" Her gray eyes squint back at him, a clear parody of his own distrust of her motives.

"Not really." Alex isn't sure how he would be a jerk to her even if he wanted to. "Definitely weird about always being the last to know,"

She laughs. "Fame will do that to you."

It's strange to Alex to hear the word so baldly. Gemma still whispers it, like *cancer*. He tells Carly that, and she laughs in delight, tossing her wavy dark hair back over her shoulder. She goes on to punctuate the rest of their conversation with inappropriate whispers of *like cancer* until Alex hurts from laughing.

Paul looks over at them and smiles. Alex blushes. When his words wind down to nothing, because the day is long and the people are many, Carly kindly squeezes his arm and tells him there's no shame in escaping upstairs to hide for a little while.

"Liam has to do that sometimes too."

18

After fifteen minutes and no Alex, Paul goes looking for him. He finds him on his side on the bed in the dim. Alex has one hand on Todd who, eyes closed and purring, is in a state of bliss in his party-exile.

"Hey," Paul says quietly as he sits down on the edge of the bed. Alex blinks before focusing on his face. He looks startled. It's still a look Paul finds incredibly appealing.

"Sorry for disappearing," Alex says.

"How are you doing?" Paul scratches behind Todd's ear, then rubs his thumb over the back of Alex's hand.

"Recharging. I'm okay."

"Do you need anything?"

Alex shakes his head.

"Stay up here as long as you need," Paul tells him. He loves having Alex next to him downstairs, but he knows Alex is strange with crowds. Paul wants to be able to give him the space he needs. "Text me if you need anything."

Alex smiles sideways at him. "Okay. I will."

Paul leans over to kiss him — gentle, sweet, and cautious — before he goes back downstairs.

At the bottom of the stairs, Paul finds Liam waiting for him.

"He cool?" Liam asks as he herds them into the kitchen and away from whatever football game most everyone is now not watching.

"General question or specific question?"

Liam laughs.

"It's a lot, I think," Paul says, squinting at Liam. They're friends, ostensibly, but they've never quite clicked. Paul knows that's less because the Carly situation is awkward and more because he and Liam just don't innately get each other, but it's still something he feels guilty about. No one should know as much intimate trivia as he does about Liam regarding someone who isn't a very close friend.

"All this luck and people think he must be designed for the results of it," Liam says. "He's really not though."

Liam trying to educate him regarding Alex feels strange, but the simple fact is that Liam has probably spent more time with Alex than anyone else — Gemma included — over the last year. Also Liam is famous, has been acting since he was a kid, and has perspective and insight on Alex's experiences that should not be ignored. Paul realizes he should probably stop trying to avoid the ever-increasing number of overlapping relationships in their mutual web of friendships and start counting them as useful. After all, Liam is the one who first suggested New York.

"Do we have you and Carly for the whole day or...?" Paul asks.

"We're due at Victor's at eight."

"Only Victor would make Thanksgiving a late-night poolside soiree." Paul isn't quite sure where Carly is and isn't tangled up with Victor and can't imagine asking. Each time he offers dry commentary about the situation in reluctant hope of finding out more, he gets nothing. Carly enjoys forcing him to ask for things directly, and Paul doesn't mind thwarting her from time to time.

Liam chuckles, but doesn't seem inclined to offer any further insight. It is, in its own way, rather sweet.

Ten minutes later Alex texts Paul from upstairs.

I'll be down soon, it reads simply. *Thank you.*

Paul knows he has a dopey look on his face as he texts with a boy in the same house with him. He doesn't really care.

"Is that him?" Liam asks.

Paul nods.

Liam gives Paul a thumbs-up and moves away. Paul wonders why Liam has chosen to appoint himself head cheerleader for Team Alex-and-Paul but decides not to question it. In the casually vicious place that Los Angeles can be, Paul is happy to take all the enthusiasm he can get.

When Alex finally reemerges, everyone is in the living room talking over the TV. Paul watches him as he comes down the stairs. His hand is wrapped tightly around the bannister like a declaration of belonging and his own right of place. Paul smiles. This house has a lot of history for him, and he loves the thought of how much of it Alex will eventually claim.

Alex takes the empty seat on the couch next to Paul and leans into his side. Paul wraps an arm around his shoulders. It's a profoundly normal moment, which is something Alex has said he's wanted badly and something Paul has done his best to give him. But moments like this are also rare and fleeting. Paul can't keep Alex next to him always.

The party goes late. Paul is relieved when everyone is gone and they can finally clean up, or at least start to. With just the two of them in an otherwise empty post-party house, Paul is reminded of the night they first hooked up. But tonight they don't fuck; once they get into bed they curl up around each other, tired and happy to do nothing more than fall asleep together.

♦

Friday is a day the world that needs nothing from them. Paul is thrilled for the break. They sleep too late and wake up just enough for sex. After Paul gets up to get a washcloth, Alex pulls him back into bed for another nap.

The day, when they face it, is mostly a haze of watching bad TV and eating turkey sandwiches. Alex drifts from his notes and books to his phone to Paul's side, tucked in and still. For some reason — maybe it's the quiet after yesterday's chaos — today feels more snug and domestic than the other weekends they've spent together. Paul feels like Alex belongs here more and more with every passing day.

In the evening Alex's quiet starts to worry Paul. It's more profound than usual, and something about his mood seems gloomy, even melancholy. When Paul, unsure of what he needs and unsure of how to get Alex to tell him, suggests they go to bed early, Alex acquiesces easily. Perhaps the anticipated separation anxiety is getting to both of them.

In bed, in the dark, Alex seems to come back to himself a little. They spend hours talking about nothing in particular. But by the time they doze off, Paul knows that Alex's favorite book as a child was *James and the Giant Peach* and that he grew up poorer than he likes to talk about.

Saturday, Alex says he needs space.

"Movie date?" Paul suggests when Alex tries to express that he needs to get out of the house.

Alex nods. "Two hours in the dark without having to talk to anyone sounds perfect."

That night in bed, Paul can't stop himself from telling Alex that he wants to fuck him, too.

Alex says, "Good thing for you that you are," with a laugh, even though Paul knows Alex knows that's not what he meant.

Alex is right of course, but to Paul it feels like a sea of things they should address even if they both lack the courage for it.

19

Alex fears the sex in the morning will be slow and thoughtful. He doesn't want this to feel like goodbye or just enough; he wants it to feel as good as it always has. But Paul seems happy to take cues and thankfully their last morning together in bed is fun and full of laughter.

They lie on the pillows catching their breath, heads together. Paul smiles when Alex laces their fingers together. Alex takes a moment to watch his face; the last chance he might ever have. At least from so close and intimate a perspective as this.

"Are you excited?" Paul asks.

Alex isn't sure. It feels churlish to say no. But he's not excited, not really. Especially not at the prospect of leaving Paul. "I will be, when I get there, I guess. But change is scary, I don't like planes, and there's a lot that could go wrong."

"With the planes?" Paul teases.

Alex shakes his head. "No. Not with the planes."

"Look, you're gonna be great. You're — "

Alex cuts him off. He doesn't need Paul's encouragement. Especially on the points he's not even worried about. "This is all new for me. I'm still working on not fucking it all up."

"You're good at new things," Paul says. He squeezes their twined hands. "I mean, you're good at this."

"This is new," Alex concedes.

"I mean, not that new — " Paul teases.

"Paul." Alex nudges at Paul's feet under the covers.

"And it's good, right?"

Alex feels his smile brighten despite his worries. "It's really good." He looks down at their clasped hands, then up at Paul again. He feels frighteningly vulnerable. "I'm going to miss you."

"I would tell you it's just a couple of months with Christmas smushed in the middle, but...." Paul takes a deep breath. Alex wonders where this is going. He has a strangely sinking feeling. "I was talking to Victor and Liam and we decided — "

"You decided?" Alex says dryly. Whatever he was expecting, this is clearly about to be some bonus WTF of epic proportion.

"We decided," Paul continues, "that maybe it would be a good idea if I came and visited you in New York."

Alex doesn't say anything for a long time. He knows the silence is ominous. "When were you going to tell me?" he finally asks, quietly, before adding, "Or, you know, ask me?"

"Before you left."

"Before I left?"

"I was nervous," Paul says carefully.

Alex goes still. "Nervous about what?"

"It's a big thing," Paul says.

"Did you think I'd say no?"

"Is this you saying no?" Paul's voice is conspicuously tight with worry.

"I'm not supposed to say no," Alex says, despite knowing that's not an answer at all. "But I need to be able to. You should have asked."

"I think this is me asking?"

"No, this is telling me something Victor and Liam apparently decided with you. One of those people is my boss."

"He's my boss too. And a friend."

"Yes, and he doesn't control how you wear your hair, when you eat, when you sleep — "

"Definitely when I sleep."

"You know what I mean."

"So I phrased it poorly."

"And sprung it on me when I'm about to leave and we can't discuss it because it was apparently never up for discussion." Alex sits up and flings the covers back.

"Hey, hey, hey." Paul sits up and grabs Alex's hands.

"Do not patronize me," Alex says. He modulates his voice carefully: Not petulant, wrathful. He doesn't yank away from Paul as he says it, though he wants to. "I have been going crazy all weekend, maybe for weeks, thinking that this was our last big hurrah, because I don't even know what we are. And I was prepared for that. I was ready to be grateful to you for this time and get drunk with my roommate, and then you had to go and do this!"

"Isn't this good news?" Paul asks.

"NOT WHEN YOU'RE MAKING ALL THE DECISIONS."

"What — what are you talking about?" Paul stammers in the silence that follows.

Alex's heart is racing and his palms are sweating. He'd trusted Paul, at least to understand how little control Alex has over anything in his life. How much he needs people in his private life to not make decisions for and about him, too.

"You came up with this and then got it cleared by Victor?" he demands. "And *Liam* — how the fuck does Liam come into this? Did you actually run it by him before you talked to me?"

"No," Paul says, clearly disoriented.

"What a relief."

◆

Alex grabs his jeans from where he'd tossed them last night as they were getting undressed together.

"How do you not know what we are?" Paul finally asks. Out of everything, that's the one that stings the most, somewhere over the hurt that Alex thought Paul would leave him.

"What are we, Paul?" Alex reaches for his shirt.

When Paul gets up on his knees on the bed and grabs his wrist, Alex stares at his hand until Paul lets go. "We're — " Paul starts, then hesitates. This feels like a moment where there are no right answers. Out of all the mistakes he's made, he should have asked Alex about this most of all.

"Nothing, apparently," Alex says, quiet again now and chillingly calm. He puts on the shirt.

Paul's mouth drops open. On some level he understands that Alex is terrified, has been terrified for days, if not weeks, if not possibly this entire year plus of his strange good fortune. It's all bursting out now, at Paul.

He tries to tell Alex as much, but all he gets for his trouble is Alex storming out of the bedroom.

Paul yanks on a pair of jeans and grabs a T-shirt out of his dresser.

"Would you stop acting like a child?" he calls down from the landing as he struggles into the shirt. He's furious.

"I don't see why I have to when you're treating me like one," Alex says.

"You are being ridiculous. This is seriously one of the craziest fights I've ever had."

"Speaking of other things you have an excellent track record with," Alex says loudly but not really to Paul as he joins him downstairs.

"Look," Paul says, "We are arguing in circles. You're pissed at me for not communicating with you about us and for making a hash of it when I tried. But you're yelling at me because you don't want this to be over while deciding it already is. Frankly, I'm fucking confused."

"You were the only person who didn't want anything from me and that I didn't owe anything to, forgive me for being upset."

"Well, there's an amazing summary of your problems with intimacy," Paul shoots back.

Alex gapes at him. "Are you writing an afterschool special? Is this really coming down to my owing it to you to take it up the ass?"

"Jesus Christ, that is not what I meant, but if you weren't so fucking terrified of — "

"No," Alex says. "You don't get to call me a coward. I have had my life pulled apart and put on display. I've had my body evaluated like fucking livestock so I could afford better jeans and stop my roommate from hating me forever because I got the big break she wanted. I have done everything in my fucking life, on my own, since I was eight. You do not get to take that from me because you're a melodramatic asshole who has decided I don't measure up to your happy fun times gay checklist."

Paul makes a noise of frustration.

"What?" Alex snaps.

Paul holds up a hand. He's trying to stop himself from making things worse.

"WHAT?" Alex repeats.

"Do you want to hear that I feel like slapping you right now so you'll shut up? That I want to hold you until you sob out whatever fucking misery has just surfaced in your head? Because neither of those impulses are appropriate or fair. So I'm going to go out for a run, get some air, and try to calm down. I suggest you do the same."

"I'm not a child."

"We've covered that," Paul snaps as he shoves his feet into the tennis shoes left by the door. "Prove it to me by still being here when I get back, and we'll hash this out. Because newsflash? While you were worried about me dumping you, I somehow skipped over *boyfriend* and went straight to *partner*, but I suppose you're probably pissed about that too."

Paul slams the door on his way out.

◆

Alex stares at the back of the door unable to make sense of what just happened.

He wants to yell, *You're fucking right I am* at Paul, because he's furious about one more decision Paul made about him that goes way beyond semantics.

He also wants to run after Paul and say *please don't leave me alone*, because the house is silent and empty in the sudden aftermath. It's frightening.

He wants to cry, and he wants to throw something, and none of those are adult responses, so he doesn't.

Alex walks back upstairs. When Todd meets him at the bedroom door and rubs against his legs, his eyes start to sting.

His suitcase is at the foot of the bed, open, half-empty, the clothes and contents scattered across the room and all over the house. He looks at the clock on the nightstand and tries to judge how much time he has before Paul gets back.

Then he starts packing.

He has to keep picking Todd up out of the suitcase.

"Hey, no," he says, when Todd tries to crawl in yet again. "You can't come, buddy. You don't want to be Divorce Cat." His voice echoes and small in the stillness of the house.

Once he gets his bag downstairs, he sees that his hat is still tossed over the back of the chair in the kitchen where he'd left it when they got in from the movie yesterday. Alex lets it stay.

And then he leaves.

♦

By the time Paul is done with his run, his head is clearer. He's now willing to admit that, for all of Alex's horrible fear and anxiety that had fueled the utter stupid of that fight, he's not blameless either.

He rounds the last corner before his street wishing they at least had more time to talk everything out before Alex has to leave for his flight.

When he gets to his house, Alex's car isn't in the driveway. When he goes inside, he calls out to him anyway, just in case it's some sort of awful, impish prank. But Alex isn't there and neither are his things, except for his beanie resting on the back of one of the kitchen chairs. If it's a sign, and Paul is sure it must be a sign, he has no damn idea what it means.

20

"Wow, man, you look like shit."

Alex makes an apologetic face to the woman at the desk who is trying to check him in to the hotel in D.C. as Liam bounces up to him. "So would you if you'd spent a cross country flight sobbing into your eye mask."

"Aww, you guys are so cute!"

Alex doesn't even have the energy to remind Liam of bystanders. At least Natalie and Raphael are in a different hotel. "We had a fight."

"Oh. Oh shit. Why?"

"Does the thing where you, Victor, and Paul made decisions for my life without consulting me ring any bells?"

Liam splutters. "Dude, that is not — "

"I've barely slept. Everything's crazy, and I'm pissed at you. Please go away?"

"Do you want to talk?"

"No, Liam. I do not want to talk. I want to drown myself in the bathtub, but a nap is going to have to do," he says as he collects his key card.

"I'm in 723 if you want to talk."

"Right." Alex walks away.

"What room are you in?" Liam shouts.

"Not one I'm going to holler across the lobby at you," Alex calls back without turning around. Fuck his life. And night shoots on top of it all.

♦

The last thing Alex wants to do is check his phone, but he's been off the grid since LAX and the task is unavoidable. Thankfully, everything in the handful of notifications can be ignored for now, but there's an email from Paul.

He stares at it for a good fifteen seconds, reading the subject line — simply, *Alex*, like he is the problem in this whole mess — over and over before he finally opens it.

It's many screens long, but the gist of it all is in the last sentence: *I adore you. I fucked up, and I'm sorry. Can we work this out?*

Six hours of misery on the plane was plenty of time for Alex to come down from his pitch of righteous anger and realize how awful and unfair he'd been. He fucked up, too, badly, and they do need to talk, but he hasn't slept and has only a few hours before he has to be at work.

Got to D.C. okay, he replies. *I know I was an asshole. I'm sorry. But I didn't know we were together and I really didn't know we were married. I'm 21 and trying to do TV and a movie a long way from home. I can't do this right now.*

Alex hits send, sets an alarm, and collapses onto the bed without bothering to take his shoes off.

◆

He's woken, not by his alarm, but by a pounding on his door so insistent he thinks for a moment the hotel is on fire. He takes a moment to lie there and consider whether or not that would actually be an awesome turn of events.

But when he gets out of bed and looks through the peephole, it's just Liam.

"What do you want?" he asks as he opens the door. He feels disgusting and has no bandwidth for whatever this is.

"We gotta talk, dude."

"Jesus Christ, if this is about Paul you've — "

"Noooooooo, it's not," Liam says, pushing his way into Alex's room. "The timing's shit, and I'm sorry. I'm still willing to listen if you wanna talk about it, but trust me, you're gonna be less pissed at me about a whole set of other things if we have this conversation now as opposed to later."

"Okaaaaay," Alex says, puzzled, as he lets the door slip closed. He retreats into the bathroom to brush his teeth and splash water on his face to prepare for whatever the hell is happening now.

Liam leans against the bathroom doorframe, ignoring Alex's glare in his direction.

"I want to tell you this now before we have to shoot the stuff tonight, because it's, you know, *stuff* and you deserve to know it, and — "

"What is it, Liam?" Alex tosses down the towel and props himself against the fake marble of the bathroom counter, folding his arms over his chest.

"So, I'm bi."

Alex cracks up.

"Dude! Hey!" Liam looks affronted.

That makes Alex stop with a hand over his mouth. "You're kidding. You are actually kidding."

Liam shoves his hands in his pockets and for once in his life says nothing.

Alex lowers the hand over his mouth slowly. "You're not actually kidding."

"Hey, man, don't stereotype."

"Liam!"

"Yeah?"

"What the actual fuck."

"I'm not in the closet. I mean — it's not a secret."

"Like fuck it isn't," Alex shoots back.

"It's complicated, okay!" Liam retorts.

"So explain it!"

"I'm trying!" Liam looks wounded. "You laughed in my face."

Alex cannot process any of this. "I'm not going to apologize for anything right now," he says carefully.

"Yeah, that's…yeah, that's probably cool. Anyway." Liam shuffles his feet and gives Alex a look Alex knows he practices. "I wanted to tell you before we had to shoot the kiss tonight."

"Thank you for the advance warning."

"You're — "

"No, seriously, Liam." Alex pushes past him out of the bathroom. "Why the fuck is it that I have no time to process anything because everyone in my life keeps waiting until the last minute to drop bombshells on me? On purpose?!"

"Dude, I'm sorry Paul — "

"Does Paul know about this?"

"What does that have to do with — "

"Does. He. Know?"

"Yes." Liam sits down cross-legged on the end of Alex's bed. "And if he didn't say anything it's 'cause he's a good guy, so don't be pissed at him for my choices, okay?"

Alex stares. "Please tell me you haven't slept with him."

"Nope."

"No you haven't or no you're not telling me?"

"No, I haven't," Liam says seriously.

"Okay."

"Okay?"

"Only about that," Alex clarifies. "I'm still pissed at you."

"You know this isn't about you, right?" Liam says in a manner that suggests he has a lot of practice pointing that out to people, whether true or not.

"And that's why you're telling me this and why the internet has spent the last year thinking we're dating."

"Look, I'm sorry about that. It's not fun for Carly and me either, but there's nothing — "

"*Bullshit.* You played that up every second you could. While saying you're straight. Who does that?"

"It's helped both of us," Liam says mildly.

"I'm the fucking twink. That's what helped you," Alex snaps, before cursing under his breath.

"Ego, ego," Liam teases in lieu of yelling back.

"You know what I mean." Alex deflates.

"Yeah. I do."

"So *why?*"

"I'm with Carly for one. For another, you wanna try explaining non-monogamy and/or bisexuality to *TV Guide?*"

"Alan Cumming," Alex replies.

"Great name, right?"

"Are you trying to get me to storm out of my own hotel room?"

"Look, it's not convenient or salient or easy. I've never lied about it. I've omitted, and I've dodged, but I have never lied about it. You can go back through every interview and check that."

"But, because it wasn't going to get you the cover of *People,* you didn't tell," Alex clarifies for him.

"Yeah," Liam says. "Like why would anyone not make that choice?"

Alex is horrified. "Do you want me to congratulate you?" He crosses his arms in front of his chest. He understands being in the closet — no matter what Liam says — but he's not going to cheer the man on for being mercenary.

"Come on, aren't there some things you want to keep out of the product?"

"Yes, and as the last twenty-four hours has demonstrated, I don't get to have any of them."

21

Paul gets Alex's reply as he's walking down the hallway to the writers' room. He nearly fumbles his phone as he tries to juggle it, his bag, and the door.

He's done reading the message by the time he gets to his desk but can't begin to think of a reply. Alex never does use very many words, but he is always devastatingly good at communicating himself.

Okay, he replies before shoving his phone back in his pocket. "Message received, darling," he mutters under his breath.

During lunch, Carly calls. Paul leaves his laptop open to where he's continuing to fail to fix a scene and walks out to the hallway.

"Does everyone know?" he asks. This information diffusion is even worse than when they'd first gotten together and a lot less happy. Paul hopes that Alex hasn't seen that there are paparazzi pictures of him from LAX on the internet. The internet, because Paul is morbidly curious enough to have checked, is in fact having an absolute field day trying to figure out why Alex looks so miserable.

That the prevailing assumption is that he finally broke up with the jackass he'd been dating instead of, or in addition to, Liam is a whole new level of horrible. And not only because they're not entirely wrong.

"Liam told me. He's worried."

"Oh."

"Are you okay, Paul?"

"I just had someone walk out on me last night for the second time in a year."

"Oh, honey."

Paul makes it to the courtyard, where he sits down on a bench and presses the phone hard against the side of his head. "Yeah."

"Do you want to come over sometime this week? Not to talk if you don't want to. Get you out of your space."

Paul thinks of his empty house, his own too-full mind, and the way Carly continues to try to help him be a functional man. "Yeah. But I know you're judging me."

"Sure, but I'm luring you in with my compassion first."

Paul puts back his head and squints against the brightness of the sky. "Why do you put up with any of us?"

"You and Liam, you mean?"

"And so many more."

"You two are my most special of special snowflakes," she says with a certain degree of weariness. Paul manages a smile anyway. "But this is what I do. I'm good at it, it's good for me, and you certainly need it."

◆

That afternoon, Victor breezes into the office and surveys his hardworking minions with satisfaction. Then his eyes land on Paul. "Is everything set for New York?"

"Come with me," Paul shoves away from the desk and stalks out of the room.

Victor follows Paul into the kitchenette. "Ooooh, drama," he drawls in the San Francisco gay accent that marks all their divides — from generational to experiential — in a way Paul finds particularly irksome in the moment.

This is not a conversation he wants to have. The subject matter is upsetting, Victor is unpredictable, and the whole matter feels like a test he doesn't know how to pass.

"New York isn't happening," he says. "I fucked up, and you let me do it. Alex may be overreacting but he isn't wrong, and I am way too used to you pulling all the strings to think how I made your friendly advice sound. You are some sort of fucked up, Victor."

"I told you to be careful of him," Victor says mildly. "And it's your life too."

"I'm aware of that," Paul snaps.

"Apparently not enough. And don't blame me for your sloppy sentence construction." Victor watches Paul intently, fascinated with how he's reacting. While Paul is used to this level of scrutiny, right now it feels more unsettling than it has in a long time.

"It would be a lot easier to feel like I wasn't one of your creations if you didn't keep treating me like one."

"You've always been a character in my story, Paul. You keep missing the point is all."

"Really? And what's that?"

"That no one cares about stories where no one ever says no and everyone always lives happily ever after."

◆

Alex is relieved to go through hair and makeup and let himself sink into the headspace of not quite existing. Sometimes he hates it, but right now he appreciates not having to worry about anything.

The sun sets earlier here and it's colder than he's gotten used to in L.A., especially with the wind off the tidal basin. It's one more strange and surreal thing in his strange and surreal life to be here in D.C. for a job he never planned on having. He never even came here when he was growing up, although he saw photos from school trips other people from better towns posted on the internet.

The Washington Monument is shorter than he thought it would be.

Alex tells Liam that, while Liam fidgets with yet another random app on his smartphone. Then he says, "Don't even." He knows the next thing to come out of Liam's mouth is going to be a dick joke.

Liam is quiet for another moment, then puts his phone away. "You're freaking out."

Alex gives him a look and tries not to see the people who are starting to cluster around the edge of the area they've got closed off for filming. All this day needs to make it better is fans. "No, I'm not."

"Yes, you are. This isn't about the thing, is it?"

"It's not about the thing."

"You're a shit liar, Alex."

"It's not lying, it's acting," Alex says haughtily.

"…Dude, that's fucked up."

"I am reminding myself that I am a professional." Alex focuses not on Liam, but on the lights on the water. Beyond them, the majestic columns of the Jefferson rise above the skeletons of the cherry trees. "And in thirty seconds I will be right with you, but currently, yes, I'm freaking out."

Liam checks his watch.

"Oh my God, seriously?"

"Shhhhhh, twenty-five seconds left. Freak out wisely,"

Alex doesn't even think he's teasing so much as respecting the process. "It's not about the thing." Alex's life is too much of a mess for Liam's bisexuality to be the centerpiece of his day.

"Is it about you being here, doing this, and having no clue what your life is right now?"

Alex hugs his arms around himself. "That, and in about fifteen minutes I have to make out with you, on camera, which officially makes this the second weirdest day of my entire life."

"Hey, I only get second place?"

"The first-weirdest day was totally half your fault too."

"Whose fault was the other half?" Liam asks curiously.

Alex isn't sure what to say. He's never told anyone about the run-in with Paul the morning his life exploded. Besides, it's easier to blame Victor.

Liam taps his watch before grabbing Alex's shoulder. "Time's up. Let's go rock this."

◆

Halfway through the night, Alex realizes that Liam didn't decide to come out to him at an incredibly inconvenient time because he suddenly felt the need to absolve himself. Yes, the burden created by the audience's preoccupation with the sex lives of *Fourth's* stars is significant. But in the scene James has his hands in his pockets and is talking — quietly, earnestly, shyly — to Zach about truth and honesty. For once, nothing he's saying has to do with journalistic ethics or even the appalling lack of them.

"Everybody here's got a lie," he says. "I don't want to lie to you anymore."

As they reset the cameras for the sixth of what feels like twelve different angles on the damn kiss, Alex realizes Liam's giving a better performance because there's truth underlying it. He wanted Alex to know that and give more because of it too. The situation is humbling, and Alex isn't sure if he has more to learn about life or acting in the face of it.

◆

Back at the hotel Liam walks with Alex from the elevator to his room.

"I'm, like, just around the corner there," he says once Alex manages to get his key out and his door open. Then Liam hugs him tightly.

"Liam, what the fuck?" Alex tries to keep his door open but it's awkward with Liam affixed to him.

"Good job tonight," Liam says, muffled over Alex's shoulder.

Liam's sudden bursts of thoughtfulness and awareness of others are as surprising and unpredictable as his need to — inconveniently, at the moment — physically express his affection for the whole word.

"…Thank you," Alex says tiredly, finally hugging Liam back. The door clicks closed again. "You too."

"There you go." Liam unwraps himself from Alex, and looks him in the eye intently for a moment before patting his cheek. "You're gonna be okay, man."

Alex has to bite his lip. Unexpected sympathy is even worse than unexpected hugs. His eyes suddenly sting. "Okay."

"I'm down the hall if you want to talk."

"*Okay.*" He's amused more than otherwise, but still. "It has been a really long day. I'm going to go sleep, and then you can bug me more in the morning, yeah?"

"Cool!" Liam bounces away.

Alex rests his forehead against the door before he manages to get the key in the lock again. It's been the longest day.

22

"So there's this thing you do, that I don't get," Paul says, kicking his socked feet against Carly's. They're in her bed — Carly in pajamas and Paul in sweatpants and a ratty T-shirt that pass for the same — with beer and a bag of ranch-flavored chips, half-heartedly watching *Jaws*.

"Yeah?"

"Why do I always have an awesome time with you when I'm miserable?"

She shoves another handful of chips into her mouth. "Because I am awesome, and most of the time we spend together has involved you being miserable, which is what happens when you date girls you shouldn't be dating."

"I'm starting to think I maybe shouldn't be dating."

"Ya think?" Carly asks.

"Thanks."

"Look, I'm just saying you didn't magically stop being nuts when you realized you liked dick the mostest."

Paul cackles. Carly is the most awful and awesome of all his friends. Even with her long, wavy hair up in a messy, lopsided ponytail and the hideous yellow and pink pajamas that completely clash with her tawny skin, she looks amazing and slightly terrifying. He's very fond of her.

"So what's your call?" he asks. "Permanently broken or temporarily broken?"

"You and dating or you and Alex?"

"Me, mainly."

Carly ponders for a moment. "Mmmmm, thoroughly broken."

"This door number three thing you do is really annoying, by the way."

"But it works. You, on the other hand, do not work. You fall in love with every good fuck that comes your way and yet can't figure out that you're the common denominator enough to love yourself? As usual, my friend, you should be smarter than your bad crazy."

"And yet...." Paul steals a handful of chips.

"And yet. So what's the plan?"

"A vow of celibacy while I convince myself maybe he wasn't the one?"

"Wait, seriously?" she asks, sitting up and clicking pause on the shark.

Paul nods solemnly.

"That's not good. Like, you can talk all you want about not fucking around, but you're too much like Liam. Just monogamous. You need someone in your bed like people need water."

Paul thunks his head back against the headboard. "No kidding."

"Why haven't you gotten blindingly drunk yet?" Carly asks.

"You mean why didn't I bring over something better than beer?"

"Yeah, this is entirely about my need for gin." Carly rolls her eyes. "You're such an asshole, answer the question."

"Because every night when I get home, I think I'm going to see his car in the driveway, or I'm going to wake up to him climbing into bed."

"Because you're delusional or because you think he wants to fix it too?"

"That's the problem," Paul says as the pause timer expires and the shark action recommences. "I can't tell."

23

When he wakes up on day two, Alex feels like a human being again. The crisis, at least for now, is past.

Zach and James kissed and the world didn't end. Alex, meanwhile, didn't combust from the horror of it. Or freeze at the feel of lips other than the ones he wants and doesn't get to have anymore. And all things considered, Liam was more decent about the whole thing than Alex expected.

Alex may not feel in control of his world, but he feels capable. The thought of going for a second day without disaster in a new city is appealing. So is a proper breakfast and a foray to a bookstore. Since they're shooting nights this week, he has his days to himself. In a city with an actual winter, Alex thinks he might even be able to remain unseen.

It doesn't work. He left his beanie at Paul's and there are fans loitering outside of the hotel. It's amazing to him what people think counts as inconspicuous. He has to offer to sign something for a girl and chitchat with her friends in order to convince them not to follow him. While he does, the Margaret in his head is telling him not to negotiate with terrorists. He winds up purchasing a new hat, acrylic and ill-fitting, from the first street vendor he sees.

D.C. isn't like L.A. at all. The buildings are shorter, and it's actually built for pedestrians. Although the spoke-and-wheel street layout complicates navigation, it's not hard to find a bookstore. Alex feels himself relax when he pushes open the door and is greeted with a burst of warmth and the smell of coffee.

He spends an hour browsing, picking up books at random and skimming through them. History, art, politics, literature, poetry, philosophy — he investigates them all. He hardly has time for leisure reading anymore, not with his life and his schedule. He misses it. When he was in Indiana, he never had the money for books and he'd soon exhausted what the public library had on offer. Even after three years in L.A. — one of them as a TV star — new books still feel like a delicious indulgent luxury.

The coffee shop is maybe half-full. The occupants look to be mostly local high school kids with laptops and textbooks, or sitting with their friends talking. Alex swallows down a stab of envy. How different his life would have been, if he'd been able to have bookstores and coffee shops and other kids like him growing up.

He should do this more often, he thinks as he finally makes a selection.

He spends the rest of the afternoon in his hotel room curled up with his book.

♦

Alex and Liam get driven in a car to location that night because no one trusts them to get to set in a city they don't know. Once they get there Liam spends as much time as he can on the edge of the shoot area, signing things for fans and smiling and waving into smart phones, while reminding everyone there will be no kissing on set tonight.

Of course, the fans have never believed Liam on this sort of point. Given what Alex and Liam filmed last night — not to mention the fact that Liam is bi — they suddenly look a hell of a lot smarter for their skepticism. Liam's repeated demurrals only seem to summon more of them. Alex considers joining Liam to see if his own overwhelming lack of enthusiasm will drive the spectators off. He decides to huddle by a heat lamp at crafty with some of the hair and makeup crew instead.

◆

"Hey, you want to get a drink after?" Liam asks, checking his watch when they call the last shot of the night.

"Everything's closed," Alex points out. It's almost three in the morning.

"I know a place."

Alex squints at him. There's a halfway decent chance Liam does know a place. But while Alex may be legal now, drinking at some illegal after-hours bar doesn't seem like the best plan in the *don't fuck up in public* sweepstakes.

"Is this place your hotel room?" Alex asks, somewhere between dubious and hopeful. Somehow, Liam's room would be the lesser of two evils. His life is damn surreal for having come to this.

"Dude. Minibar!"

◆

"This is your idea of a minibar?" Alex says when they walk in. The full-sized bottle of scotch on the dresser renders that something of an understatement.

Liam immediately snags the glass tumblers the hotel set next to a complimentary bottle of ridiculous mineral water. "Compared to the bar at home, yeah."

Alex watches Liam as he pours them both a drink and accepts his gratefully. He's been to Liam's house many times — almost exclusively for work-related parties — and considering he has a whole room full of manly leather furniture, books Alex is sure he doesn't read, and one hell of a bar set up, he can see his point.

They wind up lying on the bed, side-by-side and shoes still on. While Liam seems mesmerized with the rapidly dwindling contents of his glass, Alex balances his on his chest and stares at the ceiling while he talks about Paul — not what happened, but what it was.

"Anyone could see that," Liam says at one point, when Alex finally says the L-word.

"I didn't know that's what it felt like," Alex says.

"Like what?"

"Abject terror."

Liam laughs. Alex swats at him, knocking scotch all over them both. Alex curses and bolts upright to try to deal with it, but Liam puts out a hand for him to stay put.

"It's a hotel, so it'll get dealt with when we call for them to deal with it. It's also alcohol, so it will evaporate quickly, and neither of us is wearing anything nice enough to care about."

"This is not a life I'm used to," Alex says distantly. Liam is peculiar, and the idea of other people at his service is still a philosophical problem for him.

"Go bring us the bottle then. You'll feel better."

"Now I know why Carly refuses to live with you," Alex mutters as he fetches the bottle and restores their drinks.

"You ever let Paul see your place?"

"No."

"Then don't judge my housekeeping in a hotel when I'm trying to get drunk."

Alex arranges himself cross-legged on the bed. He stares at Liam, who always seems to be trying too hard. "Sometimes I can't figure out if you're the happiest guy I know or the saddest."

"Yes," Liam says, clinking glasses with him. "You think you're the only one who finds this life lonely regardless of who you're in it with?"

"Yes?"

"No. We're a species made to do this to people, not to have it done to us. No one will ever understand what it's like to be you. If you can remember that, you'll be less pissed all the time and less of a shit to the people you date."

"Er, thanks?"

"No problem."

"Sometimes I hate you."

"I know. Is that getting better or worse in the last forty-eight hours?"

Alex laughs and drains his glass. In this quiet late-night dark Liam is beautiful. Alex wonders if all the usual chaos of his body language and intrusiveness is meant to dull that. Being beautiful in Hollywood is so dangerous; maybe Liam knows that as well as him.

"I'll let you know," he says

He finds it odd that Liam should feel suddenly so much more like a peer. They've always been acutely different. That, combined with the age difference, has largely made it seem like Liam is cool and Alex just isn't. The reality is far more complex.

Liam is a hot mess of secrets that Victor is somehow forcing him to confess on TV. That's strange and a little bit ugly. Alex realizes he can feel victimized and exposed by his fame all he wants, but his life may always be more his own than Liam's ever will by the simple virtue of being out and not wanting to sell every single secret he has.

"I've misjudged you," Alex finally says.

"Yeah?"

"It's not a compliment." Alex lies down, and Liam flops down next to him. Alex supposes scotch and a king-sized bed and four in the morning will do that to anyone.

Liam chortles. "I like you."

Alex turns his head in what feels like movie magic slowmo to see Liam's blue eyes blinking back at him. He's not surprised at all, because Alex *knows* stories. Even if he's crap at predicting how they end, in the last year he's gotten very good at understanding how they begin.

"Yeah?" Liam is staring at him, and the whole thing feels loaded and odd.

Alex nods.

Liam kisses him.

He tastes like scotch and doesn't kiss like James. In Alex's altered state it feels easy. Liam doesn't kiss like James and it doesn't seem like a bad idea. This can't cost Alex any more than losing Paul had done.

"This is a really bad idea," Liam says against his lips.

Alex wonders why. He's single. Liam is poly. He laughs into Liam's mouth and has one terrible moment where he remembers the wine in Paul's. Maybe Liam is right.

"You don't give a remote shit, do you?" Liam asks.

Alex shakes his head, sits up, and toes off his shoes. "Now you get to prove to me you're not a liar."

"You don't actually think that," Liam says.

"I don't. But you would if it were useful," he says as he pulls his T-shirt up over his head.

"Christ, you're direct."

"Someone has to be." As with Paul, now that Alex knows he can have this, he wants to take it. And with Liam at least he knows where he stands.

"Fine," Liam says. He sits up, sets his glass down decisively on the night table. "I let you fuck me and we consider the matter of my truthfulness closed."

"I think it's already closed." Alex wrinkles up his face up at Liam's ridiculousness.

"Okay. But fuck me anyway?" Liam sounds exasperated. "Because I want you to and I'm drunk, very cute, only slightly pathetic, and asking nicely."

Alex runs a nervous hand through his hair.

Liam stares at him in until some sort of realization kicks in. "What? You don't top?"

"Think harder." Alex tries to squash the impulse to be defensive.

"Oh shit, you've never done this before." Liam scrambles to his knees and reaches for Alex. "We're going to have so much fun!"

Making out with Liam is hot and messy and fun. Alex figures out a bunch of small and specific things that get him going fast. It's good for Alex's ego, knowing to breathe just so against Liam's ear or to tell him how very good he is. It's even better for his confidence to not only have control, but to know what to do with it. He can thank Paul for that, though he tries not to dwell too long on the thought.

They get naked fast, mainly because Alex is already halfway there. Of the many things Liam is, a tease is apparently not one of them.

"God, I love that you take up so much more space than me," Liam says. Alex pins him to the bed and bites at his neck hard. He hasn't spent much time thinking about the fact that he's taller and broader than Liam, though it's obvious now.

"Twink my ass," Alex murmurs. Liam cracks up and slaps his in response.

Alex's laugh cuts off in a gasp.

"Oh really," Liam says.

"Apparently," Alex says and returns to biting across Liam's throat and shoulders and chest.

"You tell me when you want to add that to the to-do list."

Alex doesn't know what to say and doesn't want to think about it right now, so he bites harder.

When they have to pause for Liam to dig condoms and lube out of his bag, he realizes how glad he is that they are both drunk and hilarious and chatty. Alex is nervous.

He doesn't think of himself as a virgin, didn't even before Paul, and yet here he is in this absurd situation with TV star Liam Campbell's rather stunning ass staring him more or less in the face. His brain insists that this is a momentous occasion. As dumb as that is, Alex is fairly sure it's not the wrongest thought he's ever had.

Liam tosses the supplies on the bed. "It's just sex. And a little bit of technology. Relax," he says with a kiss so easy and intimate it takes Alex aback.

It's nothing, however, compared to Liam taking his hand and showing Alex how to finger him. It's weird and a little stupid, and they both giggle through it until Liam goes breathless. Alex can't remember the last time he's felt as glad to be as young as he is. The sounds Liam makes as Alex pushes one of his legs back so he can get deeper make his dick twitch.

"God, I could spend hours sucking at your thighs," he murmurs into skin.

"No one's stopping you."

Liam helps him with the condom. Alex isn't sure if that's sexy or not, but it's a great distraction now that his brain has started up with the momentous occasion nonsense again.

"You're going to stop thinking the second you're inside me," Liam says. "And then I'm going to give you too much direction, and you'll get pissed off and pound me into the mattress. Trust me, it's gonna be great."

Liam isn't wrong, despite leaving out the part where he's insanely tight and the slow push into him is some of the most exquisite torture Alex has ever experienced. Liam's on his knees, ass in the air, shoulders down on the bed and hands folded under his face as it happens. At first it's too much for Alex to look at him as he sinks inside, but then it's too much not to.

When Liam starts sucking on his fingers, Alex swears and pulls them away, replacing them with his own. "You need all the dick, don't you?"

Liam nods frantically, and Alex huffs out something of a laugh as he pistons his hips in earnest. Whatever this is about — and Alex can't think enough to even try to figure it out right now — it's no longer about who they are when they're wearing clothes or making words. While there's nothing at all surprising about Liam being needy and vulnerable in this way, Alex knows the signs of secrets by now. They make his heart go tender.

Liam comes first, frantically pumping his own cock and still sucking on Alex's fingers. Despite the relief Alex sees roll through him, Liam barely pauses in fucking back hard onto Alex's cock, spitting out his fingers and urging him on, a litany of *come on, come on, come on.*

Alex cuffs him lightly on the back of the head then digs his wet fingers into his hair. "Impatient asshole," he grits out fondly before he spills into the condom.

24

Alex is grateful, relaxed and still turning the whole thing over in his brain. But mostly, he is content.

"So what did you think? Awesome?" Liam asks as he takes the lead in getting them cleaned up. Alex can even recognize that Liam isn't fishing for compliments. He just wants to know he's done the right thing in showing someone something new.

He closes his eyes and lets himself drift a little. "Awesome."

"Good," Liam says softly. He climbs back into bed and drapes an arm, a leg, and half his body on top of Alex.

"I fuck you, and you cuddle me," Alex murmurs sleepily. "Is that how this works?"

He's making fun, but Alex is relieved for Liam's warm weight over him. Putting words together coherently is still taking some effort. He's not as broken as he was the first time Paul took him apart and then had to hold him until he put himself back together, but he's still a little fractured. It seems to be happening in slow motion this time.

"Alex," Liam says, aggrieved. "Cuddling is the best part of fucking."

Alex pushes some of Liam's curls out of his own face when Liam turns his head up to look at him. "Oh, is it now?"

"Mhmmmm." Liam works a hand under Alex's side to wrap around him. "Don't tell me this this is new too."

"No. Would you stop wiggling? No. I just, I don't know," Alex says, not able to articulate his warring feelings of comfort and claustrophobia to Liam any better than he could for Paul.

"Should I move? I can move. I'm not a dick. Not like that, anyway."

"Hey. What kind of teacher are you? Don't give up on me that easy." Alex gives him a tentative smile. Movement or words of any sort are an effort, but not an unpleasant one. For months Alex thought Paul was the only person he liked to have push his boundaries. Now there's Liam too. Maybe he just enjoys having his boundaries pushed — even when that's uncomfortable — more than he thought.

Liam smiles back and wriggles closer. "That means you're staying the night, right?"

"Presumptuous," Alex says.

"Dude, that ship sailed, like, an hour ago."

"Someone's going to notice."

"Naw. Do you have any idea how many guys I've passed out drunk with before?"

"That's encouraging." Alex considers asking for more data on the subject but decides against it. If he needs to know something, Liam will tell him. Whether he wants to know or not.

"No one's going to notice. Or care. Like, I can check the hall for you if you want, but it's five in the morning and your room is a long way away."

"Not that far," Alex protests, even though he doesn't really want to leave. Liam feels good stretched over him. With this to focus on, the memory of the fight with Paul is fading even further away.

Liam hums. Alex doesn't say anything else but also doesn't make a move to get up. Eventually,

"It's okay if you don't want to sleep alone."

"I know."

"That's new too, isn't it?"

"Be quiet and go to sleep." Alex is running out of energy to keep the conversation going. The sound of Liam breathing is soothing and his body is warm and lulling. Almost all Alex wants right now is to fall asleep.

"Okay." Liam helps get the covers up over both of them and wraps himself around Alex once again. "Sweet dreams."

"You, too." Alex wonders what there is to dream of when the world is temporarily perfect.

◆

When they wake up early in the afternoon, Alex does make Liam check the hall for him before he darts back to his room to turn into a human being who should be having regrets. But he can't bring himself to. He's tired — probably overtired, really. He hasn't slept enough in days. But after he takes a shower he wants food more than he wants more sleep.

His positive attitude lasts until he gets downstairs, because something about Liam reading *The Wall*

Street Journal over what probably, since they're shooting nights, counts as breakfast, makes him want to punch people.

"Is that an affectation or is that for real?" Alex asks as he sits down at Liam's table in the hotel restaurant without invitation.

"I like to pretend I know what's going on with my investments." Liam doesn't look up from the newsprint as he sips his coffee. "Want the *Post?*"

Alex snags the paper without comment. There's something about working on a show about fake news that has made him compulsive about keeping up with real news. Reading, however, is difficult; Liam keeps kicking his chair.

Then the fish heads make everything worse.

"What the fuck is that?" Alex asks when Liam's food arrives.

"Japanese breakfast."

"There are fish heads."

"Yes. They come with the fish."

"Do you know how often you make me wonder if I'm hallucinating?"

"Under recent circumstances that sounds suspiciously like a compliment," Liam says, still focused on his paper. It may be *The Wall Street Journal*, but Liam is reading the style section.

"Why did you order that?"

"Because it's good, and I haven't been to Japan since before the show started, and because I like it."

Alex rocks back a little at that. Liam isn't being a dick; Alex is. "What's Japan like?" he asks. "And why did you go?"

Liam lowers the paper almost suspiciously. But then, as the waitress comes to take Alex's order, he starts to tell him about a childhood Alex finds unimaginable: Early fame, deeply involved parents, and money not just for necessities, but for breakfasts anywhere in the world. Liam speaks joyfully of his travels, but with a blithe tone that Alex knows he could too easily take as cruel.

At the end of a long story about the street numbering system in Tokyo, a porn shop, and elegant gothic lolita fashion trends, Liam says, "So I just figured out a thing about you."

"What's that?"

"You're Eve."

"Pardon?" Alex is too sure he's heard wrong to even begin find his way to pissed.

"Way more interested in knowledge than consequences," Liam toys with an unused fork. "And way more intentional about it than everyone thinks."

Alex scrapes his own fork across his plate with a horrific sound, then stabs fitfully at his hash browns. Liam is astute and Alex feels seen against his will. But the oddness of the comment — and of Liam — leaves him feeling fond. "We can be friends now," he mumbles.

Liam barks with laughter. "Victory is mine."

"Don't get overexcited. You called me a chick and my memory is long."

"And that ain't all," Liam says, sliding one of the spare forks into his pocket.

Alex wants to ask what he's planning to do with it — it's better than acknowledging the dick innuendo — but decides against it, since the answer will probably make sense to Liam and absolutely no one else.

25

Alex expects being in D.C. to get easier as the days go by, but it doesn't. If anything, it gets harder. He still misses Paul desperately. Liam is being surprisingly lovely but he by himself isn't enough to absorb all the loneliness of the city.

The material they're shooting doesn't make things easier. It's all heavy and intense, and while acting is just work, the mood on-camera follows Alex off of it.

For Zach, everything is falling apart. Alex can relate uncomfortably well to his character's sense of loss even if the subject is different. More frighteningly, Alex can also relate to Zach's terrible sense of victory as he lays out to James plans he knows he shouldn't be so eager to make.

"I'm going to Iran," Zach says.

James looks horrified. He asks "Why?" with an intensity that comes either from his field experience or the personal investment James has come to have in Zach. Zach gets his concern, but doesn't back down, explaining as best he can why this is exactly what he needs to be doing. The situation and Zach's language skills James knows. Zach's passion to do right with them in a sea of the cynical and selfish, James is hearing, on some level, for the first time.

That moment of discovery is thrilling and bittersweet for both Alex and Liam to play.

They're filming in front of the Capitol, and Liam's sitting on the curb of the Reflecting Pool while Alex stands so their eye lines can be all mismatched.

"My ass is freezing," Liam complains in between takes.

Alex gives an overdramatic sigh. Liam is fishing for comments about his ass and possibly for offers to warm it up. Alex has absolutely no desire to go there while other people are around.

It's a good break from being in Zach's headspace, though, because Zach is anxious and afraid of James's reaction, whether it be anger or an attempt to stop him.

What Liam-as-James does eventually say, over and over again as they line up all the shots is, "It's my job to tell you not to. But what do you need?"

It feels like a reminder of how promises can be terrible things.

♦

By the time they wrap for the night they're both eager to get back inside a warm building. At the hotel they cross the lobby together, chattering and exchanging glances without touching.

Once the elevator doors close behind them, Alex crowds Liam into the corner. "God, I can't wait to get you upstairs." In bed, Alex won't have to think.

Liam stops him before the inevitable kiss, although barely.

"Hey, careful," he points up at the ceiling. "Security cams."

Alex blanches and reels back.

"Hey, hey, hey." Liam laughs and doesn't let him pull completely away. "They don't have sound."

"Oh," Alex says.

Liam laughs again. "So you should stop touching me, but definitely not stop talking. Seriously. How are you so paranoid and yet so bad at this?"

"It's new," Alex snaps.

"Mm, yes," Liam hums. "Let's go make it less new."

♦

"Three things," Liam says when Alex follows him into his hotel room.

"Yeah?"

"One, it's your job to tell me what you want. I don't want to assume or not assume when that's me, and I don't want you to assume or not assume that I always say yes, even though I mostly say yes."

"Text messaging is the better part of valor?" Alex teases.

"Something like that. Two, you bit the shit outta my neck."

"You loved it," Alex breathes, pushing into Liam's space a little, even as his hands on Alex's hips hold him slightly at bay.

"I did, and I have an awful reputation, so no one is ever going to think twice as to how such a thing might have happened. But you should still be aware."

"Yeah, okay," Alex nods. "What's the third thing?"

"Is there anything you don't want to do with me?"

"That sounds an awful lot like thing one."

Liam pulls Alex to him. "Sure, but it still stands."

◆

Later, when Alex is on his back and biting at the heel of his hand to muffle the sound because Liam has two fingers pressed up inside of him, he finally understands what Liam had meant earlier.

He comes like that, Liam's mouth on his cock.

Liam asks him questions afterward, too many, because Alex's brain is not online. But they're all yes or no, one or the other. Eventually, Alex manages to convey that yes it was good, that he's a little bit cold, and that he would like a glass of water.

While Liam fidgets, probably in vain, with the room's thermostat, he explains that while Alex doesn't need to be able to articulate what's going on in the moment for him during sex he really should learn how to identify and articulate it after the fact. Sure two data points is not a trend, but Liam is getting the picture. Alex didn't even know a picture was there.

"So I, or anyone, can know what you need," he says. "And you're totally not weird, that's a great place you get off to. I do it too sometimes and I love it, it's pretty much the only time my head ever feels quiet."

Alex smiles and doesn't even make a joke about how Liam so rarely shuts up. After what they've done together Alex believes him.

"And it's cool you like to hang out," Liam goes on, making a gesture that, Alex assumes, is meant to encompass the way Alex is still stretched out on the bed. "I just kinda need to do stuff for people or cuddlewhore after is all."

Alex snorts with quiet laughter. He has no idea what they're doing.

26

Victor is home, in his den, reading a book when his cell phone rings. He's not surprised it's Liam, although he is surprised by the hour. Even in L.A. it's late. With the D.C. team shooting nights, he's not sure when or if Liam is sleeping.

The second Victor picks up, Liam is already babbling. "Okay, so, I know you're gonna yell. But if I don't tell you you're gonna hear it somewhere else, like from Alex or when I'm drunk, and it's going to be a lot worse for me if you do."

"An auspicious start." Victor sets his book aside so he can focus on Liam. "What did you do, and why is Alex involved?"

"See, okay, I hooked up with him."

Victor squints at the bookshelves that line the walls of the room, full to bursting with books and DVD cases. He can't cow Liam into being less of an idiot with a glare like he could if Liam were there in person, but he can express his displeasure at the furniture.

"Hooked up with whom," he coaxes, for clarification. He's unconcerned that it sounds more than a little menacing.

"With Alex," Liam repeats.

"You did what?"

"Alex and me."

"You did *what?*" Victor doesn't often yell. He doesn't often need to. It's much easier to intimidate people with quiet. But Liam's caught him completely off-guard, and he's concerned.

"Dude! We didn't fuck on the National Mall. This isn't, like, stupid — "

"Yes it is stupid!! Jesus Christ, Liam, what kind of a fucking idiot are you?" Victor feels bad about the cruelty of the words the moment he speaks them, but he's appalled.

"Why is it stupid?" Liam's voice is distant. He's probably pulled the phone away from his ear.

"Other than the fact that you felt the need to call and confess to me, which probably ranks it ɔretty high on the list of idiotic things you have done?"

"Well, yeah."

"Does Carly know?" Victor is well-acquainted with the nature of their arrangements. If Liam is calling him, he wants to make damn sure he hasn't fucked up with someone even more important.

"Victor, seriously." Liam sounds subdued but not defensive. If experience is anything to go by, that means that this is for real. And if it is, it means Liam's done everything right, according to his understanding of his contract with life. Heaven help everyone. "You're pissed. Which, you know, not surprised. But I probably deserve to know exactly why."

"Is this going to happen again?"

"Yes. That's why I called."

"And Alex is okay?"

"Alex is fine, Victor." Liam's patience, on the rare occasions he chooses to be patient, is maddening. "Why is it dumb?"

"Alex is in D.C. right now, with you, and headed to New York next week — even if that's not one of my projects — because I pulled him out from behind a clipboard and dropped him in front of the camera."

"Yeah?"

"None of what I've done to him is anything he wanted for himself."

"No," Liam says. "He's doing pretty okay, though."

"And he just ended a very promising relationship with Paul because the three of us were making decisions about his life. According to Paul according to Alex, at least."

"Yeah, I got that lecture, too. He's not totally wrong, you know."

Victor breezes past that one; he's already told Paul everything he needed to about that, and Paul's feelings and Victor's miscalculations have nothing to do with Liam now. "And now you've hooked up with him. It's not that I don't trust you, and at least you're only five years older than him — "

"It's just that you don't trust me," Liam teases.

"No," Victor says. He doesn't trust Liam's judgement, and there's a significant difference. "The fairytale comes with costs, and I don't want this, of all things, to be one of them."

"Victor! You're worried about us." Despite everything, Victor has to smile at the glee in Liam's voice. If only more people understood his feelings more often.

"I was not built to deal with you mere mortals," he mutters.

Liam's laugh is delighted. "Careful, someone might figure out that you're human after all."

"Perish the thought."

"Alex is gonna be okay, you know."

"Alex will always be okay," Victor says firmly. "I made sure of it."

"Then why are you worried?"

"Because my favorite people are the ones who surprise me, and I adore you all."

27

Paul goes for a run before work. The sun is coming up, the streets are quiet, and it's almost peaceful.

He wishes he at least had Beau to run with, and wonders if it's worth thinking about getting another dog. He's been pining about dog jogging for over a year. But Todd is territorial and doesn't need the attention a dog would, so maybe it's best things stay as they are.

On the corner he gets flagged down by one of his neighbors, a grandfatherly man named Tom. Paul stops to say hello; Tom is the opposite of the stereotypical Los Angeles experience in so many ways and has always been amusing to interact with.

They exchange pleasantries in a way that's reflex, but Paul now recognizes as a struggle. The human impulse to tell the truth when asked how he's doing is something clearly not entirely trained out of either of them.

"I've been worse," Paul says when it's his turn. He makes himself smile, even though the fact that he's even out here indicates he's also been much, much better. Staying fit is one thing, but the pace and distances he's pushing himself for aren't healthy and he knows it. But then, that's the point.

"That's good, that's good. Got plans for the holiday?"

Paul's lost track of so much time in the last few months that, even with Thanksgiving being days ago, it's hard to believe that Christmas is a few weeks away. "Yeah. Going back home for a week. Are your kids coming out this year?"

"Yep," Tom nods. "The grandkids too. It'll be a whole swarm. If I don't see you before, be sure to have a good holiday."

Paul picks his earbuds up again. "You too. Say hi to your wife for me."

"Will do, son. Enjoy your run."

Paul still needs to cancel all his reservations regarding New York.

♦

Driving to brunch on Sunday without Alex in the car next to him is lonely, but Paul's been stuck in the house all weekend working. If he doesn't get out and interact with actual human beings he fears for the future integrity of his soul.

He misses Alex's shitty country pop music.

At the restaurant there's another seat reshuffle. He winds up with Craig and Beau on one side of him and Shawna on the other. Shawna spends the meal kicking Brian under the table whenever he starts to opine on something snarky and not at all amusing.

"What are you doing this afternoon?" Craig asks him as the meal is winding down.

"Nothing scheduled. Why?" Paul asks, because *moping over my latest ex* isn't an appropriate answer when the second-to-last ex is asking.

"Beau and I have a date at the park with a Frisbee. If you want to get out of the house, we'd love to have you."

Whether Craig is inexplicably hitting on Paul or taking pity on him, it's still a more appealing idea than going back home alone.

"Sure."

♦

The park they go to isn't the same one they used to frequent when it was Paul and Craig driving to brunch together before spending the afternoon hiking somewhere or other. There's still plenty of sun and green space, and Beau is ecstatic to run after the Frisbee as many times as they want to throw it.

Hanging out with Craig is easy, familiar, and even fun. By the end of the afternoon they're sitting side-by-side on the bench of a picnic table, getting caught up on work and families and gossiping about their friends. Beau sits at their feet and gnaws a stick he'd decided to fetch back instead of the Frisbee on his last run. If Paul lets himself think about what might happen next, it doesn't seem like a bad idea.

They get tacos for dinner without anyone having to worry about getting spotted by overenthusiastic fans. Paul is the one who suggests watching a movie together, and Craig offers his apartment.

They don't finish the movie.

They make out and jerk each other off on the couch without even bothering to hit the pause button. Paul feels vaguely guilty that his self-imposed celibacy lasted only exactly as long as he had avoided temptation. But it feels too good to lose himself in a familiar body and hands that know him.

If Paul closes his eyes he can almost fool himself into thinking Craig feels like Alex. The fantasy isn't fair to anyone, but it's there.

They curl up together on the couch while they catch their breath. Craig's apartment is smaller than Paul's house, but the leather couch and the modernist art hanging above the TV feels so much more like L.A. success.

"Want to stay the night?" Craig asks.

Paul does at least pull himself together enough to say "No. Not this time, at least," because there's dumb and then there's moronic.

"You know where to find me," Craig says.

Alone at home, even with Todd curled up at the foot of the bed snoring softly and adorably, Paul wishes he'd stayed anyway.

♦

Paul and Craig's first dinner plans get scuttled when Paul gets caught at work. He's rejiggering a plot for the third time, because the guy who's supposed to be doing this has great ideas but sucks at execution under pressure. Paul has no idea why someone who hates the fast-paced high-stakes nature of the TV game would choose to be in this business in the first place.

He texts Craig from the parking lot to meet him at the house.

This time, they skip the pretense of the movie and go straight to bed.

♦

Paul wakes up in the morning with Craig asleep next to him, Todd blinking at him from the chair, and Beau curled up in the corner that had always been his. It's exactly the way things had been for years.

The room looks as though Alex never existed, and the whole thing was just a particularly elaborate dream. The thought should be an idle one, but once it's there Paul can't get rid of it. It scares the absolute shit out of him.

Carly, when he calls her about it later that day, is absolutely unsympathetic.

"You are adding tragedy to tragedy," she says bluntly. "Seriously, Craig?"

"Would you prefer someone random?"

"This shit with Craig will only end in tears. Again. I would prefer you to get your head out of your ass and not make this so much worse for everyone involved. You're not the only one breaking over this."

"How do you know that?"

"Liam," Carly says simply.

"What's Liam doing?"

"If you want information about a relationship between two adults you are going to have to talk to either of them yourself because that is not my story to tell."

"But Liam's telling you," Paul says snidely.

"Liam is my partner," Carly says pointedly. "And you, meanwhile, need to stop fucking settling."

"Well, I can't have what I want, can I?"

"You can have a lot more than you're getting. And I don't just mean in terms of fucks."

28

After the last of the overnight shoots, Liam dismisses their car and tells Alex they're going for a walk. Alex is dismayed, but Liam seems to have a plan. He heads off down the street, giving Alex the opportunity to follow. Alex goes. There's something compelling about the offer.

Liam smiles when Alex falls in beside him, then starts talking. He narrates less what they pass than what Liam says Alex should do if he can find the time.

"Everything is haunted," he says. "And most of it doesn't want you here."

"I'm not really a believer," Alex says.

"In what?" Liam counters.

"Monsters. Ghosts. Astrology. Magic." Or God or anything else requiring belief. Religion has always been physically dangerous to Alex, a closeted gay kid with no father in the worst town in Indiana. Too many people, if they'd known what he was, would have felt the need to 'fix' him. Usually with violence and all in the name of God. It hasn't left Alex with particularly nice feelings about belief. And the rest of it — magic, monsters, or anything else — might not have hurt Alex, but they were never around to help, either. Alex keeps his faith confined to himself.

"Wow. You really haven't been paying attention."

Alex frowns but doesn't ask what Liam means. He's not sure he wants to know. And Liam's beliefs, whatever they are, at least seem benign.

They walk the length of the reflecting pool. The water shimmers in the light of the streetlamps, and ducks mutter sleepily to each other. This late, there's no one else around.

The reflecting pool is so long the Lincoln Memorial nearly takes Alex by surprise, transforming suddenly from a pale form in the distance to a massive construction of marble shining softly in the moonlight.

"Go on up," Liam tells him, when Alex hesitates at the bottom of all those steps.

"Aren't you coming?"

Liam shakes his head. "Take some time alone with it. Everyone should." Then he disappears from view.

Alex almost panics. He is outside, at night and all alone, and it's not a feeling he's had since he left Indiana. First L.A. — and then fame — made it impossible for him to be alone. This is a gift he's been given, but all it does it make him want to text Paul, so he can have it too.

He takes a selfie, joyous, awkward, blurry and poorly lit in the dark. With all the time he spends on camera for his job, and dodging the cameras of strangers, Alex doesn't take his own picture much. But this one feels important. He wants it to exist, and, what's more, he wants to share it. He sends it to Paul with a note that just says *Thank you.*

Alex hopes he'll understand that he means for the gift of a whole city that, at least for a moment, has no people in it. Alex is only here because of the stories Paul writes for him.

Half an hour passes before Liam rejoins Alex, reappearing out of the dark as suddenly as he'd disappeared. It scares the shit out of Alex.

"Don't *do* that," he scolds, clutching his heart and learning against a pillar for dramatic effect. He's been spending too much time with Liam.

"Sorry," Liam says easily.

By mutual and silent consent they walk around to the back of the monument and sit there on the wide stone ledge facing the river. Liam pulls out a flask and they pass it back and forth as they sit staring out at Virginia. Liam, without prompting and for no reason Alex can fathom, tells him about the real story behind *The Exorcist* in excruciatingly weird detail until Alex feels sore and miserable with five a.m. cold.

"I'm gonna go back," he says, standing and stretching. "Sleep for a few hours. Try to forget all the creepy shit you've told me."

"And then?" Liam asks, his agenda unclear.

"Then," Alex says, handing him his second room key, "you're going to come wake me up. Make it good."

"Cool." Liam takes the key with a wink and twirls it in his fingers.

29

Alex jogs off with a wave to find a cab before the city wakes up, and Liam pulls out his phone, thumbing through to his entries for Carly. There's a decent chance she'll still be awake, and he's glad. Good times and hard work without her by his side to share in the adventure just don't make sense any more. Alex, too, is a hefty responsibility, and she's the only one he can talk it through with. For all Victor's voyeurism, there are some details he never wants.

When he gets to Alex's room, the heat's been turned up too high. The drapes are pulled closed against the winter sun that's finally starting to rise, but the desk lamp in the corner is on, bathing the room in a soft yellow light. Alex is asleep on his stomach, naked, a sheet barely covering him.

He's beautiful, not that Liam doesn't already know that, but he's tempted to let Alex sleep. None of them ever get enough rest. Night shoots and being on the road make it worse. But Alex had asked for something very specific, even if he hadn't done so very specifically. The few agreements that exist between them boil down simply to a requirement that they take each other at their word. Liam tries to do that with everyone because then he is not responsible for their shit. But it's even more important with someone as unique and reticent as Alex.

He sets his bag down, toes off his shoes, and shrugs off his outerwear. He considers doing it noisily to wake Alex up, but he's pretty sure that's not what's wanted. When he's down to his briefs, he puts a hand on Alex's shoulder and kisses the side of his face. Alex's eyes flicker open. Liam is rewarded with a bright smile and a mumbled greeting as Alex rolls over onto his back and stretches like a cat.

Liam knows it's much permission as he's going to get until Alex is a little more awake.

"Drift as much as you want," he murmurs as he strokes his hands up and down Alex's sides. They're both already half hard.

Alex may be out of it, but he's definitely with him, humming happily as Liam drags his lips over his body. He digs his fingers tightly into Liam's hair to pull his head up and demand a kiss. Then he whines at Liam about his not being naked.

Eventually, Alex gets on his stomach with Liam half on top of him working two fingers into him as Alex ruts against the bed. He's clearly both turned on and frustrated as hell, chanting *more, more, more* at Liam.

"I can't read your mind," Liam says tight against his ear. "What do you need?"

But the only reply he gets is more frustrated, beautiful neediness. It's hot, but it's also just this side of awkward. On the list of people Liam does not need to risk making the wrong guess with, Alex is surely near the top. Or, he thinks darkly of the lecture from Victor, every single entry.

"Do you want my cock, baby?"

Alex nods frantically. Liam has to close his eyes against it for a second lest he wind up coming right then and there from the combined force of friction and fantasy.

"Where?" he barely manages to ask.

"Oh my God, Liam, where do you think?" Alex finally says in a burst of frustration.

Liam cracks up. "I want to hear you say it."

"Why?" Alex whines.

"Because it's great material for the spank bank?" Liam offers.

It's Alex's turn to laugh. After that, they're both a little more awake and a little more able to talk about it. Alex isn't being symbolic or any sort of fucked up about it, although Liam can tell he might be if he weren't so hot for it. Still, it seems like a good thing and a happy want and Liam's turned on and honored and amused to be the guy who gets to go there first.

Alex has to open the condom for him — he uses his teeth — because Liam's hands are already stupidly slick with lube. After that, they manage to keep the fumbling to a minimum, even if their lack of sleep makes up for sobriety.

Alex tenses up as soon as Liam starts pressing into him, and Liam has to talk him through it, distracting and praising and reassuring him millimeter by millimeter.

"Holy fuck," Alex finally manages once Liam is all the way in.

"Good? Bad? Indifferent?" Alex is like a vise, and Liam needs some guidance before he just takes what he wants.

"Move," Alex demands.

"I fucking love you right now," Liam says, the chuckle reverberating between and across their bodies.

It's clumsy at first, Alex hissing in uncertainty as both of them shift their hips to look for the angle that works. Then everything catches just right and *more* and *move* shift to a constant stream of *yes*, Alex jerking himself off frantically, even as he grabs at his balls to try to stave off the inevitable.

Liam's hand joins his, and then it's a litany in Alex's ear about how tight and heavy his balls are and how ready he must be, and how he needs to hold on for just a little bit longer, just until he can't anymore.

Eventually, Alex comes with a shocked-sounding moan.

Liam pulls out and strips off the condom. When he comes over Alex's back, it's with a gasp and a whimper.

♦

"That was good," Alex says, into the soft warm space that smells like Liam and sex.

Liam rubs his back. "There you go."

Alex finds it less scary — and easier — to stay down in the place where he can't process yet or even make words. Which is good, because if he tried to fight this right now he's sure he'd fly apart entirely. So he clings to Liam and lets himself sink.

It's a little bit terrifying.

♦

Twenty minutes later, Alex jerks awake in Liam's arms. For a moment he doesn't know what city he's in, or who he's with. Slowly his awareness of his body filters back in and so does the rest of the morning. He rolls out of Liam's grasp.

Liam turns over to face him. "Are you okay"

Alex scrubs his hands over his face. "I'm good," he says at random. "Just…be normal for a minute, okay?"

Liam plumps his pillow fastidiously then flops back down on it. "Normal for me, or normal for what you like dealing with?" Liam

"I still can't tell if you're the most generous asshole I know or…."

"The most asshole asshole you know?"

Alex wonders if he'll ever understand Liam's contradictions. "Yeah, that'll do."

"You can kick me out you know, if you want space for real."

Liam seems sincere in a way Alex can't quite fathom. "I'm still deciding."

"What do I have to do to earn my keep?" Liam gives him a ridiculous look that's both hopeful and suggestive.

Alex laughs. "Do not make another pass at me right now."

"What about scurrilous gossip? Does scurrilous gossip work?"

"I don't know. Depends on the gossip."

"How about me and Victor?"

"What about you and Victor."

"Me. And. Victor."

Alex would smack Liam for being so condescending, but he's busy trying to get his head around what he's just been told. He's tempted to laugh in Liam's face and call him a liar. But since last time he did that led to being bed with him right now, Alex figures he's probably better off taking this one at face value.

Still. He has to say something. "That's a giant case of what the fuck."

Liam nods.

"You know what people would say about that," Alex adds.

"You asking?"

"Yeah. Yeah, I guess I am."

"It's not a deal," Liam says defensively. "It's not, like, the casting couch."

"Okay. What the hell is it then?"

"Complicated. But also not. Like, we have date nights once a week."

"You promised me gossip and I can't decide if this is way too much or not enough."

Liam sighs heavily. "Look, Victor's a lot less interested in sex than control. We get each other, it's cool. Trust me, however you think it works, it doesn't. He's not my boyfriend or anything."

"You have date nights at his house once a week but you're not boyfriends."

"We are what we are. And we both know where we stand with each other. Also what even is your logic, you were over at Paul's way more than that."

"I have no idea how to process any of this," Alex says sharply. He very much does not want to bring Paul into whatever bizarre story time is going on right now.

"Hell of a week, huh?"

"Fuck you."

Liam cackles. "So…are you worried you're next or are you jealous?" he teases.

Alex laughs nervously. He doesn't know what to say. Victor is fascinated with him. None of them could deny that.

"Dude, I mean, you're beautiful. If that was what you wanted, Victor would find a way to give it to you, but you really don't. And that's a good thing."

Alex narrows his eyes. Liam is giving him vast swathes of information, but he can't make the pieces form into any coherent whole. "Why's that?"

"Because you don't need him. We both know you're not one of his little lost lambs."

"What then?" Alex fires back. "Am I one of yours?"

"Yeah," Liam says simply. "For now."

Alex doesn't say anything in response. As offended as he should be, *lost* and, in a way, *innocent*, have certainly been apt words for the last couple of weeks. But Liam's ongoing info dump has only added to his disorientation. For all the things he was asked and told before fame became his life, over a year later he still feels like he signed a contract made of constantly shifting words, ominously permanent and never read.

"Why are you telling me this?" he finally asks.

"One, Victor is important to me. Two, you should know how surprising you are. Three, you keep complaining that everyone is keeping you out of the loop. Now you're in the loop."

30

Paul blinks awake in the grey light of early morning. The buzzing of his alarm had woken him, but now that he's up he's not sure how he'd been able to sleep. Parrots are sitting in the tree outside, cackling up a storm.

All chance of even five more useful minutes of sleep gone, Paul rolls over to check his phone for any early morning work emergencies. Craig grumbles something sleepily at him. The familiarity is disconcerting, even if Craig isn't awake enough yet to articulate an unhappy comment about Paul's work habits.

There are no emails declaring that the world is ending via script problems, deadline issues, or another war between Victor and the studio, for which Paul is grateful. There is a picture from Alex that Paul clicks open a little warily. But he smiles when he sees Alex, flanked by D.C.'s seemingly ubiquitous marble columns, smiling up at him from the screen.

Paul locks his phone, not because he feels guilty for the thrill that Alex has given him this, but because he doesn't want to get caught.

Downstairs in the kitchen, waiting for the coffee to brew with Craig still asleep upstairs, Paul opens the picture again to stare at it more. He has no idea why Alex sent it, but Paul is glad to have it. Alex looks easy and happy. At least it's proof that Alex is real.

On his way out the door he finally replies, *You're welcome.* Even if he's not sure what he's being thanked for, he's grateful to have given Alex something.

31

New York is cold and dark and tall.

Alex arrives at night; His life no longer has any recognizable cycles to the days. He spends the car ride to the hotel looking out the windows and wishing he were anywhere else. This city is never easy for him. As often as he's been here since, the lights and the skyline and the noise always evoke for him the first time he came here, when his life was an unrecognizable whirlwind of fairytale insanity. When *Fourth* had sent him to New York for that initial round of press, he'd never even been on a plane before.

That in a couple of days he's going to start something completely new — a movie, with all the attendant glamour — makes it all that much more intense.

Alone in his hotel room, Alex turns off the lights and lies on the bed and looks out at the night. He feels small and not in a good way. Liam will be in New York in another couple of days, visiting friends and family over his own break from *Fourth*, but he's not here now. If he were, Alex would go find him and undoubtedly spend the night with him. Who he really wants, though, is Paul. Alex has been fucking Liam for the last few weeks, but it's still Paul he longs for and Paul who feels the most familiar.

It's not that late in L.A. Alex pulls out his phone.

♦

Paul's just gotten home from a long and frankly awful day at work when his phone rings. He glances at it to assure himself he can let whatever panicky writer it is go to voicemail. Seeing the name on the screen gives him almost an electric shock.

"Alex?" Paul answers. Surprised is an understatement; even with the picture Alex is the last person he expected to hear from. At least Craig isn't staying over tonight.

When Alex doesn't say anything right away, Paul says "Hello? Alex? Are you okay?"

"Tell me about your first night in L.A.," Alex finally says. It's the first time Paul has heard his voice in weeks.

"What?"

"It's home, and it's you. New York is really hard right now."

Paul isn't sure what is going on or how much stock and hope he should place in Alex's use of the word *home*. He's completely taken aback, both by Alex's unexpected call and by his question.

He also has no idea what he's supposed to do, so he does as he's told.

He sits on the loveseat by the window in the living room and looks out at the quiet street while he tells Alex about the day he'd spent moving into his first apartment here.

"I think it was as shitty as you say yours is, and my roommate was quirkier than Gemma."

Alex chuckles softly.

Paul goes on to tell him about how he'd fallen asleep that first night on his bed, just a mattress on the floor at that point. "I couldn't find where I'd packed my sheets. And then I woke up in the middle of night because the pipes were clanking. That stopped, finally, but then the streetlight outside was too bright and the crappy strip blinds were no help at all."

"I hung towels over the windows for the first couple weeks," Alex offers.

It's one of the few specific mentions Alex has ever made of his own apartment, and Paul is wary of asking for more no matter how much he still wants all of Alex's stories.

"Yeah. See, that makes sense. I went running."

"In the middle of the night?"

"My instincts for self-preservation have never been the best."

Alex asks more questions, and Paul tells him more of the story. After every question and every answer the silences get longer. Eventually, Paul watches three minutes tick by on his watch without either of them saying anything.

Finally Paul says, his voice is soft and close as if Alex were right here on the couch with him, "What time's your call tomorrow?"

"Seven."

"I'll let you get to sleep, then."

"Okay." Alex doesn't add anything else. Another thirty seconds pass before he says, his voice barely a breath, "Good night."

The line clicks silent.

Paul has no idea what the hell just happened and is sure he's never going to tell anyone about it.

♦

On the *Fourth* lot, the office starts to feel devoid of human life without the manic bustle of filming and as people take off for the holidays. The dingy hallways look even sadder than usual, and the sets and soundstages are quiet and empty.

Paul misses Alex at home and at work, where Alex never appears anywhere he shouldn't anymore. Paul can't figure out the midnight phone call and after a while he stops trying. If nothing else he's grateful for another sign that Alex was real.

A quiet office and no crises to fix means more time for his own projects. Victor finds Paul at his desk late one night with his laptop open and glasses on, working not on *Fourth* but on a pilot. For once Victor doesn't even stop to say or ask Paul anything, just nods from the doorway and moves on.

Paul leans his cheek on his fist and scrolls back through the pages he's written. At least he's doing something right.

32

Alex finds that filming *Paradise Square* is a little different from doing TV, but the essentials are the same. The familiarity of the routine is good, because it's the only thing he's used to right now. He's got a different character, and after the terror of the first few days — he can act, yes, but he's only ever acted Zach — he starts to think that this might be something he can do. It's a challenge, but a good one. He's making progress towards proving himself.

New York, however, remains hard.

The fans have found his hotel again. It's almost impossible to move around outside without them noticing and trying to follow. He thinks about sneaking out one morning before they or the city at large wakes up. He wants to walk everywhere. It's not a safe option for him and the schedule leaves no time, yet still he wishes. New York is so unlike L.A. — gritty, dark, and above all *cold*. But there's a freedom here too, that of anonymity and the promise L.A. once offered him: A new life, far from whatever troubled him in the past. But that's out of reach, at least for Alex. Fame has laid its claim; he'll never be able to reinvent himself again.

He's glad when Liam arrives in town.

Assuming nothing, Alex texts him on his way back to his hotel from set that evening. *I want to see you tonight.*

His phone buzzes while he's walking into the lobby. *Come out with us. I'll make it worth it after.*

Who's us? And I'm not bargaining with you for sex.
I'm bargaining for your time. Just wear your damn hat.

Us turns out to be a group of Liam's friends from high school, including his childhood best friend, Charles, and a bunch of film school geeks, all of whom think they're going to be the next Tarantino. Alex meets up with the group for dinner, and then they embark on a bar crawl.

As a whole, the group is almost as loud and obnoxious as Liam is, and, on the surface, are even less to Alex's taste. Yet, none of them give a shit about who he is when he's not a guy in jeans and a beanie, even if Charles watches Alex closely in a way that screams Liam-related backstory.

Alex stares back with an intensity he knows is almost confrontational. He thinks he finally understands why Liam's worked so hard to be as charming and charismatic as he is, if Charles — possessed of deep brown skin and a classical dancer's body — is what he's been competing with since he was a kid. Somehow, though, the observation only helps Alex look at Liam with a level of fondness that is probably unwise.

They're in a dive bar with red walls and too many Christmas lights, all of them grimy with being up year round, when Liam polls the group on what the word for a male starlet should be. When everyone but Alex gets distracted by a discussion of which it-girls they would, and would not, do, Liam tells him he's decided it's *starling*. They are, he notes, an invasive species.

◆

Liam and Alex end up back at Liam's parents' Brooklyn brownstone. Without any good reason to be in the same hotel anymore, Alex's accommodations are out of the question. Even with the separate garden entrance and no sign of Liam's parents, Alex worries this choice isn't any wiser.

"Don't they know Carly?" he hisses as they make their way down the hall to Liam's old room.

"Sure. They know a lot of things. It's cool."

Everything about Liam's life represents a different sort of discretion than when Alex told Paul not to hold his hand. He's trying to understand, but even right here, with his hand in Liam's, the gulf between their lives and their fears seems insurmountable.

Any worries about closets and secrets or the immense, persistent loneliness of New York are burned away once Liam shuts the door of his room behind them. He leads Alex to the bed.

They get naked, and Liam digs his fingers into Alex's bare hips. Liam makes it so easy for Alex to let go of everything. He closes his eyes and lets himself drift as Liam prepares him, then sinks down onto Liam with the same steady concentration and ruthless determination he does everything with.

"Holy shit," Liam gasps, as Alex starts to move. "You learned a new trick."

Alex shifts to brace his weight right on his thighs. "Practice makes perfect."

"Bullshit. You've never practiced a thing in your life."

"Yeah," Alex says and leans down to brace his weight on his elbows and bite at Liam's mouth. "But I still get better."

"Fuck yes, you do," Liam pants and grabs the back of his head to yank him into the kiss.

◆

Over the next few days Alex settles into a rhythm of work, Liam, and not sleeping particularly well.

Spending nights at Liam's parents' house is the best. Even if it's more lavish than anywhere he grew up, it's a home, and he's honored and touched by Liam's trust in inviting him in and letting him stay.

Alex loves his work, if not the spaces in between. Wrapping himself up in Liam, not only his body but his kindness and tenderness, makes things a little easier.

◆

"So you want to tell me what you're doing, wasting all your time in New York with me?"

Alex tenses at the question. They've gotten naked and into bed; this is not what he was expecting. It's been two weeks since he first went home with Liam, and they've spent almost every night together with no need of discussion.

He tries to ignore Liam's words now and reaches for him instead, but Liam bats his hand away. Alex isn't sure if he's supposed to be hurt, embarrassed or amused, but he does pull back a little.

Liam speaks again. "There's a whole city out there full of guys prettier — and probably less annoying to you — than me. So what gives?"

Even with the self-deprecation, Liam's charisma is still stunning. "I told you I changed my mind about you," Alex says, knowing he sounds like he's acting.

"Mmmmm, yeah, I know." Liam plays with Alex's hair. "I'm trying to figure out how much."

Alex rolls onto his back and stares at the ceiling. Glow-in-the-dark stars are stuck to it from, presumably, when Liam was a kid. But they've left the light on, so Alex can only see their outlines.

"Fuck," he says to himself. Liam has always been able to see through him. When Alex first met him that was a nuisance. Then it became a comfort — Liam was one less person Alex had to explain himself to. Now it's a threat. He can't hide from Liam.

Liam says nothing, but continues to pet his arm.

"This is the thing where I have to tell you the truth because of one of your stupid lists of things, isn't it?" Alex says, still not looking at him. He could evade and avoid, but it wouldn't work. Not for long enough. And it wouldn't change what both of them know.

"It would help."

"Should I go?"

"No. Talk."

"But I don't talk, Liam."

"You do to me."

"Because you're annoying and won't shut up." That's not exactly why. But what else can Alex say?

Liam grabs his hand and squeezes.

"This is so good," Alex says, anguish bubbling up with the words. He doesn't understand why everything — even his respite from other pains — has to be so hard.

"It really is. The best, even." Liam brings Alex's hand up to his mouth to kiss. "But I can't be for you the way you want right now."

"Carly."

"Not Carly. Not really. Although, yes." Liam shifts and turns to Alex. Having the man's full attention, which is so often so scattered, on him is strange. "Look, you're not the only one people are hard for. Like, *love* — awesome. But don't fall for me. 'Cause I can't, okay? I love you, and I don't work that way, and you're just being fucked up over Paul anyway. So...okay?"

"You're not making sense."

"You've understood every word I've said." Liam's eyes dart between Alex's, like he's making sure he's paying attention. "And you're an asshole for making me say them without confessing first."

"You're still holding my hand."

"So?"

For a long time, Alex says nothing. When he finally turns his head to look at Liam, Liam is looking at their hands. He asks to stay.

"Yes, yes, totally, thank God." Liam sounds as buoyant as ever. "You're an idiot," he adds. He grabs the back of Alex's head and kisses him hard.

It's surprising and funny before it shifts into something else, slow and strange and difficult.

Liam rolls on top of him, tells him he's going to fuck him, and takes forever getting to it. Normally, Alex likes this sort of thing. With Liam, he usually banters through it; with Paul, he begged. But this here and now feels like Liam memorizing him, mourning him. Alex knows he'll soon do the same in return.

But it's hard to believe or behave as if it's truly the end. After *Fourth's* winter break is over, they'll be back to being paid to kiss each other as two men who don't even exist.

Right now, this is the most of Liam Alex is ever going to have. In a moment whatever they've been doing with each other is going to be more than it's ever been before. After that they will become less forever. It's an awful feeling.

When Liam finally pushes into him, Alex is on his back, folded in half. He's never been fucked like this before. The angle's insane, and the claustrophobia of the position is only working for him because everything else is such a mess. His throat is tight with tears and he's not even hard.

It feels good anyway. Arousal, as he's used to understanding it, creeps up on him eventually.

Liam's face above him is beautiful, shuttered and pained. He's clearly trying to make this last. When his eyes open, it startles Alex badly. He tries to push his head further back into the pillow to get some space from the other man's gaze.

But there's no space to get. Liam whispers "No," in his ear softly when Alex closes his eyes.

So he does as he's told. This is a gift, and Alex knows enough to take it on the terms it's being offered.

Liam says, "I promise you I'll miss this," and shoves his hands, grabbing sharp and tight, into his hair.

Alex comes.

Liam lets him close his eyes then as he works towards his own orgasm. His panting in Alex's ear sounds not quite like exertion, but the soothing noises made toward children and wounded animals.

Other than dealing with the condom, Liam doesn't even bother to clean them up after. He pulls Alex close, tangles their legs, and presses their foreheads together. Alex is reminded of Paul, and that's when he breaks.

Liam takes his hand again and kisses his palm.

◆

When Alex wakes up the next morning he finds Liam on his side, dressed now and watching him. When he sees he's awake, Liam squeezes his hand and silently slides out of the bed.

There are very few other options, and none of them are good. Alex drags on his clothes and follows him upstairs where the deep silence of the morning is suddenly broken by Liam's mom. Her unexpected presence in the kitchen may be the strangest thing to happen to Alex all month.

She greets them both with hugs and with pancakes. Surrealism, apparently, comes with chocolate chips. Alex says *yes, please* to orange juice and wonders how many broken hearts she's nursed for Liam in mornings-after through the years.

He doesn't feel heartbroken, though, not exactly, as he pours syrup and listens to their friendly chatter. Heartbreak was walking out of Paul's house. This is something else, something profound and deeply aching.

His relationship with Liam only ever had a name as it was ending, and maybe even only because it was ending. Alex is still not sure what that name even *is*. This doesn't feel like anything he thought it would except for the grief that he's holding, precious and odd.

But then, Paul never felt like anything Alex expected either. That was different than this, but maybe part of the point. All Alex is sure about right now is that of everything Liam has taught him, the least important has been the mechanics.

Liam and his mom don't require much from him in the way of conversation, and Alex is glad for the chance to simply sit with his thoughts. There will be more of that, later, when he's well and truly alone. For now it's enough to be here, where it's warm and home-feeling, and watch out the windows as the snow start to fall.

33

The night after Liam breaks up with him, Alex goes out with some of the cast and crew of *Paradise*. He's never socialized this way before, never wanted to, but his options are limited to going out or staying in his hotel room alone and moping over both Paul and Liam.

Alex is tired of feeling sorry for himself. He's never been one to wallow in his pain; he likes to take action to solve his problems. And if a bar in Tribeca has never been his particular poison, well, he's been trying a lot of new things lately.

There's a guy there, a friend of somebody in the cast, who stares at Alex from the moment Alex walks in. For the first half of the night, Alex avoids the looks. Nobody looked at him like that before his life changed, and now it feels like everyone does. Alex never trusts the sincerity of it. People like to look at the things TV shows them, but it doesn't mean they're truly interested. Alex has also never known how to look back.

Paul never stared at Alex that way, not in a manner that was about assumed possession. Neither did Liam. But now Alex doesn't get to have either of them. A hookup with a guy he hasn't known for at least a year was unthinkable a few months ago. Now, it feels like the inevitable outcome of the math of misery and strategy.

The next time the guy tries to catch his eye, Alex lets him.

He knows people are watching them when they leave the party. He doesn't have the energy to care.

In the hotel room — not Alex's — Alex tells him exactly what he wants, closes his eyes, and gets it.

The next night it's somebody else. The night after that isn't much different.

Busy now he sends Liam when his phone buzzes halfway through the fifth evening, or maybe the sixth.

Is he someone I know?

Who says it's only been one?

Alex wonders if Liam is simply incapable of letting go of people no matter how the relationship changes.

♦

When Alex gets off work the next day, there's another text from Liam. *We need to talk.*

I thought we already did that, Alex types back.

Come by the house tonight.

No.

We're having this conversation. I really don't think you want to have it at your hotel.

Alex knows Liam is going to call him on his recent extracurricular activities. He also knows that isn't going to be about them getting back together. Why Liam feels the need to intervene in Alex's promiscuity when Liam is just as wide-ranging in his habits, Alex doesn't know. But for all Liam is baffling and often irritating, he never pushes Alex in any way Alex doesn't like. For that, Alex types back, somewhere between angry and meek, *Fine.*

◆

They end up in Liam's parents' tiny backyard, bundled in their coats, in ass-numbing patio chairs.

"All right," Liam says. "You want to tell me what you've been up to the past few nights?"

"It's none of your business," Alex says shortly.

"Dude. We're friends. You said so!"

"So?" Just because Alex agreed to come here doesn't mean he's going to make it easy on Liam. Too much of this moment is his fault.

"So I care, and you tell me this shit."

"No, I don't." Alex understands everyone rewrites the past. And while he accepts that he might have an overly romanticized version of what happened between him and Liam, he is one hundred percent sure it didn't involve any of the confessions Liam now seems sure he made.

"You did when it was Paul."

"No, I didn't." Alex protests.

"Yeah, you did. You just didn't realize it."

"That makes this better how?" Maybe Liam isn't wrong. Maybe he really did worm himself into Alex's life not just as a lover, but as a confidante. Alex doesn't like the idea that he revealed himself to Liam without knowing it, but he supposes that's what sex does. At least the advice — and encouragement — Liam has always given in response hasn't steered him wrong yet.

Liam kicks his shoe against the edge of a loose flagstone. It's an oddly soothing rhythm. "I want to hear you tell me what you think you're doing.

Because you don't know your own power, and that's fine when it's just you being neurotic about fame, and it can also be really fucking hot — "

"Thank you?"

" — but right now you're fucking around with random dudes, and I have no idea what that's about."

Alex tips his head to the side and studies the patterns the shadows of the bare tree branches make against the fence. "You told me to find shinier toys in New York."

"I did. And now you're playing with rusty cans."

"They're not utter strangers, they're industry — "

"And in the closet."

" — and it's not going to wind up on the internet."

Liam blows out a tense breath. "This is not about the internet. You and I? This? This is fucked up, but we have trust. What the hell do you have with these people? Mutually assured destruction?"

"Apparently the closet has advantages for both of us," Alex snaps. "Also, what the fuck? You sleep around."

"Alex."

Alex turns toward him. Liam gives him an absolutely devastating look and counts off on his fingers. "One. I fuck friends. And your choices are your choices but I'm careful."

"Which is why you sucked my dick without a condom or a conversation?"

"Yeah. So. I get to make mistakes too. Also, you keep complaining that everyone talks about you without you present. Where do you think that stops exactly?"

Alex stares. He'd never even considered the possibility that Paul would talk about their time in bed together with anyone. Much less Liam, or anyone who would talk to Liam. Carly, maybe?

"Sorry?" Liam offers.

"Who do I yell at first?" Alex says to the universe at large. Suddenly everything that's happened seems small and funny and terrible.

"Can we get back to that? I was counting."

"Uh…." Alex will never understand the things Liam chooses to care about from moment to moment.

"Two." Liam holds up another finger. "I have watched you from the beginning of this. I know you. You deal with your shit by making shit harder for yourself. And that can be awesome. That's how you get better. But, three." He holds up a third. "You're not fucking around with random people to learn something new about yourself. You're fucking around to make shit hard for yourself, because it makes you miserable. You think you should be miserable, because you're not getting what you actually want. That's fucked up. Because, four — " Liam holds up a fourth finger before pointing his whole hand at Alex accusingly, " — if you keep this up in the direction I think you're going, you're going to wind up chasing the kind of destruction that isn't about being on the cover of *Us.*"

"What are you talking about?" Alex asks. He's never seen Liam look this serious.

"Look, I know you grew up in a tiny town in the middle of nowhere and there's all sorts of history that seems really abstract to you. But you can't sit here in New York City and ask me that question."

"Don't you think that's kind of alarmist? Especially now." Alex asks faintly through his own dawning horror.

"I'm not sleeping with you now, and I know how to be careful. Also, that's kind of the point. Alarms are for before the house burns down."

Alex sits very still, doesn't look at Liam, and doesn't say anything. He's pissed at Liam, but he's also self-aware enough to know that's because Liam's right. Alex is embarrassed and ashamed. His fingertips prickle, cold, maybe, but also perhaps the tingle of adrenaline at whatever near miss he's had.

"Look. Alex. You scare the absolute shit out of me— "

"I get it," Alex says tightly.

"You do?"

"Yeah."

"Okay," Liam says, still kicking the flagstone. "Are you pissed at me?"

"Yeah." Alex folds his arms over his chest. He wishes Liam would hug him. Among other things, he's cold. But he needs to sit with this by himself for a while.

"I figured. It's cool."

Alex laughs, tense and a little watery. "This has been the weirdest fucking week."

34

In his mother's kitchen in South Carolina, Paul is on drying duty. His sister Sarah is washing and hands him wet and still slightly soapy, dishes. Mike, Paul's brother-in-law, is upstairs putting the baby down for a nap. His mom sits at the kitchen table fidgeting with a pack of cigarettes. Eventually she'll go outside onto the verandah to have what she'll swear is just one but is always two.

In his pocket, Paul's phone rings. The chime makes Paul jump, and he almost drops a dish trying to fish his phone out of his pocket. The call is unlikely to be important, but L.A. has long trained him never to ignore what could be an opportunity. Sometimes he's not even wrong.

A glance at the caller ID surprises him. "Alex?" he says, fumbling the phone to his ear.

Alex, if it is indeed him and not a misdial, doesn't say anything.

"Let me step outside," Paul adds when he sees his mother and sister exchanging meaningful and somewhat smug looks.

Alex still doesn't say anything.

Paul turns off the light by the front door so moths don't keep flying at his head. "Are you still there?" He doesn't mean to sound annoyed, but what other options are there?

"Yeah," Alex says.

"Are you — "

"In New York."

"I was going to say okay."

"That's annoying," Alex says, more directly than Paul is used to.

"I'm sorry."

"I've had a really fucked up week."

"Yeah?" Paul asks, hoping for any sort of story that will help him understand. Alex has so often been all sharp edges and dark spaces.

"Yeah."

"Is *Paradise* okay?" He doubts work is the problem, but Paul suspects it's the safest thing to ask about.

"That's great, actually. Turns out I can act." Alex giggles. "I died yesterday."

"…What?"

"My character," Alex says. That should have been obvious; Paul wonders what it is about Alex that makes it not. "Death scenes are fun."

The conversation, like so many he's had with Alex, is nothing like normal. Paul realizes, too late now, that very little with him ever will be.

"…Okay," he finally says. "I don't know why you're calling, and I don't know what to say to you."

Alex is being marginally less frightening than the last time he called out of the blue, even if no less strange. That, as well as whatever he and Craig are trying to do, makes Paul feel a little bit bolder, as if he can survive all possible answers, even though he's not sure that's true.

"So," Alex takes a loud breath like he's going to explain but then stays silent, having apparently thought the better of it.

"Alex."

"Liam and I had a thing," he blurts. "And then he dumped me. At his parents' house. With some advice I sort of intentionally took in a really stupid way, so he spent last night yelling at me for my bad choices and wow, you were right about closeted guys. I don't mean Liam, by the way, and I'm sort of freaked out, and I hate New York. My life got taken away from me eighteen months ago and was given back to me changed. My mom gets here tomorrow too, and I just…hi. I didn't know who else to call."

The words tumble out of Alex like a flood. It's a lot to take in. There are several items Paul desperately wants more information about from the Liam thing, which stings, to the demise of it, which honestly has him a little bit worried.

"What do you need me to do?" he asks.

"I'm not having a crisis." Alex sighs. "Just stay on the line."

"Okay," Paul says. "Okay. Do you want to talk about any of it?"

"Not really. Not now. Not yet."

"Right." Paul feels a little guilty for how bitchy he sounds, but Christ, *Liam?* "Tell me about your first night in New York then," he says, flipping the tables on Alex after their last late-night call. "Not this time, I mean. The first time." Paul still knows so little about Alex's life before they got involved. Even now, when he has no claim on Alex's stories or his time, he wants more. Also, Alex called him.

Alex laughs weakly. "I'd never been in a hotel before. Other than the motels on the drive out to L.A., I mean. The windows were too big."

Paul sits down on the steps and settles in to listen.

35

Alex's mom arrives the afternoon before Christmas Eve. For the first couple of hours it's bizarre. This is not Alex's city, he hardly knows what his life is, and being with his mother makes him feel vividly like who he was before. He tries to see himself through her eyes but doesn't know what to make of himself.

They haven't seen each other since last Christmas when Alex flew her out to L.A. Despite the time they spend on the phone together, they're both unsure around each other for the first few hours. Alex feels embarrassed by the hotel room he got for her, which is possibly bigger and definitely nicer than the trailer he grew up in. Laura is either mirroring his discomfort or likewise doesn't quite know what to do when confronted with her strange son in a strange new city.

They make awkward small talk about her flight and the traffic from the airport while she unpacks her suitcase. Alex, finally desperate to get out of a room where he feels — wrongly, he knows — that neither of them belong, asks if she wants to get a drink.

"It's two in the afternoon," Laura says reproachfully, but her eyes shine with mischief and delight.

"It's even earlier in L.A."

"Oh, I have missed you, Alex," she exclaims and hugs him tight.

In the hotel bar downstairs they both get a beer and sit in a corner at a high-top table for two. Now that they both have something to do, the silence is less awkward. They spent a lot of evenings like this when Alex was in high school — not sitting in hotel bars, of course; such places didn't exist in Paragon except on TV. But on the nights when neither of them had to work, they'd sit on the back steps of the trailer, each nursing a beer. Sometimes they talked, sometimes they didn't. Those evenings, peaceful and with a comforting sense of solidarity between them, are some of the few memories Alex has of Indiana that aren't awful.

For several minutes they both sit in contemplative silence. Alex wonders if his mom is remembering the same things he is.

Laura finally says, "Are you seeing anyone?"

Alex looks up at her sharply, not offended, but surprised. She's never asked him anything of the sort before. That she's asking now is either an indication that he's not a child in her eyes anymore, or a reassurance that he can tell her about all the things he never talked about when he was growing up.

He wishes he had a simpler, happier answer for her. "No. Yes. I mean. I don't know. It got messed up." He doesn't even know if he means Paul or Liam.

She frowns at that and asks a couple of vague questions Alex doesn't know how to answer. She's clearly trying to suss out if the problem was Alex's inexperience or Alex's gay and famous life. He in no way feels comfortable telling her that the answer is obviously both.

Not that that's anything new. He didn't even come out to his mom until five minutes before he got into his shitty Dodge Neon to leave Indiana forever. In retrospect, he is sure his mother always knew. Now, he feels more than a little ashamed of his cowardice. This, however, is not that. Rather, he doesn't want her to worry any more than he wants to let the air touch the recent disasters of his heart. They feel as embarrassing as they do sacred.

When she asks if he's happy in the face of so much unsaid, he confesses that he hates New York. It isn't much of a confession until he tells her why, and then her face goes gentle. He's never told her he was scared, not once, not even when this life was beginning.

♦

They have tickets, thanks to the connections Alex now has, to midnight mass at St. Patrick's. Religion was never an issue with his mom growing up, which was one of the mercies of his childhood. But this is a different kind of thing, ritual and community for the sake of it and an opportunity he's supposed to take simply because he can. Even though it would probably mean more to someone else who has less ability to access it.

For all those reasons, he hadn't been sure if it was a good idea to go. But Margaret and his mother had cooed about it over the phone. Once they're there he's glad they did, if only for the warm bustle of the crowd on a cold night and the enchanted look on his mother's face.

Alex can't wear his hat but he's also not the most interesting figure in this particular crowd, filled with local politicians and celebrities way more famous than he. The cathedral and its patrons make him feel small, like the beach does.

They muddle through the service — they're not Catholic, only theoretically Methodist, but when getting them the tickets Margaret had insisted that was a trivial detail. The service is showy, and if his mom were more religious she'd probably be uncomfortable with it. As it is, Alex finds the pomp and ceremony fascinating. And after a month of playing an Irish Catholic immigrant to the city on film, there's something to be said for seeing the rituals up close and personal.

He spares a thought to wonder if Liam is here too, somewhere in the crowd. Liam hadn't mentioned it, but they haven't spoken since that night in Liam's parents' backyard. But Liam is Catholic — Alex knows from one of his bizarre rambles about 16th century saints and canonization laws — and certainly would be more at ease here. He wonders what Liam would think about his own attendance. Probably nothing more than that it was good Alex was having yet another new experience, and one very unlikely to get him into any sort of trouble at that.

When they are asked to exchange the sign of peace with those around them, Alex laughs at his mother's delight in strangers and finds a certain relief that no one's eyes flicker over him in any way that marks him out from the actually faithful. Between the actor thing and the ever so gay thing, he had been slightly worried.

They emerge from the overheated church into the snapping cold outside to the peal of bells and the sky dark beyond the glow of the city. Looking up, Alex realizes that it is, in fact, Christmas. He threads his arm through his mom's as they walk and feels at peace.

They cross the street to Rockefeller Center, which is crowded with tourists when and the people spilling out of the Cathedral. After half an hour, the crowds ebb, and it becomes as quiet as New York ever does.

Alex buys them both hotdogs and sodas at a cart, and they sit on one of the benches that line the walkway down to the viewing area for the skating rink. In the midst of the lights and noise of the city, his mother's presence, from the lines on her face to the way she brushes her hair out of her eyes, feels familiar and comforting.

"I'm buying a house," Alex says without looking at his her when they've been quiet for too long. "We should talk about what to do about yours."

"What's that supposed to mean?" she asks.

"It means I have money I don't even know how to spend, and Indiana is cheap. I've been too freaked out by everything to solve my own housing crisis much less do right by you. But…I don't know. Just tell me what needs doing, and we'll get it done. Or, I mean, if you want to move. Just. You know. Merry Christmas or something." He hunches his shoulders almost up to his ears, awkward and embarrassed all over again.

"Alex."

He's glad she doesn't manage anything more. The Midwest is good for that. The whole conversation is hitting a raw place he doesn't want to think about. Sitting here, he feels like the sheepish, sullen, and occasionally funny teenager he was not all that long ago. "Don't worry about it," he says. "I forgot to go shopping."

36

Liam greets Carly at the door with a wild hug and an enthusiastic kiss, then grabs her hand and drags her into the room. New Year's with Liam's family — all generations of it, all packed into a reconstructed black box theatre on 42nd Street — is a must for the holidays and completely worth flying out for.

When she finally finds Alex she wraps him in a hug too and rocks a little until he finally relaxes and hugs her back. It's good to see him; she's been more than a little worried about him. She didn't sign up to take care of Alex on top of everyone else in her life, but sharing advice won't cost her anything and he could use it.

"Hi, Carly," he says, his voice drily amused, when she lets him go.

"Hello, Alex."

"…That's not a good voice."

"Come with me," she says and hooks an arm through his elbow. She has an agenda and nothing to gain by delaying.

She drags him to the back of the room, where it's darker and quieter and there's less chance of an audience. None of this needs one, and Alex has always functioned better outside a crowd.

"Okay, real talk time," she says.

"Yes?" Alex looks a little scared.

For a moment, Carly feels bad for him. Alex has nothing to fear from her, but he doesn't seem to know that, and she doesn't have the energy to explain it. "So, the genius thing where you called Paul about Liam? Total asshole move. I mean, I am sorry you were messed up about that, because Liam really does adore you. You guys are good now, right?"

"I thought that's what you were going to yell at me for."

Carly waves that off. "Oh, no, honey. I'm glad you had a good time." She loves Liam's affectionate heart that wants to care for all the world, and she's glad whenever he finds someone who makes him happy. "I am going to yell at you about Paul, though, because he's fucking Craig again which is more bullshit than you thinking Liam should be your boyfriend — "

"I didn't — "

"Rounding up! Let me finish, then you can talk." Men need to stop talking over her when she is, as usual, the only adult on deck. "Look. We are all fucked up, but we also all adore you. And you're being fucking nuts and also an asshole, so you should decide what you're doing so you have a plan when Paul is done with his self-injury routine."

Alex's eyes go a little wide. It's the exact opposite of the cute squinty thing he does when he smiles.

"Oh, sweetie," Carly grabs his hand to squeeze it. She wonders how much Paul has told him, but he's a smart kid in any case. "Paul's fine. He's just stupid. But please, figure out what you're doing with him."

"He's back with Craig?" Alex asks.

"Total bullshit," she says firmly. She squeezes his hand again before she drops it. "Which is why you need to figure your shit out. Now come on, baby boy, you need a drink."

◆

A drink he gets, more than one, because the showdown with Carly, no matter how harmless, was sort of scary, and the Craig information is additionally unpleasant at best.

The family atmosphere — and the fact that he's now apparently part of that family — is excessive. Within a couple of hours he feels like he's being passed around the room, not as J. Alex Cook, actor, but as Carly's friend, Liam's coworker, and *I heard you had Kathleen's pancakes the other day*. Alex wonder if the whole planet knows what that's a euphemism for.

Charles is there, as well as the rest of the crew Liam dragged him out drinking with on their first night in New York. He nods across the room to Alex at one point and only says hello much later. Alex is glad he's not more drunk when it happens; this time he might have asked him if he's fucked Liam too.

Alex also notices two girls he's seen random tabloid gossip about Liam hooking up with at various points. Carly seems super chummy with one of them but slightly and unkindly amused towards the other. He kind of wants that story, if only because it has nothing to do with him.

Liam comes to check on him periodically between stints at bartending, but it's nothing more than playing the good host. Alex appreciates the opportunity to be just like everyone else, introversion and recent excursions by his dick aside.

At eight, as platters of food are set out, there's an announcement that they are all now officially locked in, as the street has been closed for emergency vehicle traffic only.

When Alex finds himself in a conversation with Liam's father that's probably only awkward in his head, he winds up blurting something about how they should throw one of these shindigs in the event of zombie apocalypse. Luckily, Liam's father laughs, probably because no matter how awkward Alex is being, it'll never live up to Liam's weird.

Fifteen minutes before midnight, Liam wraps an arm around Alex's waist and tells him to be by the doors by five to twelve. When he asks why, Liam says, "Trust me."

Two minutes before the ball drops, Liam leads Carly, Charles, the two girls, and Alex outside into an empty 42nd Street, just east of Times Square.

"Look up," he whispers in Alex's ear.

The ball, all lasers and glitter, is right there and the massive and miserable crowds are at least fifty feet away.

"Oh my God."

"Right?!" Liam says smugly as the countdown from sixty starts.

By the time they get to thirty, Carly has an arm around Alex's waist, and Liam's half climbing on his back. Alex doesn't have eyes for any of them. All he can do is watch the spectacle.

"One day, I am going to host this thing," Liam whispers into his ear at twenty, jerking his chin towards one of the many stages covered with celebrities and cameras.

At ten, Alex wonders what it says about a city that it marks a new year with a fall, but he shakes it off to shout the last numbers with the rest of them.

Midnight comes, and Liam kisses Carly, long and wet. Alex keeps staring at the ball, as if making sure it won't fall any further, through buildings and concrete. He only tears his gaze away when Liam grabs his face and kisses him too. Alex laughs at the hint of tongue.

When he gets through the line of them — because Liam kisses everyone with varying degrees of enthusiasm — he pulls out his phone to text someone. As Carly catches his eye, Alex does the same: Gemma, because it's a decent thing to do, and he loves her. Paul, because the truth is that he is Alex's wish for the new year.

♦

Paul is kissing Craig, the sound of the crowd in Times Square a roar from the TV, when his phone vibrates in his pocket. He knows it's Alex.

It takes him a moment to disentangle himself from Craig and from the rest of the group crowded around Brian's living room. Out in the hallway he checks the text. It is, in fact, from Alex. All it says is *Happy New Year*, but even with everything that is fraught between them it makes Paul smile.

Happy New Year to you, too, he sends back. *Hope you have magic.*

He stares at the screen for another few seconds to watch the message send and wonders what Alex is up to tonight. Can he ask? Does he even want to know the answer?

Before he can decide, a reply comes back. *I already do.* And then, a picture: An empty street in front of the crowd and the air full of confetti. *Wish you could see it.*

Paul melts a little. He thumbs back *It looked pretty cool on TV.*

"Paul?"

Paul looks up from the phone to see Craig leaning in from the doorway.

"I was wondering where you went." He looks at the phone in Paul's hands but doesn't ask.

"I'll be right there," Paul says. Craig nods but doesn't move from the doorway, so he has time to see but not reply to Alex's next text. *Carly says hi, by the way*, God knows what that might mean.

They trade sporadic messages over the course of the next three hours. Craig doesn't look thrilled whenever he sees Paul with his phone out, but doesn't say anything.

At actual midnight Craig has his hand on Paul's hip as he kisses him again. Paul's phone buzzes in his pocket, and he knows Craig can feel it.

He's not judicious and doesn't move away from Craig as he checks the text. *Happy *real* new year*, Alex has sent. *Magic to you, too, but beware.*

Of what?

Paul doesn't get to see Alex's answer, because Craig grabs his hand and gives him a look that's a little pissed, which is probably fair. Alex is going to have to wait. Paul hates that, but he also believes he will. There's still some thread connecting him and Alex, and it's not going to snap tonight.

Paul's out on the back porch, escaping the loud and getting-too-drunk crowd, when he finally checks his phone again.

Do I really need to tell you?

37

After the holidays, the return to life at *Fourth* is a slow trickle, with production and writers filtering in a couple of weeks before the actors are back on set. Paul's one of the first there simply because he's in town, and it's become increasingly easier for him to write — whether for the show or his own projects — in the office.

Outside of his own house, Paul is less haunted by an Alex that was his and less dogged by a Craig who is trying to get him to be a better boyfriend this time around. Even after over a year's intermission, the habits of his work and his inability to negotiate with Craig about them successfully seem to remain.

He's the only one there one afternoon when Victor strolls in and spins a chair around to sit in front of his desk.

Paul looks at him over the top of his laptop. He hits save but doesn't say anything. He also doesn't stop typing. Victor hasn't even said hello yet.

"So," Victor finally says, crossing an ankle over his knee. "You're here. Liam's back in town, and Alex is going to be back in a few weeks. Are there going to be explosions?"

"Which particular set of circumstances are you referring to?"

"Whichever one is going to end in pyrotechnics."

"Liam and I?" Paul is sure that Victor knows at least part of that story. If it involved anyone else it would be reasonable to assume its conclusion would end, not just in vicious gossip, but somebody taking a swing at someone.

"Is that the one?" Victor asks mildly.

Paul isn't fooled. This isn't Victor in search of entertainment. This is Victor desperately concerned and checking in on his people. He's rarely so obvious about it, but he's seen it before regarding Liam, and, increasingly, Alex. Paul wonders what he's come to, that he's now on Victor's Needs Care list.

Paul looks at his computer screen. The cursor flashing at the end of a sentence is easier to endure than the other man's stare. "I don't know."

"I'm very aware," Victor says carefully, "that none of you are exactly okay at the moment, and that you and Liam have never been as close as would be convenient."

Paul isn't sure how to take that.

"I'm not thrilled about that," Victor adds into the silence.

Paul snaps his laptop shut. He is done with taking advice, or instruction, or whatever it is from Victor. "Yes, because I planned for Alex to walk out on me and then fuck Liam because he was pissed at me for conspiring with the two of you. Nobody's thrilled, Victor. Sometimes that happens, and I have to tell you, it would be a lot easier to be an adult about this if you weren't so sure none of us are up to the task. Just so you know, I heard about Liam from Alex, which was a pretty damn adult thing for him to do even if I don't understand the why about any of it."

"If it helps, I had rather considerable words with Liam about it."

"That's your business," Paul says.

"Why do you always shut down when — "

"Because you're my friend and my mentor and my boss, and I did not volunteer to hold Liam's secrets, especially when they are continuously provided to me without his consent or mine. It's a pain in my ass, and more unwelcome today than usual."

"Would you rather I said I was worried about you?" Victor asks.

"It would at least be relevant, so yes."

"Fine, I am worried about you. And I don't understand your choices."

"And what choices are those?"

"You've been working on my projects for how long now? Seven years?"

"Eight." Paul has no idea how this conversation has suddenly shifted into a discussion of his career.

"Eight years. I know you have ambition, but you've never even tried to move on. Add in Alex and Craig and whoever else — you can yell at me about being in control of your own destiny all you want, but you're trying to serve too many masters and not one of them is yourself."

"I have a plan," Paul says more than a little defensively.

"It's not working for you," Victor says.

"It was starting to."

"Then what is it you're so damn afraid of?"

Paul laughs sharply. "You, Alex. Everyone keeps telling me be careful what I wish for. And I wish for a lot. But I am also surrounded by the costs of success. I don't ever want to be you."

"Paul," Victor says reprovingly. "None of us here are fucked up because of success. That's the fun icing on the cake. I am the way I am because this is the way I am. Just because my life would not make you happy, does not mean it makes me unhappy. Quite the contrary. You should know better."

"Who's unhappy?"

Paul turns towards the voice.

There, in the doorway of the writers' room, Liam lounges. Paul has no idea how long he's been standing there. He assumes not very — Liam isn't known for quiet or still — but it's hard to be sure.

They all stare at each other for a moment.

"How is he?" Paul asks Liam.

"I'm going to assume you mean that in the least pornographic way possible."

Liam is exhausting, but Paul makes a gesture for him to continue.

"Better than he was, I think."

Paul nods. "Okay. Good." There's a part of him that can't stop picturing Liam and Alex together now. He wants to believe Alex never connected with Liam the way he did with Paul, but that's probably not true. Certainly, it's not fair and not his business.

"How are you?" Victor asks Liam pointedly.

"It's been a month," Liam says wearily. "How's Paul?" he asks back.

"Right here," Paul says sharply. He's less than amused with whatever double act is playing out in front of him. "And I've been better."

"Alex is totally fucked up over you," Liam informs him, like Paul wants that information in front of Victor. Or from Liam at all.

"Is that supposed to be comforting? I don't want him to be fucked up. I want him to be happy." Paul means it, but he also wishes the situation was less of a mess for all of them.

"With you," Liam says.

Paul shakes his head. "I'm in a relationship."

"Give him some time."

Paul doesn't know if Liam means Craig or Alex and has no interest in asking. He sighs heavily.

Victor, done with this drama, tosses his keys to Liam. "Go wait in my office. I'll cook you dinner."

Liam beams, gives a little salute, and is gone.

Victor puts a hand Paul's shoulder as he stands. "You need to stop being so nice about your desires."

"You have no idea." Victor underestimates him. Because there was nothing nice and everything glorious about the way he and Alex devoured each other. And, unless he can get it together and make it work, there probably isn't anything nice — in an entirely different way — about what he's doing to Craig either.

38

By the weekend Paul attempts to put all thoughts of Alex and Liam — and Alex *and* Liam, because that image is vivid and pretty and awful and odd — out of his head. He and Craig have beach plans.

It's overcast out when they wake up — late, because they've both been working a lot and sleep and sex are good — and nowhere near the forecast eighty. The beach is one of their good places, though, and they've been looking forward to this all week, so they go anyway.

They park in their usual lot and Craig frowns when Paul pulls a sweatshirt on over his T-shirt. Skin may be awesome but the wind is off the water and it's January. It's cold. Beau, no longer Divorce Dog, is thrilled to be out of the house and trots happily alongside them as they walk hand-in-hand above the surf line.

For long stretches of beach they're alone. It's wonderful, though, despite the gray, to walk and let their shoulders bump together, as they banter and laugh about utterly stupid shit. A string of breakups and actual divorces split up their social group early on in their relationship. In the isolating aftermath they'd learned to be very good company for each other. Carly always used to say they were boring, but sometimes Paul looks at her life, and this mess he's coming out of with Alex, and thinks boring is great.

When the afternoon starts to close in they build a fire on the beach and sit tucked close next to each other. Craig runs back to the car for a blanket when the temperature drops again. Beau naps next to them, twitching his ears whenever the fire pops.

They fall quiet eventually. With his head on Craig's shoulder Paul looks out at the water through the translucent tongues of flame. The water is grey and choppy, but the fire is warm, and the rush of the surf is soothing. Eventually, he drifts off.

He wakes a little while later. The sky is a shade darker, and the fire is a little lower.

Craig presses a kiss to the top of his head. "Hey baby, how're you doing?"

Paul assesses. He's a little cold, a little stiff, and getting hungry. This part of the day is just about over, but he doesn't want to go yet. "Really good."

Craig hums, "Good." He settles his arm more snugly around Paul's back. Beau yawns and nestles his head back down on his paws to drowse.

39

When everyone returns to *Paradise Square*, Alex feels better than he has in a long time. Everyone's rested from the break, and shooting outside in sub-freezing weather feels slightly more tolerable than it did before.

For whatever reason, everyone is treating him less like an interloper now. As much as he doesn't want to admit it to himself, that's probably because he's spending less time running off to Liam, who returned to L.A. late on New Year's Day with Carly in tow. He's also no longer fucking people's friends he met at the few cast gatherings he went to just before the holidays.

Press for *Fourth* is looms, which is slightly terrifying. Doing print interviews during the hurry up and wait on set is one thing. Doing the big morning shows with the screaming fans outside and the insipid banter inside is something else. Especially when all they want him to do is talk about kissing Liam. Some days it seems no one gives a shit about Zach and James — or TV shows having actual plots — at all.

Meanwhile, photos of his mother and him after midnight mass have emerged, and there's a dark sort of hilarity to being seen eating a hotdog quite so all over the internet. It's absurd enough to be funny, and if his fans are going to be intrusive, at least they are also cooing over his mom.

But on the whole things are fine — or at least more fine — than they've been in a long while. So when one of the A.D.s throws a fit at the extras and his walkie into a pile of suspiciously colored snow, it's awful and yet hilarious in just the right kind of way.

The day brings back memories of the horror stories he and Paul had delighted each other with about everything that could and did go wrong in the day-to-day of their existences. So when he's back in his room that evening, he leaves his Farsi notes on the nightstand and pulls out his phone.

◆

Paul's at home on the couch, Todd snoring softly from the chair in the corner, when his phone rings. A glance at the caller ID shows that it's Alex. After the few calls Paul has gotten from him over the past month Paul is less surprised as he's been before, but he is worried. Alex calling hasn't meant anything good for him yet.

"Hey," he says. "Are you — " Remembering Alex's admonishment, he cuts himself off. "How are you?"

Craig's won the miserable schedule sweepstakes this week so Paul has the house to himself, a fact for which he is grateful as he closes his laptop and braces himself for whatever insane adventure Alex has had this time.

"Hi, Paul," Alex says, like his name is enough of an answer. Then he dives into his story.

He's not broken or lost or upset, which are all good things but throw Paul badly. If he's meant to mend or soothe, he can try that and make sense of it. But Alex is laughing, and the only thing Paul can do to that is lose himself in the happiness of the sound.

"I miss you," Paul says softly when the story winds up. He doesn't mean to, because then they're going to have to talk about things, and that's probably unlikely to end well. But every fiber of his being wishes he were in the same room with Alex right now.

There's a long silence as Alex doesn't reply. Paul has to force himself not to fill up the space with apology or nervous chatter.

"I know about Craig," eventually comes his response.

"Carly?" Paul asks.

"Carly," Alex confirms. Then, "I miss you too."

♦

Alex should stop calling, but Paul keeps answering the phone. Whether that's because he wants him or wants him back — or thinks they can be one more version of the strange friends they've been since they first met — Alex has no idea. But he can feel himself being a little nuts, because when it comes to Paul he is a being of pure want. It's new in its way, a sort of desire and longing only made possible by too many disasters and his recent education less at Liam's hands than at his heart.

They talk about none of it, however. Not the fight, not Liam, and certainly not Craig. They don't say *I miss you* again, they just talk, mostly about nothing in particular while Alex tries to wind down from his days on set. It's oddly domestic. When they don't connect by phone, because Craig is over or Alex has been spending social time with some of the *Paradise Square* crew, they text.

The times Paul doesn't reply right away, when Craig's asked him to put the phone away or they're otherwise busy, make Alex antsy. He still has bad days, and while it makes things better when he can look forward to calling Paul at night, their unspoken *do not go* list gets in the way.

He can't say why when he's exhausted or heartsick or feeling fucked up or confused about everything, and Paul doesn't try to pry it out of him. It makes Alex snappish and sullen because as much as he wants Paul, he needs him to be his rock. But Alex can't have that. The absence of it and the reasons for it make him crazy.

◆

Paul should stop answering the phone. But he can't bring himself to. Alex's pull on him is as magnetic as it's ever been, even when he's three thousand miles away and continued contact is an extremely bad idea.

As eager as he is for Alex always, he's not always successful at reigning in his own temper and snappishness when Alex gets reticent and bitchy. But the nights when Alex isn't happy and doesn't get pissed and doesn't *talk* — when he's just a distant breath on the other end of the line — are the worst.

Sometimes Paul hangs up at the end of a call wondering if he'll get another. Somehow, he always does.

The night the phone rings around two a.m., Paul is grateful Craig is a sound sleeper, and he slips out of bed with a kiss to his shoulder. While Alex often calls late, it's usually not excessive and Paul learned long before Alex not to ignore middle-of-the-night calls.

When he answers, Alex immediately starts in on a story. He's not babbling. The story is precise and well formulated, like he thought about how he was going to tell it in the cab back to his hotel. Even so, Paul can tell he's drunk and trying to extend the moment through the pleasure of an audience.

"So why didn't you go home with him?" Paul eventually asks, amused, after Alex has run out of glowing adjectives for the very cute and very flirty boy at whatever party he's been at.

"Because I am trying to make better choices."

"Like staying out until five a.m. and calling me in the middle of the night?"

"I said better, Paul. Not good."

Paul laughs at that. Alex is in no condition for the alternative. "What would you have done to him?" he asks, before he can think the better of it.

"Maybe I wanted to be done to."

"Well, that's precise and informative," Paul says carefully.

"What? Maybe I just wanted some head."

"I know you, Alex. You wouldn't be that coy about wanting your dick sucked," Paul says.

"Yeah. Okay…. Look. Repertoires expand, okay?"

Paul laughs and shakes his head. Alex's economy and choice of words always surprises him. "Tell me about it," he says in the wrong tone for it to be meant as a phrase of agreement.

Shockingly, Alex does. He goes on and on about how tight this guy's jeans were and how much he wanted everyone to leave so he could say *stay right there, honey* and sit on his dick. Eventually Paul finds he has to ask the obvious question.

"Have you?" he asks.

"Have I what?"

"Alex — "

"Your breath is ragged. Are you touching yourself?" Alex says.

Paul can't tell if his tone deflection or indictment. "I am trying not to. My *boyfriend* is upstairs," he hisses.

"Yes," Alex shoots back.

"Yes, what?"

"Yes I had Liam's cock in me and I miss it." Alex pops each word.

"You're more drunk or more vicious than I realized," Paul tells him.

"Maybe I'm just learning how to say things," Alex retorts. "Or maybe, I'm finally figuring out how to want things."

"Do you always do everything in the wrong order?"

"I don't know. Do you always go from zero to married in your relationships? Or do you stop short of that and just have really sketchy interactions with your crazy exes who are totally not over you?"

Paul has no idea if Alex means Craig or himself. He's afraid to ask.

"Go back to the boy," Paul says. That's safe compared to everything else.

"Man," Alex says pointedly. "More hung than me. Can we take a minute to celebrate skinny jeans?"

"We can until I have to get them off someone," Paul says.

"I didn't know you didn't approve of my clothing choices."

"I don't think I approve of clothing on you at all."

The way Alex's breath punches out of him in response is shockingly hot. It also encourages Paul to keep going, like he's as drunk as this very dangerous creature he can't seem to let go of.

"Would you like that?" he asks. "The world where either of us has enough days off for me to keep you naked all the time?"

"It sounds terrifying," Alex says.

"Why?"

"Because you overwhelm me. Because you're asking me if I'd like to not have to think or speak or do anything but suck your cock. How am I supposed to give any answer to that other than yes?"

It's not the most Alex has ever said to him in a sexual context, but it might be the most coherent thing Alex has ever said to him in a sexual context. All Paul can grapple with right now though is that little whine creeping into Alex's voice, the one that begs and pleads and always tells Paul it's all too much even as Alex asks for more.

"Are you touching yourself?" Paul asks.

"No."

"Well, maybe you should be."

"Fuck," Alex says. "I don't have enough hands."

Paul can tell when he's dropped his phone onto his hotel bed and is fumbling with his clothes.

"I told you skinny jeans suck," he says when Alex returns.

"Say something useful," Alex demands.

This time Paul can't stop the laugh, and he smiles when he hears Alex chuckle in sheepish reply.

"So we're going to make this real simple," Paul says as he wanders into the kitchen to put even more distance between what he's doing and what he should be doing. "In part because you need to go to sleep, and I need to not get busted."

"Yeah?"

"Yeah. You jerk off, and when I say stop, stop."

"Paul — "

"Did you think I was going to stop teasing you?"

"No," Alex says once and then again. It sounds like relief.

Paul doesn't come — he wants this to be all about Alex — but by the end of the call he's relieved too. Climbing back into bed beside Craig he feels no guilt, just the exquisite torture of Alex's breathless whine still ringing in his ear. But they'd acknowledged every one of their red lines only by storming recklessly past them.

Alex doesn't call the next night, and Paul is glad because he has no idea what he's meant to say.

When days stretch out into a week without any word at all, Paul wonders if Alex had gotten out of him the last hurrah he'd been looking for since November and really is gone now. It's a dark thought, and may be unfair to both of them, but neither of them have ever been fair to each other, or themselves, in any of this.

40

Filming in New York is starting to wrap up, which means both even more press for *Fourth*, and the looming prospect of returning to home. L.A., City of Angels and also Paul, and Craig, and the whole giant mess that Alex was happy to pretend was a little less real than he knows it is so long as he was attached to it only via a phone line.

The seeming unreality of it is nothing like an excuse for not calling now, though, as much as Alex might want it to be. As many times as Alex thinks about it, and as much as he wants to, in the end he doesn't reach for the phone again. There's nothing he can say that he would mean.

The interviewers (the less professional ones, at least) and the internet still want to know about him and Liam. The newest pet idea — there aren't any credible rumors, but fans like to spin bullshit — is that they somehow hate each other.

Spend five minutes with him, Alex wants to say, with an overwhelming fondness. *You'd want to strangle him too.*

When he gets asked, the third or fourth time, about how well everyone in the cast gets along, with the unspoken but obvious subtext of *how do you and Liam get along?* he's tired enough and annoyed enough to put on his sly smile.

"Oh, everybody's great friends. Yeah, Liam and I did New Year's together here in New York. It was amazing."

The internet goes insane.

That's bad enough as it is. The fact that Alex has only his own stupidity and impatience to blame for handing that line to the maniacs makes it worse. But New Year's was a good night, and he could maybe have shrugged it off, if it weren't for the pictures.

I wasn't sure if I should post these, the captions online read. *But after what Alex said about Liam, it's not like they're hiding anything ;)*

It's not pictures from New York. They're from D.C. The shimmer of the reflecting pool and the stabbing column of the Monument glow behind two figures that are unmistakably the two of them.

None of the hyperventilating fan girls and boys on the internet know it, but he and Liam were on their way to the Lincoln Memorial that night. The more-than-grain of truth in all the suppositions about what they were up to that are also so fucking far from the truth is — after everything — heartbreaking.

In a way, Alex is glad to have the pictures, creepy and fucked up as that is. They are his only souvenir of something he still doesn't know how to classify. *Relationship* is far too tight a box now that it's over. *Affair* seems too open. But what Alex does know, even from this short distance, is that he was happy during what were also probably some of the worst weeks of his adult life. It makes him furious that people have decided to intrude on that.

Margaret gives him grief over the interview. Not because it was bad, but because he wasn't in control of himself to have offered up that tidbit of information — not that she knows the full story of it either. Liam sends him a few texts that Alex suspects are at least intended to be annoying.

Eventually he gets Liam to shut up with, *New Year's really was great* and *Paul and I had phone sex.*

When Liam doesn't have a response beyond *Cool!* Alex knows he's probably making more of a mess of everything than anyone wants to deal with.

That night, he lets himself be dragged to a party at Soho House by a couple of the wardrobe girls on *Paradise.* The second he's there, it feels like the worst choice ever. He just wants to talk to his friends, not hang out with their friends of friends of friends who desperately need to feel like they're getting their $900 per month's worth in celebrity hobnobbing. The whole winter rooftop with heat lamps thing is also more ridiculous than Alex can stand.

A drink doesn't make it better, and he feels good about his decision to leave until he tells his companions and actually goes. There are paparazzi outside — not just for him, never just for him, thank God — and they're loud, shouting for his attention. On one hand, it's less creepy, because unlike the fans with smartphones sneaking pictures of him, he knows they're there. On the other, it's harder to remain calm and firm in his need to treat them as invisible.

When one of them grabs his arm, it becomes impossible. A flash goes off too close to his face. He's physically unbalanced by resisting the unwelcome hand he can't yank away from without looking like the worst sort of asshole (not that he doesn't already by virtue of the venue). Someone is shouting a question at him about Liam.

"We were with his girlfriend," Alex replies to the question he's only half-heard about New Year's. "His parents were around too. Opposite of scandal!"

He tugs away from the hand on his arm and somehow finds his way into a cab, despite the spots from the flash still going off in front of his eyes. It takes a moment for him to even remember to give the driver an address.

As the car finally starts moving, he slumps against the door. None of that is anything that hasn't happened to him before, and while he never likes it, right now he feels shaken by the clamor far more than he usually does. The detached place he can usually fall back into when the world is too much isn't there. He doesn't understand how there can be real people these things happen to any more than he understands how he can be one of them.

Somehow he gets back to his room, where he shuts the city out behind the drapes and flicks on all the lights. It's still not enough for comfort, and in spite of the bucket of bad ideas it probably is, it's easy to reach for his phone for what he knows will be.

Paul has always picked up. He does tonight, too.

He sounds wary, at first, until Alex starts talking. Then he sounds worried. Alex tells him everything — the poorly calculated interview, the photos, the party, the paparazzi and how his most tender secrets are somehow currency.

"I wanted to hit them," he confesses.

He closes his eyes with a different sort of relief entirely when Paul responds, strangely gentle, "Wouldn't anyone?"

"I want to come home." Alex hates himself for how pathetic it sounds.

Paul hums, and it's soothing. "You will be soon."

"I know," Alex says. It's a little sad. But then he keeps talking.

◆

Paul listens with as much shock as concern; this isn't banter or ill-advised innuendo. This is Alex scared and broken again in ways Paul's only just coming to understand. At first he keeps an eye on the clock; he and Craig have plans tonight and honest to God he's trying. But Alex needs him, and Paul needs more than anything to be here for him. So at one point, dangerously close to the line when cancelling is going to become standing up, he interrupts Alex and says he's got to do something.

"I promise I'll call you right back. Just stay by the phone."

There's a rustle that he's pretty sure is Alex nodding. His heart aches for him. So do his hands.

He gets Craig's voicemail; he's probably in the car already. Paul should probably feel worse about that then he does.

"Hey," he says, when Alex answers on the first ring. "Back now. I'm yours all night."

Alex says, "Good."

◆

In the morning, Paul has a text from Craig which, given the voicemail, not to mention everything else, is probably fair: *I think we need to talk.*

They meet for dinner at the same sushi restaurant Paul had first been spotted at with Alex. It's Craig's suggestion and Paul can't tell him no without telling him why. There's so much writing on the wall already that there's absolutely no point in adding any more.

"So, about last night," Craig begins, once they've gotten their drinks.

"I'm sorry," Paul says. He is, though not in a way that's useful.

"No, it's — " Craig stops himself and shakes his head. "It was Alex, wasn't it?"

Paul nods, once. "Yeah. It was."

Craig looks at his glass and bites his top lip in the way Paul remembers falling in love with, when they'd first been together. He looks up at Paul. "I don't think this is going to work."

"I — " Paul starts, but stops at Craig's resigned look.

"I'm glad we tried again," Craig says. He doesn't sound angry. Just so tired. "I always would have wondered, otherwise."

Paul nods. He doesn't trust his voice right now. "Me too," he says. He's not sure if it's true, but he owes Craig the kindness.

"I'm sorry I took Beau."

The laugh, watery and sharp, bursts out of Paul before he realizes it's going to. He presses his closed hand to his mouth and looks over Craig's shoulder at a spot on the wall until he's sure he can look at Craig and hold himself together at the same time. As inevitable as this outcome probably is, he really had tried. If any number of things had been different, he and Craig still could have been very good together. He's mourning the loss already.

"I'm sorry I'm an asshole," is what he finally says when he's sure looking at Craig isn't going to crack him a little.

Craig smiles, but it's strained. "Only when you try to be."

Paul isn't sure if he means about the sorry or the asshole; he's pretty sure Craig's right about both.

They finish the meal talking about small, quiet things. They split the check, hug goodbye in the parking lot, and go their separate ways.

In his car, Paul sits with his phone balanced on the steering wheel as he types a message to Carly. *Free tonight? I need to get blindingly drunk right now.*

41

The flight back to L.A. is almost nothing like the flight out to D.C, for which Alex is infinitely grateful. He's glad to spend it sleeping, instead of trying not to cry. But while he's definitely less miserable, Alex feels just as uncertain.

As the plane circles LAX on its descent, Alex braces for the moment the wheels hit the tarmac. It's his least favorite part of flying; it feels so close to a crash.

The plane lands safely, though, and as it taxis to the gate Alex turns his phone back on and scrolls through the notifications. Emails from Margaret; a late exhortation from Gemma to have a good flight and call her when he lands; and a text from Carly.

Paul and Craig are done, it reads. *Got a plan?*

What the fuck am I supposed to do with that information? he types back, stunned, as the jet way rolls out to meet the plane.

The reply comes back sooner than he expects as he waits for the people ahead of him to shuffle down the aisle. *Whatever you want. That's the point.*

When he wheels his suitcase into what is still, for a few more days, their shitty apartment, Gemma's on the couch with a giant bowl of popcorn. The fact that it's all like he never left is faintly irritating. He's changed; the world hasn't; and now he's expected to sit down and eat popcorn.

"Hey, stranger," Gemma says as he takes off his jacket.

"Hey."

"I know you were making a movie and all, but way to keep in touch."

"Gem...." Alex starts guiltily. He's barely contacted Gemma at all since he left over a month ago, which makes him the worst of roommates and friends. But he could hardly talk about what he was doing with the people he was doing it *with*. Explaining things to a third party was beyond his capacity.

Something in Alex's tone makes Gemma sit up straight and pats the seat next to her. "Oh my God, what happened, and tell me everything." Interpersonal drama is for Gemma what certain high frequencies are for dogs.

"Um." Alex sits down next to her cautiously. "This is all like...like you can't tell anyone ever. I know I tell you to keep secrets all the time, and I'm sure you don't and that whoever you tell is trustworthy or at least batshit crazy enough that no one would believe them if they talked, but this is like orders of magnitude, okay?"

She frowns. "What did you do?"

"Liam."

She squeals and kicks her feet so that the popcorn spills everywhere.

"Okay, the sudden feeling I have that you've been reading porn about me and a colleague on the internet is extremely uncomfortable."

"He's so charming," she whines.

"Not really," he says dryly. "I mean, yes. But not the person you think he is."

"Obviously."

"Look, you can't tell. And not just for my sake. He's in the closet, the thing with Carly is very real and very serious, she knows, it's all fine, but not for the world, okay?"

While she agrees to keep the secret, Alex makes her swear again and again to silence in the course of a conversation that covers about eighty percent of the madness. After Gemma's curiosity and his own need to tell someone outside of that mess about it has been satiated, the conversation culminates in a planning session regarding the impending move. If everything goes as expected, closing is happening the day after next.

"You seem different," she says, when they get to the end.

"I'm a beautiful person who goes to beautiful parties with beautiful people now," he says sharply although only a tiny bit unkindly. He tries to pick some of the spilled popcorn out of the couch. "What's your story?" he asks.

"I'm the girl who used to want to be famous," she says. She doesn't even sound like she's lying.

♦

Moving does not go smoothly, not that they had any right to expect it to. The paperwork is fine, and signing the final dotted lines is a lot less scary than it seemed when Alex was first planning this. But there are boxes everywhere, first at the old apartment and then at the new house, which is open and echoing and bare. By the end of moving day Alex is sore and cranky and exhausted and feels homesick for their old place.

"This feels like a museum," he says, sitting cross-legged on the rug in what will probably be the living room.

"It needs furniture," Gemma says, lips pursed and hands on her hips as she surveys the space thoughtfully.

Alex groans and flops onto his back on the floor.

◆

That night in his new bedroom, Alex lies staring at the ceiling for far too long. This is a moment, and maybe after all the other moments he's had recently, this one should feel less by comparison. It doesn't.

He pulls out his phone to reread the text from Carly, then scrolls to Paul's name in his contacts. Now that there's no reason he shouldn't call and nothing stopping him from getting in his car and driving to Paul's house, doing any of that feels impossible.

The idea of being with Paul again had been lovely as a fantasy and an abstraction. Here, in unfamiliar surroundings in a familiar place it's too easy to remember all the things that had gone wrong.

But with Gemma down in the loft instead on the other side of the wall Alex is lonely in the vast expanse of his new house. He's never been any good at backing down from challenges anyway. He hits the call button.

"Alex?" Paul always answers with his name. Some things, at least, don't change.

"Hi," Alex says. "It's my first night in the new house. I feel like I should tell you a story."

"That sounds dangerous," Paul says.

Alex laughs. The assessment is certainly fair. "The movers weren't hot, and I didn't fuck any of them. Also, why do I hurt all over when I hired people?"

"I broke up with Craig," is Paul's incredibly not helpful answer.

"I know."

"Carly?" Paul asks.

"It would be nice for once to get some of this news from you," Alex says mildly even as he's aware that maybe Paul doesn't owe him anything anymore.

"I think you need to blame other people for that," Paul says cautiously. "Time and place. And it only just happened."

"Was it because of me?"

"Yes. No. I mean, yeah, but Craig and I have always had plenty of issues before I knew you existed. So…whatever makes you feel better."

"I'm willing to feel guilty about Thanksgiving. I'm not willing to feel guilty about Craig. Believe it or not, I'm trying to be an adult here," Alex says.

"What do you want me to say, Alex?"

"I want you to stop babying me. 'Whatever makes me feel better,' what the fuck?"

"You may be trying, but you have none of your shit together," Paul says wearily.

"Thank you," Alex says sharply.

"It's got nothing to do with your age. It's your life," Paul continues. "It's insane."

"I appreciate the vote of confidence."

"This from the guy who spent so much time at my house because it felt normal."

"So what if I did?"

"Alex," Paul says, his voice placating. "I'm not...." He stops and starts again. "I'm just saying. Your life is strange and hard. It would be strange and hard for anyone. But there are resources. You know there are people you could talk to."

"You mean therapy."

"I mean — yeah. Yes. I do," he says firmly.

"Paul?"

"Yeah?"

"What happened to your wrists?" Alex says. Paul may have a valid point, but Alex is so not the only one of them who is screwed up.

"What does that have to do with this?"

"My life is fucked up, but I never tried to make myself disappear."

There's silence for two terrible seconds. Paul snaps, "Why did *no one* notice you until Victor picked you up and dropped you in front of a camera? Now they've seen you, and they can't look away."

"Victor's a wizard."

"He didn't create you, Alex."

There's silence for a moment. Alex says softly, "Somebody noticed me before Victor did."

"What are you talking about?"

"You did."

"Well, arguably, Nick did then," Paul says.

"No. Not the way you did."

"And what way was that?"

Alex takes a breath. "Like I wasn't invisible. Like I wasn't an interchangeable part of the L.A. monster."

"Alex — "

"You still do. My invisibility's just different now, is all. Paul," he says. "And maybe you're not wrong. But you're fucked up too, and I can't be the kind of adult you need me to be. Not now. Not when you can't be single for seven whole days in a row."

"What does that mean?"

"It means it's my first night in a house I bought, my room is full of boxes, and I go back to work tomorrow, which means I'm going into the desert," Alex says, annoyed but also a little proud of what he's managed to accomplish.

"That's not a helpful answer, although I'm sure that's the point," Paul snaps. "What are we doing?" he asks, more softly.

"Me? I'm working on being twenty-one and not being late to work. What are you doing?"

Paul snorts. "Yeah. Okay. Fair, I guess. You should get some sleep."

Alex sighs. "Okay, Paul? New rule. You don't ask me what we're doing 'til you can get your head around me setting my own bedtime."

◆

The sun's not even up when the van comes to take him to location. There're some guys from the crew too, and Alex is fine with that. He doesn't want a car, and he doesn't want a hotel closer to the site. He just wants his own bed as much as he can have it and a few hours passed out in the back row of seats when he can't.

The weather out at Kelso is variable in the extreme — cold as fuck when they get there with a rapid climb to uncomfortable heat during the late morning — but Alex likes the labor and ordeal of it. It's a welcome change from all the parts of his life that are supposed to be easy and aren't.

Other than having strangers constantly reapply his sunblock between takes, the desert is mostly good. Even the absence of familiar faces helps a little bit. The idea of being at the lot with Paul or Liam isn't awful, but he can't say he minds putting that reunion off for a little while longer.

The desert is also beautiful. The sky is massive and endless, and as much as Alex does love the work, he wishes he had time alone on the dunes, watching the sun come up without anyone else around. He takes some amazing pictures that he emails to his mom.

42

Alex hasn't been to brunch in weeks, so there's no particular reason to miss him more this Sunday than all the previous ones. Paul goes anyway, even if he's glad Alex is most likely sleeping off a long week in the comfort of his own home not that far away.

Paul ends up talking to Shawna, who it transpires has been in much closer contact with Alex since he hit the desert. Paul is genuinely trying to figure out where he's been misstepping. Maybe part of treating Alex like an adult is to get his head around the fact that he has plenty of relationships that aren't mediated by him. Or Victor.

Paul probably won't ever not feel a little protective of Alex, but Shawna's frank assumption of Alex's ferociousness as they talk about the work he's doing is a little chagrining. Alex may be more broken than the rest of the world knows, but maybe the rest of the world also knows a little more about how strong he is than Paul does.

At home, Paul works on being single. It's easier to let go of Craig than he might have expected. Some of that is because Paul hasn't managed to let go of Alex at all, which brings its own guilt, but Paul is grateful for at least one loss that doesn't sting any more.

Paul starts working out again and this time paces himself, running around the neighborhood without pushing himself too hard or trying to constantly make life painful for himself.

When he gets back from his runs he makes dinner and then spends the evenings on the couch or on his bed or at the kitchen table writing with just Todd for company. The house still feels empty, but at least it's not unbearable anymore.

That said, the other downsides to being alone make themselves evident quickly as well. But it's not all bad; one night, he jerks off not to memory or fantasy of Craig or Alex or anyone else he's ever been with, but to straight-up porn. Paul realizes it's kind of awesome to get off and have it not be about anyone else for a change.

♦

Back on the lot, filming carries on with everyone else. Paul keeps an eye on social media and is amused by fan speculation about what a film crew for a show ostensibly set in D.C. is doing out in the desert. The fans know Alex is there too, which leads to other speculation Paul finds a lot less amusing.

The fans who assume Liam and Alex are dating are as dedicated in that belief now as they were before Christmas, and they're taking that theory to some strange conclusions. For instance, they assume that Liam is driving out to the desert every evening to visit Alex, which makes no sense whatsoever on any number of levels. Liam's on the lot and is spending at least half the time he's not working irritating Paul.

Late one evening he looks up from his desk in the writers' room to see Liam hanging in the doorway.

"Working. Out!" Paul snaps without bothering to make any inquiry as to what Liam wants. He's in no mood for conversation, and Liam usually responds best to simple and direct. But Liam doesn't leave.

"Hey, man, just wondering…" Liam swings a little on the doorframe. "Have you heard from him?"

"Yes," Paul says shortly. There have been a few texts back and forth since the phone call the night Alex got back to town. Paul braces himself for further questioning, but none is forthcoming.

Liam nods with satisfaction, and Paul wonders what the other man knows that he doesn't. Before he can work up the patience to ask, Liam turns on his heel and is gone.

43

Alex finally reaches that familiarity with Kelso that he can forget the trailers and equipment and everyone else and focus on the dunes and the mountains beyond them. The eight-year-old in him who spent summer wandering through woods and fields is endlessly fascinated by the sand, rocks and shifting shadows on the dunes. He desperately wants to explore.

Today at least, the rest of the crew doesn't share his calm or his joy. No one's been sleeping enough, things keep going wrong with the equipment, and tempers pop and simmer. None of it is helped by the heat, which skyrockets as the morning wears on.

Even Alex starts to feel shitty as he sweats through his costume and his sunblock in record time. By midmorning he's fighting a headache. The glare of the sun off the sand does not help with that. When he stands up from the crouch where Zach's been bent over some of his equipment the blood rushes disconcertingly out of his head.

Lunch makes him nauseated, and the headache doesn't get better. Eventually he throws up. He pushes aside the flutter of concern from the both the director and the safety monitor to insist that he's fine, that he can keep going, that people have worked through worse before. It's not untrue.

He goes back to do the take again and wishes his mouth was less dry. Even the thought of water makes his stomach unhappy. He also wishes the breeze was doing more to keep him cool.

◆

With two units shooting this week, it's less that Liam has more free time, and more that the *Fourth* schedule has been a little bit more flexible to accommodate everyone else's other interests. While most of the cast is either sleeping in or whining at their agents about wanting more, more, more — as if they have the time or stamina for it — Liam's doing a brunch for an arts education charity. There are fans outside, but then there always are, especially at stuff like this that easily features half a dozen people someone cares about.

Carly has begged off. Doing sound editing on commercials is generally way more nine-to-five than his job, and she's always been insistent about keeping it that way. Another random charity lunch decorating his arm isn't worth the later hours to her. Liam can understand that; he's always been more than happy to do whatever is necessary to make sure she gets the space for the life and career she wants. He feels honored that he gets to be a part of that.

Besides, as of two days ago she has an engagement ring on her finger and they haven't told anyone outside of their most immediate circle. Her attending an event with him without announcing it first would instigate a media feeding frenzy that is unlikely to be pleasant. And while Liam's usual impulse with anything that makes him happy is to share — Carly saying yes has made him happier than anything else ever — he's enjoying these few days of having their engagement belong just to them.

After the lunch, since he's not in any rush and the fans are pretty much the only people who don't find him too excitable, Liam stops to chat. He finds it strange when people want him to talk to their smartphones as opposed to them.

There are lots of awkward questions which generally fall into three categories: *Marry me*, *marry Alex*, and inappropriate requests for various forms of physical contact. While Liam has no objection to physical contact in principle, getting involved with fans is a bad idea. And given what happened between him and Alex, all those questions cut a little too close to the bone.

Somehow, in one of those awful moments when all the questions hit at once, Liam manages to get everyone to shut up for half a second. Later, he'll wonder if this was the gift of big hand gestures or simple bad luck.

"Three things, which should cover all the questions," he says into the nearest cellphone camera. "One, Alex is a dear and awesome friend and that's it. Don't badger him about it, 'cause it pisses him off, and I hate when he's mad at me. Two, but yes, I also like boys — no, no, no shut up and let me finish — I am only telling you this because, three, Carly and I got engaged two days ago. And she likes me better when I'm not asking her to keep my secrets."

With that Liam smiles smugly, waves, and tells everyone to have a beautiful day, before getting into the waiting car. It only takes about five minutes before he starts wondering if that was one of his really bad ideas that's going to cause Victor to yell. Then he realizes he should probably call his publicist. Ten seconds later, as he's still trying to figure out the appropriate chain of next events, his phone starts ringing and doesn't stop.

♦

The day on set is fairly quiet. Between meetings Victor is in his office going over plans for *Fourth's* next cycle when his phone goes off. The voice on the other end of the line is concerned, and after a few sharp questions Victor asks several more, all worried.

It's the A.D. on location in Kelso. Alex collapsed during filming, and is being taken to the hospital now. Heat stroke, is the unconfirmed verdict. His temperature had been far too high and he wasn't sweating. Whatever the case, his condition is definitely not anything to be fucked around with and is scary as hell for everyone involved.

Victor knows he'll react later — the thought of anything happening to any of his people is devastating. The thought of it being Alex, who never even asked for this life, is worse. But an emotional response now would be self-indulgent; too many people are relying on him. There's delegation to do, because a principal getting rushed to the hospital from set disrupts everything. There's insurance to deal with, because even if today is all they lose in filming time that's still a day gone. And there are calls to be made. Alex's emergency contact is his mother.

Victor calls her himself, because fuck policy. She takes the news that her son is hospitalized with the sort of calm crisis management that tells Victor as much about Alex as it does about her. Victor lets her know what's going on as best he can and gives her the contact information for the hospital. There's press to yell at too. Somehow this has gotten out instantly — Victor wonders darkly if the EMTs are on Twitter — and no, heat stroke is not a euphemism for drugs or a nervous breakdown; it's fucking hot in the desert, and Alex has always pushed himself hard.

When everything that needs to be dealt with immediately has been dealt with, Victor heads downstairs to the writers' room. Word spreads fast and he wants to get to Paul before anyone else does. Paul deserves to know what's going on, but Victor also knows he's going to want to do something stupid about it, and he would prefer to head that off.

While he's en route, his phone goes off again. His heart lurches badly at the ring. He answers, expecting a possibly awful update on Alex. Instead, his assistant informs him that Liam has chosen this day and hour to suddenly come out of the closet and that it's all over Twitter.

It is some magic of Alex, Victor thinks, that everything he touches seems to explode all at once.

His instructions to his assistant are simple: Get Liam on the phone, be gentle with him, tell him to expect a call from Victor in fifteen minutes and do *nothing* in the meantime.

"Tell him I'm not pissed," Victor says before he hangs up. Worried, yes; this wasn't planned, and he wants to make sure Liam is okay. But angry? Not in the least. Liam finding his own way is his favorite thing in the world.

When he gets to the writer's room and shares the news, he nearly has to staple Paul to his chair to keep him from going to the hospital to be with Alex.

"Why can't I go?" Paul sounds closer to anger about it than Victor has ever heard him about anything.

"Alex is fine," Victor tells him firmly. "He's stable; he's recovering; and he needs rest. You are not restful. I will take the blame for you not being there if he's pissed, and I will keep you updated myself, but you are to stay here, and then you are not to get into your car tonight except to go home. Do you understand me?"

Paul blanches a little at the word *stable*. Victor can't blame him. It's supposed to be a good word, but all it does is remind people how anyone it gets applied to very recently wasn't.

Victor puts a hand on Paul's arm. "He's going to be fine."

Paul nods rapidly. This is why Victor has to stay calm. If he isn't calm, he can't force his people to be.

"Stay by your phone," Victor tells him, already on his way out the door. "I'll call you as soon as I can."

◆

Victor waits to go to the hospital until that evening. As much as his impulse is to get to Alex first, there's not much he can do but get in the way. Once he knows he's no longer packed in ice, he heads to the set first to see how people are and talk to the A.D. and the safety captain. On top of everything else they'll have to deal with the union, and Victor wants to make sure no one was pushing Alex but Alex before that particular headache begins.

At one point he finds himself yelling at everyone for being afraid of him before he thanks them for being so damn excellent at doing everything right in a terrible situation. Before he goes, he exhorts everyone to check the internet at their earliest possible convenience, so they can know just how bizarre this day has been. It's not quite gallows humor, since everything is going to be okay, but it's close.

Alex is asleep when Victor gets to his room at the hospital. He looks like shit and fragile in a way that he usually doesn't. Then again, everyone looks like shit when they're in a hospital bed, and there's something to be said for situation normal.

Eventually, after Victor stares at him for fifteen minutes, Alex's eyelids flutter open.

"Could you feel me staring at you?" Victor asks.

Alex huffs a sound that might be a laugh but might be pain. Victor takes it as invitation to pull a chair over to the bed and sit down.

"Are you pissed?" Alex asks. He doesn't sound scared so much as faintly amused.

"No. We have good insurance. And you're not dead. If I'm pissed, it's only a little at myself."

"Then why are you here?" Alex asks.

"Because someone should be, and I already told Paul no. Also Liam."

"Why?"

"Because this one is my job. I gave you this life, and if you ever need help because of it, I have to be the first and last person in line to provide it. Also because Paul is still working on seeing you as an adult, and I know Liam drives you bugfuck."

Alex laughs, but it's weak and scratchy. "I feel bad about that."

"Don't. In either case." Victor reaches towards Alex briefly, but pulls back before touching him. "Are you up to talking for a little bit?"

Alex nods, and as much as his eyes don't quite want to focus or stay open — Victor knows that's the muscle relaxants to stop the shivering that went with the ice — there's a hint of trepidation there now.

"Good. So, there's some other stuff going on, that I'd rather you know about sooner than later."

"Okay?" Alex says.

"Liam came out today."

"What?" Alex tries to sit up, but his muscles won't support him. Victor does touch him then — he grabs Alex's shoulders, gently, and presses him back to the bed.

"To the entire internet via a random fan's smartphone. Don't worry, he's implicated exactly no one but Carly, to whom he is now engaged, by the way."

"Tell me I'm hallucinating."

"Would that make it better?" Victor asks. He's always been fond of Alex, but never so much as now.

"No, but…that's an insane choice."

"A little bit, yes."

"What was he thinking?"

"That he wants to be a good man. Can you imagine how I feel?" Victor feels as exhausted as Alex looks. The admission is nothing Alex could be expecting, so he makes his voice quiet, kind, and private.

"I can't answer that," Alex says.

"I know you know," Victor says, enjoying confirming, in the midst of all this, what are probably some of Alex's worst fears.

"Proud," Alex says.

Victor smiles. Alex, his best student, has found the only possible answer. He puts a hand to Alex's hair and leans forward in his chair to kiss him on the forehead. "And that's why I'm not pissed at you."

44

Once Alex has slept for approximately a year he feels less like death. As a bonus, they finally let him have his phone back. There are more or less a million things on it to check, and he's bored enough to tackle at least the important ones first. He happily takes the excuse of heat stroke and hospital to ignore the rest.

He calls his mom and spends a blissful twenty minutes being chatted to; it's exactly the comfort that he wants right now.

Gemma, worried, offers to come visit.

He texts back, *Thanks, but I'm exhausted. And completely fine. I'll see you on Thursday.* Talking on the phone is one thing, but he's not up to people yet. He's being kept for observation another night because apparently one of the perks of fame is more hospital food.

Liam he texts too. *Congrats on the engagement. And everything else.* Alex means it. Deeply. But that doesn't mean it doesn't also hurt on multiple fronts, not that these things have happened, but that he has, once again, been the last to know.

Paul, he calls.

"Hi," he says, a little sheepishly, when Paul picks up.

"Jesus fucking Christ, Alex," Paul breathes.

"Yeah. Hi." Alex grins at the ceiling.

"How are you doing?"

"To be honest, I feel terrible. But they tell me that's normal."

Alex can hear Paul shoo Todd off his chair so he can sit down. "Should you be doing anything other than resting?"

"I'm bored."

"So am I, but I also want you to get better."

"I notice you're not telling me to sleep."

"I also notice you told me you feel like shit and why, but we can talk later," Paul says softly. "Look, Alex, the longer I stay on the line the more likely I am to say things I really shouldn't say, especially not over the phone. And I want to come see you, but Victor would kill me."

"Okay," Alex says easily. He recognizes that they're stepping into a dance with each other again. A little more cautiously than the first time, to be sure, but with no less intensity. "I get it. I just wanted to say hi."

"I'm glad you did."

♦

After he's made his phone calls, Alex has little to occupy him other than social media. He knows he should avoid it, since it's never given him anything but a headache even before he was in the hospital, but he can't look away from the train wreck of *Fourth* fandom as it unfolds. Liam has come out and has gotten engaged, to a woman no less; and Alex almost died. The internet has devolved into incoherent key mashing and internecine conspiracy theories. Also, a lot of people are angry.

Very, *very* angry. Angry at Liam for lying for so long while also being off the market. Angry at Carly Amadahy, alleged beard, for existing. Angry at *The Fourth Estate* and Victor for putting Alex at risk. And then angry at Alex and Liam by turns for upstaging each other with their ridiculously well-synchronized media crises. That part is nearly funny, except for how it's somewhat true. Everyone's PR teams are furious.

Predictably, the media the next day is a mess. Alex's publicist issues a statement for him. Victor issues statements about everything for everyone. Liam does a ridiculously lovely daytime talk show interview: Focused and kind and as straightforward as he can be on the burdens his choices have placed on others.

Alex watches it all from his hospital bed. The interview goes a long way towards easing whatever regrets he's been nursing about his affair with Liam, no matter how complicated it remains in his head. He doesn't like the idea of feeling so vulnerable to someone he's so not fucking ever again.

◆

Alex gets discharged at noon the next day and is relieved when only a few paparazzi are outside the hospital. Gemma, bless her, is there to pick him up and does not immediately throw herself at him in a rib-crushing hug, for which he is grateful.

"I need a Big Mac or I'm going to die," he says as soon as he's waved to the photogs before sliding into

Gemma's car. Hospital food is horrific and he finally feels like he wants to eat again besides.

She cackles and throws his hat at him.

He spends the rest of the day drinking Gatorade and sleeping off the last of the horrible either in his room or on the couch that they desperately need to replace. He finally snaps at Gemma to stop hovering the eighth time she checks in on him, and they both enjoy the quarter hour of bickering that follows. After, they look at furniture websites while leaning against each other companionably. Alex emails Yancy to ask how necessary it really is to see furniture in person before purchase.

Ultimately, in the absence of much else to do, and with a wealth of new data that makes him finally realize that he's not the only one who has ever found public life challenging, Alex also spends a lot of time thinking. He wants Paul, he has no doubt about that. But he also wants a life that he chose for himself, not one that he stumbled into by accident or magic. And if he's going to get it, he needs to start making some serious, thoughtful decisions.

The scope of what he's trying to achieve is frightening. The chance of failure is non-negligible. But Alex is determined.

45

For Paul, at work, everything is strange all over. The offices have to churn through all of the rescheduling necessary in the wake of a three-day delay in second unit filming. Not to mention the general insanity that Liam can't seem to stop trailing in his wake. Every time it feels like the world has adjusted, another country is heard from.

At one point a particularly odious televangelist escaped from the eighties suggests *The Fourth Estate* is forcibly turning its stars gay. Victor thinks it's hilarious, but Paul finds himself angry and unsettled. Liam, meanwhile, wants life to go back to normal. Paul feels a little bad for him. He clearly had no idea his admission would be this disruptive for this many people for more than twenty-four hours.

It's a relief when the weekend finally comes, and Paul skips his run to sleep obscenely late on Saturday. It's easier to stay in bed than get up and be tempted to do things. Like call Alex, or go visit him. They're working toward something, slowly but surely, and Paul can't get ahead of himself. If he does, he's afraid he'll break the spell and lose everything.

He only gets out of bed when hunger makes further sleep impossible. He's in the kitchen, trying to decide what to make for lunch that requires the least possible amount of effort, when there's a knock at the door.

"Wanna hear a story?" Alex says, when he opens it.

Paul stares at him. He's got a new hat on and his messenger bag slung over his shoulder. Paul realizes he's remembered every freckle on his face perfectly.

"I know the adult thing to do would have been to call, but I decided I didn't care," Alex says.

Paul knows he should be more measured but after the last few days he no longer cares. He takes Alex's face in his hands and kisses him as hard and with as much tongue as possible. Alex isn't startled at all and doesn't seem to care that they're doing this in Paul's open doorway in broad daylight. His feet aren't even over the threshold of the house, but on the concrete just outside.

Alex gasps as the kiss breaks only enough for Paul to turn his attention to mouthing at his jaw. He pushes Paul back slightly. "Can we fuck and then talk?"

"We should — "

"We should do a lot of things." Alex walks Paul backwards into the house. "But can we have this? No matter what happens?"

A month ago, or even a week ago, Paul would have told Alex he was being immature. That he was using sex to solve problems that were much bigger than he realized. But a lot has happened since then. From the sad, quiet closure of the final ending with Craig to Liam's public admission and Alex's scare in the desert, it seems like the most reasonable, elegant, and mature request in the world. They've earned this.

"Yeah." Paul stands aside and Alex slips past him, surreptitiously waving to the cat as they head upstairs.

The sex isn't as frantic or as complicated as it could be. Alex asks if he has condoms as opposed to rifling through his drawers. Paul's heart aches that he no longer feels completely at home in this room. He also doesn't help Paul undress or give Paul any chance to undress him. His whole attitude is almost clinical until he kicks aside his socks and finally looks at Paul.

They devour each other. Paul has never seen the Alex who backs him onto his bed before. He has all the power of his anger and the intensity of the gaze that he usually gives the camera. But Alex isn't unhappy and his eyes are only for Paul.

Alex sinks down onto his cock with a relieved little laugh. Paul chastises himself for assuming Alex's earlier murmur of "I'm going to fuck you now" had meant something else. Although that too is definitely on his to-do list, now that they can, apparently, have this again. The second Alex starts to move, that thought, and every other thought Paul has ever had, is gone.

Somewhere in the heat of it, when his hands are tight around Alex's hips helping to slam him down around his dick over and over, Paul asks, "Why are we so good at everything?"

"Because I'm awesome," Alex manages.

Paul is delighted by the teasing look he gets and by the loveliness of laughing again in bed with this boy who can be so funny but, with the rest of the world at least, is usually too sharp for joy.

"The thing is," he says, getting his hands under Alex's thighs and hitching his legs further up the bed, "So am I."

Alex keens.

Paul makes soothing noises at him even as he fucks up into him, Alex fists his hands hard into Paul's hair and stares him down. "Not here to be soothed," he says.

"Yeah?"

"Yeah," Alex says, punctuating the sentiment by biting at Paul's lower lip.

"Does that mean I get to fuck you into the mattress?"

"Break the fucking bed."

Paul damn well tries. He has wanted this, in this way, for so long. Alex being delighted and challenging is completely enchanting. Paul comes when Alex grabs his own dick with both hands and jerks himself.

"Jesus Christ, let go already," Paul growls as he starts to come back to himself. It's enough to do the trick.

♦

Alex grabs Paul's hand, pulls him down to lie facing him, and presses their foreheads together. For the first time since he got on the plane to fly to D.C., he feels like he can breathe. He knows that's largely endorphins talking; not all the time without Paul has been bad. Indeed, a lot of it was necessary. But the relief of being here in Paul's arms is overwhelming. There's no guarantee of this working in the long run, Alex knows enough to be sure of that, but he also knows enough now to savor this moment for what it is.

Paul tangles their fingers and kisses the back of Alex's hand. "I missed you."

"Yeah," Alex breathes. "I missed you too."

"So can I ask why?"

Alex twists onto his back, looks at the ceiling for a moment, then makes himself look back at Paul. They've come this far, and they need to have this conversation, but he's still buzzing with afterglow and wishes they could put it off just a little longer. But that's not the adult thing to do and he wants so badly to get it right this time. He doesn't say anything right away.

Paul squeezes his hand. "Hey," he says gently. "It's me."

"How do you do that?" Alex searches Paul's face. "Do what?"

"Fuck me like that and then hold me. Like this," he says. It's not a question he could have asked — or an admission he could have made — three months ago. But all sorts of things feel possible now that didn't before.

Paul grins. "Because we're amazing at everything."

"It's been a long week," Alex says eventually, when the silence stretches out. Apparently Paul is willing to wait for an answer. Alex is grateful. "And yet somehow I ended up with a lot of time on my hands. After the desert, and then after Liam…."

"How did you hear about that, by the way?"

Alex rubs a thumb over the back of Paul's hand. "Victor showed up at the hospital. I was still really out of it. I woke up, and there he was hovering by my bed like the goddamn angel of death. It was slightly terrifying," he says sheepishly.

"Well, there's a way to get the news," Paul says.

"Yeah. He was…he was very human too in that moment. I can't imagine what that day was for him." Alex feels ill at ease talking about his new found — and likely temporary — empathy for Victor. He worries Paul will tease him about it, but the other man remains silent.

"Liam was very brave," Alex finally says. "And he did something he's never wanted to do because he wanted something else more. It made me think about what I could get, if I bent a little."

"Alex…."

"Shhhh, let me finish," Alex says gently, even as has to look away from Paul in order to be able to continue. "My life is messed up and it's never as much in my control as I need it to be. I'm twenty-one and new at everything. You noticed that. You didn't always react to that the way I wanted you to, but you weren't wrong."

He is lightened by the admission, but he still feels frightened of whatever comes next. Despite what he said to Paul on his doorstep, he doesn't want only this. He wants so much more.

"You've changed. Since you got back. And I don't mean the sex thing," Paul says, his voice quiet and close. "You clearly have a plan. And I never want to let you out of my sight again,"

Alex tries not to be smug, but the praise for his focus and Paul's need for him is everything he's wanted to hear since he stormed out of this house all those weeks ago. "You're not the same either," Alex says thoughtfully. "I've learned a lot."

"It's been a long winter," Paul says with a weariness Alex feels certain they've both earned. "I want you to know. I adore you, you drive me crazy, and if we're having the conversation I think we're having, you need to know how very high the stakes are. Because I can't do anything else. It's not in me."

Alex nods, letting the thought settle. "I know." He is overwhelmed by Paul's declarations, spoken and not, but, like much else with this man, so good. Still, Alex has no intention of letting this conversation linger only on his own wounds. "You have problems too, and I can't be the fix for them. You've been holding yourself back, and I have no idea why."

"Victor asked me the same thing, you know."

"Did he?" Alex asks, vindicated and amused.

"Yeah."

"What did you tell him?"

"That I was scared of turning into him."

Alex giggles. Victor is a laser. Paul is a softer light, still electronic but more diffuse. "I don't think that's possible."

"I'm scared of getting what I want." Paul says abruptly.

"Why?" Alex is baffled.

"Afraid of losing what I have, I guess."

Alex frowns. "You can't live like that, Paul."

"You are not, as you've so eloquently stated, the only one with problems. And I know you know that, but — I can't always be perfect for you. It's not fair to me for you expect it. But, fuck, I need you to talk to me."

"I'm learning how," Alex says seriously. He knows that logistics, not feelings, are the limiting factor here, and that he owes Paul all the effort he can give.

"I'm noticing."

Alex squeezes Paul's hand. "We're both fucked up. But I want you, and I want to make this work. I think that means I'm willing to be the adult I'm not ready to be, if you can be the ambitious adult I know you already are. Because I'm going to take over the world whether I want to or not, apparently."

"You want to," Paul says, matter-of-factly.

"I do. If I'm going to pay the price for this life, I am going to make it everything I can. But I need you to stand on your own two feet beside me for it or you're going to blame me, and that won't end well."

They talk for hours. Most of it's about identifying problems instead of solving them, but it's a start. They break only to order Thai food, which they eat in bed.

"I'm not normally this much of a slob," Paul says at one point after accidentally dropping noodles on the duvet. "But you inspire me."

Alex laughs.

"I can see doing this forever," Paul admits with his mouth full.

"You know I won't always be this young, right?" Alex can't wait until that's true, but he also knows his youth and presumed inexperience is part of his appeal to some of his fans and, probably, some of his friends. "Things won't always be new, and I won't always be the one with less experience."

"That makes you more appealing. Not less."

"Oh. Okay," Alex says softly when he can find his voice again.

"See, not quite as fucked up as you think," Paul says. "Now, can we talk about how I like people and you hate them? Because that's going to be a thing."

Alex thinks that's a not a particularly fair assessment of a real problem, but it breaks the ice on what Alex knows is a very necessary public/private discussion.

He watches curiously as Paul fumbles for words to explain why things Alex has already decided are trivial and impossible matter so desperately for him. "It's like asking me not to write," Paul says. "If I don't, I can't see."

Alex refrains from asking what happens if Paul can't see — whatever the answer, he is not ready to hear it. Instead agrees to have dinner with Paul once a week out in the world. He reserves the right, however, to wear one of his hats.

"Was I supposed to assume you were coming back, when you left it?" Paul asks.

"I don't know," Alex says. "Maybe I just knew I wasn't going to be safe without you anyway."

46

The first time Paul goes over to Alex's house is a momentous occasion of an unexpected sort. Paul's never seen Alex's old apartment, though he'd been curious enough about the place Alex spent the rest of his life. Alex always seemed embarrassed about the place. But when he calls Paul and invites him over to his house now he sounds eager and excited.

Paul spends the whole drive over wondering what Alex's space is like and how he'll fit into it.

When Alex answers the door, smiling shyly, Paul forgets about everything but him. When Alex pulls him across the threshold and kisses him before the door is even closed he laughs with astonishment.

Gemma is perched on a barstool in the kitchen looking like a particularly protective mother bird. Paul met Gemma back when Alex had taken her to visit the set, but once they had started hooking up Paul and Alex had been too wrapped up in each other to spend time with anyone's friends beyond those few awkward group brunches.

Paul turns on all of his charm for her, and is pleased to see her soften.

"He's dreamy," she hisses, not quietly at all, as she sweeps past them on the way to her part of the house. "Well done."

"Gemma!" Alex protests, his cheeks flaming with embarrassment.

Gemma laughs at him.

"Are you saying I'm not dreamy?" Paul asks once she's gone.

Alex's cheeks are still scarlet. "I hate both of you."

Upstairs, Paul steps into Alex's room and instantly feels like he belongs there. He looks around for a moment, then realizes Alex is still hovering in the doorway. Paul gives him a confused look.

"What are you doing?" Paul asks.

"Looking at you in my space."

"Possessive." Paul chuckles and lures Alex in, snaking an arm around his waist.

Alex doesn't budge, but he does smile. "After all the time I've spent in yours, it seems fair."

"Thank you for letting me in." Paul presses forward to kiss him. Alex finally steps forward to meet him halfway.

Paul winds his arm around Alex's waist and pushes the door closed, swings him around and pushes Alex towards the bed.

They try to be quiet because Gemma is still in the house, but Paul doesn't hesitate to kneel in front of Alex to help him out of his jeans, before crawling up the bed to hover over him.

Alex reaches an arm over to fish condoms out of the bedside table.

"You know," he says, while he helps Paul with one. "I've never had a guy in my own bed before."

"...Really," Paul says. After so long, it feels ridiculous to get confirmation of old suspicions that don't even matter anymore.

"Mhmm." Alex pets a hand over Paul's hip. "So no pressure or anything."

They're both laughing when Paul finally pushes into him. But then they go quiet.

Paul leans his forehead against Alex's, and Alex loops his arms around Paul's neck to hold him close. They move careful and slow and breathy quiet with an intensity that is so exquisite Paul has to kiss Alex to cover the sound of their soft whimpers.

♦

Tangled up on their sides, in the strange too-much mood that settles over them once Alex crawls back under the covers from cleaning them up, Paul asks, "Is this what it was like with him?"

He knows he shouldn't. But Paul's self-destructive tendencies have always gotten the better of him at the worst possible moments.

Alex goes very still. "Paul. Are you really asking me this?"

"You fucked him when you wouldn't fuck me."

"I was fucking you," Alex says, a little sharply, though he doesn't pull his hand away.

"You know what I mean," Paul says.

"Yes, and you're being gross. My choice to have sex with someone didn't obligate me to make sure that person was you." Alex hesitates, then says slowly, "The thing with Liam — when it was offered — was lower stakes than you and I were. Or are."

"Did doing that make it higher stakes?" Paul knows he's lucky Alex hasn't started yelling at him. But he needs to know. Even if he shouldn't need to about any of this.

"No. No, that's not what made it higher stakes."

"Alex."

"Paul?"

Paul tries to smile, but it's strained. Sometimes it still feels like every time he thinks that Alex is going to talk to him, he stops abruptly. "Come on, give me something here."

"I don't know what to say to you. I feel like the things that will make you feel better aren't true."

"I should worry about it less than I am," Paul admits.

"Yes. You should." Alex squeezes his hand a little too tightly.

He's quiet for a long time, and Paul thinks that's all he's going to say. He is at least grateful that Alex isn't yelling when he finally speaks again, rubbing his thumb along the side of Paul's wrist.

"I know it's hard for you. God, it isn't easy for me. I'm still trying to learn how to talk about it." Alex takes a breath and flicks his eyes up to Paul's. He holds his gaze intently. "Most relevant to you," Alex says quietly, "it is a thing that is profoundly over. But I'm grateful for it. It was important to me. And it was important to him too, I think. I need you to respect that."

As heart wrenching as what Alex is — and is not — telling him is, there's a quiet certitude to it that somehow neutralizes his fear in a way nothing else has managed to yet. His words echo what Liam has said to him on the matter. Even if Paul doesn't know if he'll ever be able to understand exactly what happened between them, he knows something about the value of experiences as mementos.

47

Liam isn't sure if Alex is avoiding him in the days leading up to filming James and Zach's big reunion for actorly reasons or because there's going to be drama about their history and Paul's reaction to it. Liam refrains from working too hard to figure it out, only because there's not much he can do; their work schedules aren't meshing at all right now. The logistics of it alone are incredibly odd.

The set isn't closed because it's just a kiss, but people are quieter than usual, something which seems to come from Alex, who has dragged his chair into a corner and jammed his headphones into his ears. Even Liam can read the clear *do not approach* of Alex's body language, and it's not something that changes once they're in front of the director and the camera.

The moment they start rolling, as Alex's eyes meet his for the first time that day, he understands. This is the work, and sometimes, you have to use your fucked up life to get it done. Zach and James are never anything but right with each other, even when things are terrible and full of fear.

"The guy in my head is in love with the guy in your head," Alex says without ceremony when Liam drops down next to him at lunch.

"Awesome," Liam says. He can't imagine Alex wants to hear more: About how monogamy is a myth; about how everyone, not just actors, are a thousand different people; about how the best things in life always hurt just a little, and that's how you know they're real. Alex relies on him to be happy and blithe, and today, Liam can provide.

48

Of their many agreements over the next several weeks — Alex wonders sometimes if he should go to law school when the world changes again and he isn't famous anymore — doing things in the world with Paul is the hardest. The difficulty doesn't stem from Alex having issues. The fact is that Los Angeles is a legitimate pain in the ass. Fan interactions feel easier with Paul by his side, but also, his boyfriend has a hashtag. They don't even go to that sushi place that often, but as far as the world is concerned Paul is #sushiguy. No one finds this funnier than Carly.

The brunch crew, which Alex returns to tentatively, is also amused. Alex even smiles when Brian starts crowing about *stories of Paul's heterosexual past* the day after he makes the mistake of tweeting a picture of the whole group. It finds its way to the fans via somebody's ex's sister's kid's teenaged babysitter. The barrage of internet communications Alex receives in response runs the gamut from bizarre to hilarious, and they're made better by Paul's recitation of the greatest hits the following week.

A few days later, Margaret utters the dreaded words, *We need to talk.* Apparently Paul now merits his own strategy, or at least the discussion of one.

"I don't want to keep him secret," Alex says to her. "I just want to keep him mine."

Ultimately the plan amounts to little more than refusing media questions on the matter and strategically holding hands in public so that people get the message.

The whole thing makes Alex grind his teeth. He still, and probably always will, resent a public that thinks it has any right to any part of his story, but Paul's pleased for how the plan works out in his favor. Which helps. Alex doesn't want to take away Paul's ridiculous adolescent joy about finally being able to show the world he has a boyfriend. Besides, it's a thing he's wanted for a long time, too.

◆

In June they start talking about living together. It's way too soon; they've only been back together for six months. But they've gotten in the habit of negotiating their way through questions and potential obstacles. There seems to be no need to stop now. Plus they're bad at spending time apart even living across the city from each other. At least Alex now has a place Paul can come to, and after he gets used to having someone else in his space he can't let go of it.

Gemma is a complicating factor, but in the end she makes things easier. The conversation is a strange one. Alex sits on the chair across the living room from her like nothing in their life has changed, telling her what he and Paul had discussed the night before and asking if she'd consider it.

Finally Gemma asks, "You want to know if I mind moving to Paul's house so you can shack up with your boyfriend here and be disgustingly domestic together?"

"Pretty much."

Gemma frowns as she considers it. "Do I get the cat?"

"No. The cat comes with Paul."

More seriously, Gemma asks, "Are we going to have some official rent deal written on paper, or is this all going to be verbal so you can screw me over at some future point?"

"I really hope you know I would never screw you over." Alex knows he's often a shitty friend with a sharp tongue, but cruel he is not. Still, trying harder and being kinder will also need to be a part of his ongoing attempts to grow up.

"One *hopes*, but we should still make it official."

"That's fair." Compared to the papers he signed for *Fourth*, this will be easy.

Gemma squeals and launches herself at Alex. "Then of course! But you're helping me move."

"I'm not helping you do shit. We're hiring people. Hopefully people who are hot this time and that we can ogle."

"That totally counts as helping."

49

Paul sits at the Alex's kitchen island looking over the last details of the pilot pitch he's been working on forever. He started working on this pitch at the kitchen table of his old house, the one he used to share with Craig. Alex's house is bigger than that house was and newer. The kitchen is brighter, even with late afternoon shadows stretching over the backyard and into the canyon behind the house. Some of the appliances on the counters came with Paul. Some are new. Todd, who acceded to the change of habitation with the grudging acquiescence of a benign dictator, sits in front of the sliding door that leads out to the deck. His tail twitches as he watches a bird alight on the railing.

Alex sits on the other side of the kitchen island, his own laptop open in front of him. He's pretending to catch up on the news, but every time Paul looks up, Alex's eyes are fixed on him.

Finally Paul puts the binder-clipped packaged in his bag for tomorrow. Alex slides off his stool, kisses Paul fiercely, and takes him to bed.

In the morning, Paul goes to Victor.

"Can we talk?" Paul asks, standing in the doorway of Victor's office. Whenever he imagined this moment in the past, he thought he'd feel nervous. But this is a moment that's been a long time coming. He knows Victor's been waiting for him to do this. What's more, Paul wants this.

Victor waves him in.

"Okay." Paul lays out his timeline for an exit — he's committed to the current cycle and will definitely see it through — but after that…. Victor watches him through it all with hawk-eyed fascination.

"I've been loyal, and I've done my time." Paul pushes the treatment and pilot script across the desk at Victor. It's ballsy, to spell out the plan before Victor has even looked at his work. But this is the time to go all in. "And I've written this. So help me get a pilot ordered and get the hell out of here."

Victor sits back in his chair and regards Paul for a long moment. Then he smiles. "It's about time. Should I thank Alex for putting you up to this?"

"No. He just reminded me to get around to doing what I've been meaning to do all along. Not everyone has his luck. Not everyone wants it. So this is me asking."

"You didn't ask," Victor notes. "You told. But this is still me saying yes. We'll make it happen." He reaches for the package. "I'm proud of you, Paul. Both of you."

50

In July Alex finishes filming for the summer cycle of *Fourth*, and Paul finishes writing for it forever.

They don't have much time to relax, though. Paul's house needs to be packed up so Gemma can move in and Paul and Alex can finally, officially live together. The process takes longer than moving out of Alex's old apartment did. Paul had a life there for years before Alex was even in L.A. He owns furniture that deserves a fate other than burning.

"I'm going to miss this place," Paul says, looking around at his room that's been reduced to boxes and a disassembled bed frame. Afternoon light streams through the windows unfiltered by curtains and paints yellow rectangles on the floor. The room seems oddly smaller now, the way rooms do when they're empty and stripped of all the equipment of life they once held. Paul hasn't seen it like this since he first moved in, years ago. There will be other houses, of course, and hopefully with Alex, but this is the first one that Paul owned himself. The prospect of leaving is unavoidably bittersweet.

"Mm." Alex says from where he's sitting cross-legged on the floor, sorting screws. "You can always come back and visit." His shorts are dusty, and there's a smudge of dirt or grease or something on his cheek. He's impossibly beautiful.

"It won't be the same," Paul says. It comes out sadder than he means it to.

Alex looks up at him, his dark eyes squinted against the sunbeam inching its way over him. "What's it like? To leave a place you know you'll miss?"

Paul considers it. Not only the question, but the idea that, in Alex's mind at least, everywhere he goes is better and makes him happier than where he's been. His heart gives a little flutter of joy that he gets to be a part of Alex's better future.

"It hurts a little," Paul admits. "But not as much as it could."

"Why's that?"

Paul crosses to where he's sitting and crouches in front of him. When Alex gives him a confused look, Paul can't help but kiss him. "Because my favorite thing about it is coming with me."

Acknowledgements

Thanks to Ben and Patty for putting up with us as we wrote this; Becca for being our first first-reader; Jude for being our first cheerleader; and all of them for sticking by us through the many books since. Also thanks to Victoria Cooper for cover design.

More by These Authors

Visit www.Avian30.com to join Erin and Racheline's mailing list and get information about new releases!

The Love in Los Angeles Series

Starling, Book 1
Doves, Book 2
Phoenix, Book 3
More coming soon!

Love in Los Angeles is a queer romance series, with elements of magical realism, set in and around the TV and movie industry.

When J. Alex Cook, a production assistant on *The Fourth Estate* (one of network TV's hottest shows), is accidentally catapulted to stardom, he finds himself struggling to navigate both fame and a relationship with Paul, one of Fourth's key writers. *Love in Los Angeles* is the story of Paul and Alex — and of their friends and family — as they navigate love, and life, both in and beyond Los Angeles.

A Queen from the North

A widowed prince in need of an heir, a not-so-united kingdom in need of healing, and an ancient prophecy that still lingers in the modern world are about to conspire to make Lady Amelia Brockett A Queen from the North.

The Art of Three

Two men. One woman. No love triangles.

The Love's Labours Series

Midsummer, Book 1
Twelfth Night, Book 2
More coming soon!

42-year-old John Lyonel has never been attracted to men before, but falling for 25-year-old Michael Hilliard is actually the least screwed up thing that's happened to him in years. Even if sometimes he thinks Michael's a changeling.

Short stories:

Sample and Hold
Off-Kilter
Lake Effect
Snare:
The Omega's Reluctant Alpha
Alpha Bodyguard
The Hart and the Hound